I hope this doesn't find you

Also by Ann Liang

If You Could See the Sun
This Time It's Real
I Am Not Jessica Chen
A Song to Drown Rivers

I hope this doesn't find you

ANN LIANG

Scholastic Inc.

If you purchased this book without a cover, you should be aware that this book is stolen property. It was reported as "unsold and destroyed" to the publisher, and neither the author nor the publisher has received any payment for this "stripped book."

Copyright © 2024 by Ann Liang

This book was originally published in hardcover by Scholastic Press in 2024.

All rights reserved. Published by Scholastic Inc., *Publishers since 1920*. SCHOLASTIC and associated logos are trademarks and/or registered trademarks of Scholastic Inc.

The publisher does not have any control over and does not assume any responsibility for author or third-party websites or their content.

No part of this publication may be reproduced, stored in a retrieval system, or transmitted in any form or by any means, electronic, mechanical, photocopying, recording, or otherwise, or used to train any artificial intelligence technologies, without written permission of the publisher. For information regarding permission, write to Scholastic Inc., Attention: Permissions Department, 557 Broadway, New York, NY 10012.

This book is a work of fiction. Names, characters, places, and incidents are either the product of the author's imagination or are used fictitiously, and any resemblance to actual persons, living or dead, business establishments, events, or locales is entirely coincidental.

ISBN 978-1-338-82717-0

10 9 8 7 6 5 4 3 2 1   25 26 27 28 29

Printed in the U.S.A. 40
This edition first printing 2025

Book design by Maeve Norton

FOR MY FAMILY

CHAPTER ONE

It's an honor to be waiting outside the school gates in the winter cold.

This is what I've been telling myself for the past hour as I shiver in my ironed blazer and watch my fingernails turn a concerning shade of purple. It's an immense honor. A privilege. A *joy*. It's exactly what I envisioned when Ms. Hedge, the year level coordinator, called for me in the middle of my math honors class yesterday and asked that I show a few visiting parents around the school.

"I trust that you're the right person to do it," she'd said with a wide smile, her gnarled hands folded neatly across her desk. "As school captain, you can tell them about how much Woodvale Academy cares for its students, and how well we've set you up for success. Feel free to also mention all the extracurriculars you're involved in and your many achievements—like how you recently came in first in the track-and-field regional finals. The parents will love that."

I'd smiled back at her and nodded along with so much fake enthusiasm I gave myself a neck cramp.

My neck is still stiff as I straighten the badges pinned to my front pocket, stamping my feet hard to ward off what feels like imminent frostbite. My best friend, Abigail Ong, always jokes that I collect badges like a magpie. She's not wrong, exactly, but I'm not just admiring how the gold lettering for *school captain* catches the pale morning light. It's also a matter of symbolism. Every single badge I own is proof of something: that I have perfect grades, that I'm the MVP of every sports team I'm on, that I'm an active member of the school community, that I help out at the local library. That I'm smart and successful and have a good future ahead of me—

Footsteps crunch on the dry grass.

I jerk my head up and squint into the distance. It's so early that the parking lot is still empty, save for a rusted brown Toyota that's probably been there since before the school was built. All the redbrick buildings on campus are quiet, the windows closed, the clouds rising over the bare trees painted a soft watercolor pink.

No sign of any lost-looking parents.

Instead, a terribly familiar face comes into view, and out of habit, all the muscles in my body tense. Black eyes, sharp angles, a smile like a blade. That single, ridiculous strand of dark hair falling over his forehead. The school blazer draped around his shoulders like he's posing for a high-fashion magazine.

Julius Gong.

My cocaptain, and the most prominent source of pain in my life.

At the mere sight of him, I experience a rush of loathing so pure and visceral it feels akin to wonder. It's hard to believe that someone with such an awful personality could have such pleasing looks—or that someone with such pleasing looks could have such an awful personality. The equivalent of opening up a gift box with gorgeous silk ribbons and confetti and foil packaging and finding inside it a poisonous snake.

The snake in question stops three solid feet away from me. The patchy, yellowing grass stretched out between us is no-man's-land.

"You're early," he says in his usual slow drawl, as if he can barely be bothered delivering the whole sentence. In the entire decade I've been unfortunate enough to know him, Julius has never started a single conversation with a proper greeting.

"Earlier than you," I tell him, like it's a major point of victory that I've been standing here so long I can't feel my toes.

"Yes, well, *I* was busy with other things."

I catch the implication: *I'm busier than you. I have more important things to do because I'm a more important person.*

"I'm busy too," I say immediately. "Very busy. My whole morning has been one urgent matter after another. In fact, I came here straight from my workout—"

"That does sound like a very urgent matter. I fear the nation's economy would collapse if you didn't get your daily push-ups in."

You're just bitter because I proved in our last PE class that I can do more push-ups than you. The words are perched right on the tip of my tongue. They would be so satisfying to say out loud, almost as satisfying as beating him in another fitness test, but I swallow them down. Stuff my hands in my pockets. The chill seems to be spreading through my bone marrow in the particularly unpleasant kind of way I've come to associate with winters here in Melbourne.

Julius smiles with one side of his mouth, an expression so insincere I would rather he scowl. "Cold?"

"Nope," I say through chattering teeth. "Not at all."

"Your skin is blue, Sadie."

"Must be the lighting."

"You're also shaking."

"With anticipation," I insist.

"You do realize we only needed to get here at seven thirty, right?" He rolls back his sleeve, consults his watch. It's a brand too expensive for me to recognize, but fancy enough for me to know it's expensive. I actually wouldn't be surprised if he was checking the time for the sole purpose of showing it off. "It's seven twenty now. How long exactly have you been standing out here like an honorary human statue?"

I ignore his question. "Of course I realize. I was there when Ms. Hedge told us." Because after Ms. Hedge had given me her cheerful little speech about representing the school, Julius had shown up in her office too, and to my acute annoyance, she'd given him the exact same task. I'd then vowed that I would beat him in this—I would rock up to school way earlier, a hundred times more prepared, in case anyone else arrived early too, and make an incredible first impression on the parents before he could. I'm aware that this isn't something we'll be *graded* on, but that doesn't matter.

In my head, I like to keep a running mental scoreboard of every test, competition, and opportunity in which Julius and I have clashed since we were seven, complete with its own specific point system that makes sense only to me:

Plus three points for earning one of Mr. Kaye's rare approving smiles.

Plus five points for hitting a fundraiser goal.

Plus six points for coming first in the school basketball tournament.

Plus eight points for winning a class debate.

As of now, Julius is at 490 points. I'm at 495, thanks to the history test I came first in last week. Still, I can't be complacent. Complacency is for losers.

"They better arrive soon," Julius says, checking his watch again. The vaguely American curl of his words has a way of making the disdain in his voice more pronounced. For some time now, I've suspected that his accent is fake. He's only ever set foot in the States for campus tours; there's no logical reason why he'd sound like that, except to seem special. "I have no interest in freezing."

I roll my eyes. *The world isn't made to serve you*, I want to snap at him. But the world must have been made to laugh in my face, because right on cue, as if he's manifested them into existence, four cars roll into the parking lot. The doors click open, one by one, and an auntie steps out from each vehicle.

Auntie is the most accurate descriptor I can think of. I don't mean it in the blood-relative kind of way (though my own aunts are definitely all aunties), but as a state of mind, a particular mode of existence. It can be felt, it can be seen, but it can't be strictly defined. It has its unique markers: like the massive perms, the tattooed eyebrows, the Chanel bags, the valuable jade pendant tied together with a cheap red string. But there are also noticeable variations among them.

For instance, the first auntie to strut up to the gates is wearing six-inch heels and a neon-green scarf so bright it could function as a traffic light. The auntie in line after her is dressed in more subdued colors and has naturally stern features that remind me of my mom.

I'm not surprised that the parents interested in sending their kids to our school all happen to be Asian. We make up at least 90 percent of the student population at Woodvale Academy, and that's just a conservative estimate. *How* it came to be this way is sort of a chicken-and-egg question. Are the Asian kids here because their parents wanted them to attend a selective high school for gifted students? Or were their parents drawn to this school because they heard there were a bunch of Asian kids here?

I know for my mom it was the latter. A week after my dad left, she withdrew me from the practically all-white Catholic primary school I was in at the time and moved us to the other side of town. *It's good to be surrounded by community*, she told me, her voice so weary I couldn't think of anything except to go along with whatever she wanted, that day and every day afterward. *People who will understand.*

Julius shifts beside me, and I jolt back to the present. When he moves forward, I step out faster in front of him, my model-student smile snapping into place. I practice it in front of the mirror every day.

"Ayi, shi lai canguan xuexiao de ma?" I say in my very best Mandarin. *Are you here to tour the school?*

The first auntie blinks at me, then replies in smooth English, with an American accent that could put Julius's to shame, "Yes. I am."

Heat shoots up my face. Without even having to look, I can sense Julius's quiet glee, his delight at my embarrassment. And before I can recover, he's already made his grand entrance, his spine straight, chin up, the smug curve of his lips broadening into a warm grin.

"Hello," he says, because he never has any problem greeting *other* people. "I'm Julius Gong, the school captain, and I'll be showing you around campus this morning."

I clear my throat.

He raises a dark brow at me but adds nothing.

I clear my throat again, louder.

"And this is Sadie," he says after a beat, waving a loose hand at me. "The other captain."

"School captain," I can't help emphasizing. My smile is starting to hurt my face. "I'm school captain. I'm also set to be valedictorian."

"I honestly don't think they care," Julius murmurs into my ear, his voice low enough for only me to hear, his breath warm despite the freezing weather.

I try to act like he doesn't exist. This is made somewhat difficult by the fact that all four aunties are busy scanning Julius from head to toe, like they're trying to pick out their future son-in-law.

"How old are you?" one of the auntie asks.

"Seventeen," Julius says readily.

"You look very tall," another auntie says. "What's your height?"

Julius regards her with all the patience in the world. "Six foot one."

"That *is* tall," she says, like this is an impressive feat on par with curing cancer. *It's just genetics*, I'm tempted to point out, though of course I restrain myself. *He literally didn't even have to do anything.* "And you've been at this school for how long now?"

"Ten years," he replies. "Almost my entire life."

I press my tongue down against the sharp edge of my teeth. This part I could answer for him. By either curse or coincidence—and I'm increasingly leaning toward *curse*—we entered Woodvale Academy in the same year. I had been the quiet girl, the shy one, the new kid nobody really wanted anything to do with, while *he* was interesting, mysterious, effortlessly cool. He had acted as if he already knew he would one day rule the place, taking everything in with that calculating black gaze of his. Then in PE, we were placed on opposing teams for a game of dodgeball. The second he had the ball in his hands, his eyes slid to me. Pinned me down. It was like those David Attenborough animal documentaries where you watch in slow motion as the serpent closes in on its prey. I was the rabbit; he was the snake.

Somehow, out of the thirty-something kids in that sweaty, poorly ventilated gym, he had picked *me* as the person to beat. But I was exceptionally good at dodging, light and fast on my feet. Each time he aimed at me, I swerved out of the way. In the end, it was only the two of us left. He kept throwing. I kept ducking. It probably would have gone on like that until the very last period, but the other kids in our class were getting tired of standing around, and the teacher had to step in and call it a tie.

From that point on, Julius Gong became the bane of my existence. The issue is that nobody else seems to share my frustrations, because he only ever bares his fangs at me.

In fact, the aunties are already in love with him. He's still smiling and nodding, asking the aunties about their health and their cooking and some upcoming farmer's market (when I'm certain Julius has never set foot into anything that starts with *farmer* in his life), and they're all just eating it up. As one of the aunties asks him about his grades, he pauses, turns his head just a fraction toward me, and his smile twists into a smirk I alone can see.

"They're okay," he says, with false modesty. "I did receive the Top Achiever's Award for English just last semester. And chemistry. And economics. And physics."

"*Wah,*" the aunties gush in sync. They couldn't be more cooperative if he'd paid them. "That's incredible."

"You're so smart."

"To do so well at such a competitive school? You must be a genius."

"Both handsome *and* intelligent. Your parents really raised you well."

I can imagine my own blood boiling inside me, the steam scorching my throat. To the rest of the world, he might be an angel, a perfect student with a pretty face. But I know what he really is, what he's like.

"We should get the tour going," I say sweetly, clenching my teeth behind my fake beam. "There's lots for us to see. Since there are four of you . . . I can show you two around." I gesture to the aunties standing closest to me. Neither of them looks particularly happy about this arrangement. The auntie with the green scarf actually heaves an audible sigh of disappointment, which is always encouraging. "And Julius can lead the way for the others."

The remaining two women step behind him at once, and

Julius pushes open the wrought iron gates with all the ease of a host at his own party. "Gladly," he says. "Follow me."

In the back of my mind, the numbers flash like a warning sign:

Three points to Julius.

CHAPTER TWO

I spend the next hour talking until my throat hurts.

It's not as if the school campus is even that big: We have three buildings in total, all designed in the same boring, rectangular style with white-framed windows and gable roofs, and spread out around the main oval.

The issue is more that there's a lot of explaining to do.

Like: why photos of the senior teachers have been cut out and glued to the ceiling. "It's a gesture of appreciation and respect," I tell them, because *prank* is not the right word here. "At Woodvale, teachers and students are on very close terms, and we're encouraged to express ourselves in, ah, creative ways. Every time we walk through these beautiful halls, we're reminded that our teachers are always looking down on us from above. Like, um, angels. Or God."

Or why there's a massive statue of a green donkey in the middle of the hall when our mascot is meant to be a horse and our school colors are blue and white. "Donkeys are symbolic," I lie on the spot. In truth, our deputy principal, who'd ordered the cursed statue, apparently just isn't very sensitive to either colors or animals. It could have been worse, I guess; she could have ordered a statue of a cow. "They stand for determination and hard work and grit: all crucial school values we take to heart."

Or why the schedule on the bulletin board says our next assembly will be happening at 9:00 a.m., 10:00 a.m., 10:20 a.m., 3:00 p.m., 3:35 p.m., and somehow also 8:00 p.m. "We like to be very flexible," I say, ushering them along. "Obviously there is only *one* time for the assembly that everyone knows about. Obviously this has been communicated well, because the communication at this school is flawless. Now, have you seen our drinking fountains? We have a *great* filtration system . . ."

Or why there's a construction site next to the cafeteria.

"I remember reading about this on the school website," the green-scarf auntie says with a small frown. We've stopped just outside the wire fences, and even I have to admit, the view isn't great. There's nothing but rubble and plastic coverings and a few scattered poles. As we stare, a literal tumbleweed rolls across the dirt. "It's for the new sports and recreation center, no? I thought it was meant to be finished two years ago."

"Right. *That.*" My smile widens in direct proportion to my panic. I don't know how to tell her that, yes, the sports and recreation center was finished two years ago. But then there came a minor issue with the bathrooms. To be specific, the toilets were all built facing the side, instead of the door, so you couldn't sit down on them without banging your nose. At first the school asked us to be grateful and flexible and view it as a learning experience, but after Georgina Wilkins got a bruise from the stalls and threatened to sue, they decided it was better to rebuild the center from the ground up after all. "There were some small delays," I say, "but only so they could make it even bigger and better. There are some *truly* exciting features coming, including a mini golf course on the roof, a swimming pool, and three private gyms. But as you know, excellence takes time."

The auntie considers this for a moment and, to my relief, moves on.

We've circled our way back to the school gates now. The students have started to trickle in, yelling goodbye to their parents from the curb, swinging their bags over their shoulders and messaging their friends. Julius is also there. He's standing before the aunties, his styled hair glinting in the rising orange light, with his perfect skin and perfect uniform and perfect posture. Just seeing him makes me want to put my fist through something hard—ideally, his jaw.

"We'll definitely be sending our daughter here," one of the aunties is saying. "If you're the standard for the students at Woodvale, then this is the perfect school."

I feel a black thunderbolt of rage, the electricity crackling down my spine. It's made worse when Julius catches my eye, like he wants to make sure I'm listening.

"It's been a pleasure," he says smoothly.

"No, no, the pleasure is all mine," the auntie returns in Mandarin, and my jaw unhinges. She was the one who'd used

English with me earlier. It probably means nothing. Or it definitely means she likes Julius more and feels more familiar with him and trusts him even though there are pyramid scheme leaders more trustworthy than he is. "We couldn't have asked for a better tour guide. Really."

Still looking at me, Julius smiles. "I'm *so* happy to hear it."

I bite my tongue, swallow all impulses for violence, and wave to the aunties as they leave. The second their clacking heels have faded into the distance, I rush off to my first class: history. Unfortunately this is also the first of my shared classes with Julius, and it's not long before his footsteps catch up to mine.

"That went well, didn't it?" he says, his voice drifting just over my shoulder.

"Did it?" I say, shoving the glass doors to the humanities building open with maybe a bit more force than necessary. I'm kind of hoping that it'll swing back and hit him, but of course, he catches the door easily with one hand and slides in after me.

"I mean that it went well for *me*," he clarifies. "Both of them are sending their children here. I bet Ms. Hedge will be pleased. She must have known I was the best person for this task, though I suppose you made some limited contributions as well."

I mutter something unrepeatable under my breath.

"What was that?" I can almost hear the gloating smile in his voice.

"Nothing. I just said we're going to be late if we keep talking."

"Well, unlike you, I have no problem with multitasking."

Go to your happy place, I will myself as I push open the next set of doors. In my mind, I'm no longer walking these crowded halls, listening to the warning bell chime. No longer in this town, even. I've graduated, undefeated, as valedictorian and school captain, and gotten my degree from Berkeley, and I've bought a huge house in a big city for my mom and my older brother, Max (ideally, he would have managed to actually find a job on his own after finishing his expensive sports university, but this is meant to be an achievable dream, not an alternate reality). In the new house, there are more windows than walls and at dawn the sunlight turns everything into gold. We'll have vases full of fresh jasmines, and chocolate-covered strawberries for dessert, and lunches outside in our own gardens. My mom will still run her bakery, but she won't have to work twelve hours a day, and we won't be understaffed anymore, and we'll only go to sneak out taro buns and tuna rolls warm from the oven.

It'll be just us, and we won't need anyone else. Our lives will be better than they used to be with my dad around. I'll do everything he should've done, provide everything he should have provided. I'll do so much that nobody will feel his absence lingering in our living room like a silent ghost anymore. Maybe Mom will even start smiling again.

All I have to do to make that life happen is push through these last few months. Turn in all my homework on time and ace every remaining test and make my teachers happy so I can keep my conditional offer of admission to Berkeley. Abigail always enjoys placing emphasis on the *admission* part, but I'm more concerned about the *conditional* part.

So. Just a few more months of this.

Which sounds simple enough, but at the thought, I feel a pressure that's almost like a physical force, crushing my ribs. I have to steady myself before entering the classroom, breathe in through my nostrils, bounce up and down slightly on the balls of my feet, the way I do before running a race. It doesn't help that the room is too bright, too loud, everyone lounging around the clusters of desks and talking at full volume.

Julius pauses beside me. "What, not going in?" The corners of his lips are curved in their usual condescending manner, but he studies me for an extra beat, like he's trying to figure something out.

"I am," I say, ignoring the tightness in my chest and pushing past him.

I've made it all of two steps inside when a freckled face jumps into my vision. Rosie Wilson-Wang. She's one of those people who know exactly how pretty they are, and uses it to her full advantage. She's also the girl who copied my science fair project last year without telling me, then went on to receive an A-plus for "innovation" and "creativity."

"Sadie," she gushes, which is a bad sign right away. Science project aside, Rosie and I are on amicable terms, but that's because I've made it my mission to be on amicable terms with everyone. Or at least appear to be.

"Hey," I say.

"Did you come in with Julius?" She peers over at him with what feels like unnecessary appreciation, then adds, "He's so great, isn't he?"

I don't know whether to laugh or cough up blood. I guess it's a testament to how well I hide my true feelings that nobody other than Abigail would even suspect how much I hate him. "Mm," I muster.

"His hair looks really good today." Her eyes trail after him as he takes his seat at the front of the classroom. "Like, it looks so soft?" It's somewhat concerning that she's chosen to vocalize this as a question. It implies a desire to find out the answer.

"Sorry," I say, trying not to look too disturbed. "Were you going to ask me something?"

"Right, yeah." She beams at me. "I was just wondering if you could send me your notes."

"Oh. Sure. For history, you mean, or—"

"For all our history classes so far this semester," she says quickly. "You know, because of that exam coming up next month? And, like, sure, I could technically use my own notes, but your notes are so much more comprehensive and organized."

"Oh," I say again. "Yeah, I guess I could—"

"Perfect," she says, squeezing my wrist. Her long acrylic nails scratch my skin, but I stay still. "You're such a saint, Sadie. A true lifesaver."

The compliment goes down my throat like syrup,

warming me up from within. It's embarrassing how tight I latch on to these little pieces of validation, how much I want to be liked, to make everyone happy. Sometimes I think I would give them one of my own arms if they asked very nicely.

Rosie moves to her desk by the window where her tight-knit circle of friends are sitting. All of them are gorgeous, most of them are dancers, and a significant, overlapping portion of them are influencers. Yesterday, one of them posted a ten-second video of themselves standing before a mirror and bobbing their head. It received seventy thousand likes, and the comments were flooded with people begging to be adopted or run over by her Porsche. "By the way," Rosie calls over her shoulder, "could you scan your notes in color and sort them by date and topic? And could you add in your practice essays too? Just send it all over to my school email by tonight—"

"Hey, could you send it to me too?" Her friend, the head-bobbing influencer herself, winks at me.

"Me too, please, while you're at it," her other friend chimes in.

I nod once, weakly, and they all turn their heads back to giggle about something on their phones.

"Thanks," Rosie says, without glancing up again. "Much love."

I swallow, her previous compliment threatening to make its way back up. But that's fine. It's no big deal. Certainly no reason to get worked up. I make a mental note to run to the school printers this afternoon before I head off to my mom's bakery. It'll push back my already tight schedule by about thirty minutes, which means I'll have to shorten my evening run to only five miles or eat dinner while I work or maybe both, but really, it's not an issue.

I take another deep breath, though it sounds strained to my own ears, and a little frantic, like someone who's been underwater too long coming up for air right before diving down again.

No big deal at all.

I've already pulled out my notebooks and written down today's date when Abigail Ong waltzes in as if she isn't seven minutes late.

I would ask her to at least *try* and be more subtle, but that would be asking the impossible. Abigail is basically a walking glow-in-the-dark exclamation mark, with her platinum-silver hair and rolled-up skirt and platform combat boots, which are really just stylish stilts. They thud over the carpet as she makes her way toward me. Ms. Hedge has told her off multiple times for not wearing proper school shoes, but then Abigail ended up writing a five-page thesis about why her boots *did* in fact meet all the requirements for school shoes, complete with a proper bibliography and everything. I don't think she's ever put so much effort into any of her actual essays before.

"I've arrived," Abigail announces to the class in general.

Our history teacher, Ms. Rachel, glances up from her desk. "That's nice. Take your seat, Abigail." No other teacher would be so chill about it, but that's one of the reasons why Ms. Rachel is universally adored. The other reasons being that she's in her twenties, she throws Christmas-themed pizza parties at the end of every school year, and her surname sounds like a first name, thereby creating the illusion that we're on a casual first-name basis with her.

"I'm giving you half of this period to work on your group projects," Ms. Rachel tells Abigail. "Of course, seeing as it's *due* by nine o'clock, I would assume that you're pretty much finished. But I like to be generous."

Abigail offers the teacher a mock salute, then drops into the chair beside me.

"Hello, darling," she says. She started calling people *darling* ironically last year, but it seems to have entered her permanent vocabulary. The same goes for *bamboozled*, *vexed*, and the random, self-invented phrase *fumbled the birdie*.

I finish underlining the date with my ruler so it's perfectly straight. This is like my version of drugs. "Hi," I say. "Do I really want to know why you're late?"

"Why else? My sister got into a fight with Liam again, so he canceled last minute. I had to walk two-point-five miles here in these heels." She kicks out her boots for emphasis.

"Have you considered, I don't know, *not* relying on your sister's on-and-off boyfriend for your daily commute?"

"Liam drives a Lamborghini."

"So?"

"So I'm a fan of expensive cars."

I snort. "You're such a capitalist."

"I like to think I'm supporting the people contributing to our economy."

"I rest my case. And it's not like he bought that car with his own money," I point out. "He's a fuerdai; his parents probably gave it to him for his twentieth birthday as a little bonus to go with his new villa in Sanya. But money aside, I just feel like he's sort of a red flag."

Abigail raises a hand in protest. "He is *not*—"

"He has a literal red flag hanging in his car."

"Okay, but you say that about all men, everywhere," Abigail says. "You don't trust any of them."

Maybe she's right. I definitely don't trust Liam, but I guess I should also give him some credit: He's the only reason Abigail and I are friends in the first place. When he started dropping Abigail off at school three years ago, someone had misunderstood the situation and spread the rumor that Abigail was dating a guy way older than her for money. As with anything else at Woodvale, it'd traveled to basically everyone—including the receptionists—by the end of second period. Even though we'd never exchanged more than a few words with each other before, I hadn't been able to resist stopping by her locker during a break to ask if she was okay.

She was, shockingly. In fact, she found the whole thing hilarious. I was surprised someone could genuinely not care what other people thought of her when her situation was my very worst nightmare; she was surprised that someone could genuinely care about a random stranger and sacrifice their own free time to comfort them.

So we spent recess chatting, and then the next period, and then the last hour of school, at which point it only made sense for us to exchange numbers and continue the conversation at home.

"I'm telling you, he's not a bad person. I have, like, perfect gut instincts when it comes to this stuff. I've correctly predicted the breakup of every couple in our year level so far, haven't I?" she's saying. She rummages through her bag—I swear I hear something cracking inside it—and tugs out a blunt pencil, a crumpled worksheet from last year, a bag of sour worms, and her lunch for the day. It must have been packed by her mom; the bread crusts are removed, the carrots are cut in the shape of hearts, and there's a sticky note that says *You're a star!* Her parents are big believers in positive messages, but they're also just big believers in Abigail. Before visiting her house, I'd assumed that kind of unconditional love and support only existed in old sitcoms. "Oh, how was the parents' tour, by the way?"

"I lost," I say bitterly. I keep my voice as quiet as possible, because I'd rather die than let Julius overhear me admitting defeat.

"You lost?" Abigail repeats, laughing. "You can't *lose* a tour—"

"I can. I did. I have."

"You're so ridiculous," she says. I would be affronted if it came from anyone else, but Abigail only teases a very select number of people she deems important. Everyone else might as well be background noise, flies, motes of dust; in her eyes, they simply don't exist. "Well, at least you don't have to worry about the group project anymore. You're done already, I gather, like the unreasonably organized person you are?"

"Of course. You know my policy." Anytime I receive a deadline, I'll set myself my own deadline at least a week before it. That's why I spent the first two days of winter break completing my part of the project on China's Warlord Era, which includes a four-thousand-word research essay, a hand-drawn animation of the Zhili-Anhui War, and an interactive map of the various cliques. The workload itself was stressful, yes, but I'm only calm when I'm ahead. "I just need my group to give me their summaries, and then we can submit it."

Abigail glances up and points at my group members, Georgina Wilkins and Ray Suzuki, who are coming over to our desk. "Uh, they don't look like they're holding anything. Should you be concerned?"

I frown. They *are* both empty-handed, and as they squeeze closer past the desks, I can make out the sheepish smile on Georgina's face.

A bad feeling digs into my gut.

Still, I'm willing to give them the benefit of the doubt. "Hey, how are you?" I ask, because it feels rude to demand to see their summaries right away.

But Ray doesn't seem to have any qualms about rudeness. "We didn't do it," he says bluntly.

I blink. He might as well have punched me in the stomach. "I— You didn't do . . . the summary?"

"Nope," he says, sticking his hands into his pockets.

"Okay." I can hear a faint ringing sound in my ears, building into a screech. I do my best to recalibrate. Stay calm. Stay friendly. Stay focused. "Okay. Okay, um. It's okay if you didn't finish—maybe just show me what you have and—"

"I didn't do any of it," he says.

Another punch, even harder than the last. If I were standing up, I'd be staggering back.

"Right. And is there a reason *why*, or . . ."

He looks me straight in the eye. "I don't know. Guess I just wasn't sure how. Or, like, what we were meant to be doing, you feel?"

"The summary," I get out. *The summary I already wrote out for you*, I add inside my head. *Word for word. The one I asked you to copy down onto the template that I predesigned and printed and personally delivered to your house in the winter rain on the first day of the midyear break so you could do it when you had time. That summary?* "I thought . . . I mean, sure," I say, seeing his blank stare. "That's okay. What about you, Georgina?"

Georgina makes a gesture that reminds me of a flower wilting. "I'm sorry," she says, pouting. "I tried to start, I promise, but, like, my face still hurts from when I hit my nose against the bathroom wall?"

"I thought you said you were fine," Ray says.

Georgina shoots him a quick, pointed look, then turns back to me, her dark eyes shining with emotion. "I feel worse whenever I have to work on an assignment. It's, like, super unfortunate. I wish I could do more to help, but . . ."

Stay calm, I remind myself. I clench the muscles in my arm so hard they hurt and then, very slowly, force them to relax again. I repeat this until I no longer feel like committing murder. "It's not your fault," I tell her, eyeing the clock. Only eighteen minutes left until the deadline. I have two summaries to write up, which leaves just nine minutes for each. Eight minutes, if I want to take time to double-check everything before submitting. "You know what? I can just do the rest myself. Totally cool."

I expect more resistance, but they retreat rapidly, as if they've just dropped a grenade in my lap.

But no time to worry about them. This is *my* project. This is my grade on the line. One mistake and my whole average will drop, and Berkeley won't want me anymore. I push my sleeves up as high as they'll go, then open up my school laptop to find my notes. Just seventeen minutes left. Briefly, as I stare at the tiny words loaded onto the screen, the dozens of tabs pulled open, I feel so overwhelmed I could choke. The words fade in and out; my vision blurs.

Nothing gets in.

Then I notice Julius watching me in my peripheral vision, and it's like I've been zapped. Everything sharpens back into focus. I won't give him the satisfaction of seeing me struggle. I refuse to.

With deliberate, feigned calm, I pick up my pen and begin copying the summary down.

For those next seventeen minutes, I don't move or speak or even lift my head until I've written down the last word. Then I release a sigh that travels all the way through my bones, down to my sore muscles and stiff fingers. That was too close. *Way* too close. Next time it might be safer to just do everything myself.

"Thanks, Sadie," Ms. Rachel says as she collects our project. "I can't wait to read through this one; the Warlord Era is absolutely *fascinating*. It was one of my favorite subjects in college."

I act like this is news to me, a happy coincidence. Like I didn't spend hours searching her up online and reading through an old interview she did for her alma mater's student magazine, where she mentioned her interest in the Warlord Era. Like I didn't choose this specific topic for the very purpose of appealing to her personal tastes.

Abigail would affectionately refer to such behavior as my *sociopathic tendencies*.

"I'm just going to pop into my office to put this away," Ms. Rachel tells me, nodding toward the pile of papers gathered in her arms. "I'll be five minutes. Could you keep an eye on the class for me while I'm gone?"

"Of course."

"Great. I can always count on you." Ms. Rachel smiles at everyone like they're special, but somehow it still manages to feel genuine when she's smiling at me.

The second she steps out the door, the class dissolves into chaos. People slump back in their seats, kick their feet on desks, stretch their arms out in loud, open-mouthed yawns. Muffled conversations give way to open hoots of laughter and shouts across the room.

Before I can do anything about it, an alert pops up from my school inbox.

One new email.

My heart leaps. I'm praying it's a reply from Mr. Kaye, our math teacher; I sent him a desperate email after midnight yesterday about one of the bonus questions. Unfortunately I still have all my tabs open, and my aging laptop is clearly protesting; I have to click my inbox about twenty times before the rainbow spinning wheel disappears. Then I glance at the name of the sender, and my hope whittles away into rage.

It's from Julius.

Just so you know, Ms. Rachel took a peek at our group project earlier and said it looked—and I quote—"phenomenal." I'm saying this now so you're not too shocked when our grades come back and mine's higher than yours. I know how upset you get every time I win.
Best regards,
Julius Gong, School Captain

I snap my head up, my eyes going straight to him, but he's turned away, chatting to the pretty girl sitting next to him. As he laughs, I'm gripped by the visceral urge to march up there and shake him by the shoulders, dig my nails into his smooth skin. I want to leave a permanent mark. I want him to *feel* it, to hurt. I want to destroy him.

"Sadie." Abigail's voice sounds a thousand miles away, even though she's sitting right next to me. "Um, there's a vein in your temple that looks like it should be examined by a health professional."

When I don't reply, she leans over me and reads the email on my screen.

"Damn," she breathes. "That boy's really making it his life mission to get on your nerves."

I squeeze out a scoff that sounds more like I'm being strangled.

Across the classroom, he's still laughing with the other girl.

Happy place, I remind myself. *Remember your happy place. Your future.*

But when I try to summon up the image of the giant house with the sunlit rooms and soft curtains, all that materializes is Julius's sneering face, his pitch-black eyes and haughty cheekbones and curved lips. Beautiful and horrible, like those vivid flowers you find blooming in the wild that are actually carnivorous.

So instead I spread my fingers over the keyboard and begin to type in a furious rush, stabbing out each letter with my nails. This is my last resort, my sanctuary, the antidote to my anger. Because I know better than anyone that I'm not really a saint.

Nowhere close. I simply like to unleash all my rage in my email drafts, where I can be as harsh and petty and unforgiving as I want, because I also know that I'll never have the nerve to send them out. When I write, I write anything and everything that comes to mind.

Julius,

Just so YOU know, I'm keeping your email as evidence so that when our grades come back and mine's obviously higher, you'll understand how it feels to be slapped by your own hand. I can't wait for the day to arrive. But also, even if it were a tie, I don't think you have any reason to gloat. You managed to complete your project only because you have smart people like Adam in your group, and you have Adam in your group only because you gave the teacher that complete rubbish speech about wanting to switch things up and bond with new peers and so she let you choose.

Maybe the teacher and the parents you showed around this morning and everyone else at this school buy your bullshit, but I can see right through you, Julius Gong. You're attention starved and self-obsessed and unbearably vain and you wear your cynicism like a crown; you're the kind of kid on the playground who steals a toy not because you want it but because somebody else does.

Also, your hairstyle is ridiculous. You might think it looks all natural and effortless, but I bet you spend entire hours of your morning styling it with a tiny comb so that the one singular strand falls over your left eye at the perfect angle. From the bottom of my heart, I really hope your comb breaks and you run out of whatever expensive hair products you've been using to make your hair appear deceptively soft when I'm sure it's not, because there's nothing soft about you, anywhere at all—

"Morning, Mr. Kaye!"

The name jolts me back to reality. I peel my eyes from my laptop and spot Mr. Kaye walking past us down the corridor, a hand lifted in greeting.

I quickly save the draft. It's the fifty-seventh draft email I have; the majority of them are dedicated to Julius, but there are a few others written for classmates and teachers who've made my life especially difficult in the past.

"Mr. Kaye," I call, shooting up from my seat so fast I bang my knee against the desk. "Mr. Kaye, wait—" I suppress a wince and rush out into the corridor after him.

"Sadie," he says, regarding me with the strained patience of a grandparent humoring their overenergetic grandchild. He's probably old enough to be my grandpa, though it's hard to tell, with his dyed black hair.

"Sorry to bother you," I say. "But did you get that—"

"Email you sent?" he finishes for me. Unlike his hair, his brows are a peppery gray. They rise slowly up his wide forehead. "Yes, I did. Are you often up at one in the morning?"

"No, of course not." I often go to sleep later than that, but there's no reason to raise alarm. And the last thing I need is for this to devolve into a conversation about my unhealthy sleeping habits. I just want to know if my answer was correct or not. "For question six . . ."

"The textbook was wrong," he tells me. "Don't worry, Sadie, your calculations were completely right. The answer should have been ninety-two. I'll make a note of it in class, though I doubt anyone else except Julius has even touched the bonus questions."

The textbook was wrong. The most beautiful arrangement of words to ever exist. It's like someone's injected sunlight directly into my veins. I'm so relieved, so euphoric, that I don't even mind the mention of Julius.

"Oh my god, that's amazing," I say, completely sincere for once. "That's— Thank you so much, Mr. Kaye. I redid my calculations so many times; I tried, like, eight different methods—"

"I'll bet you did," he says, and this time the corners of his lips rise too, with mild amusement. "Was that all?"

"Yes," I babble, my face splitting into a beam. "Yes, thanks again. You have no idea—this just made my entire day."

I'm still beaming as I head back, my high bun bouncing, my footsteps light. So maybe the morning was off to a bit of a rough start. That's fine. Things are good now.

I don't even mind the fact that the classroom situation has deteriorated further, or that Rosie and her friends have pushed back a few of the tables—including mine—to shoot a video of themselves spinning on the spot for god knows what reason. I simply wait until they're done and rearrange the tables myself.

"Your mood changed fast," Abigail says, seeing my face. "Did Mr. Kaye give you a cash prize or something?"

"Even better: The textbook was wrong." I let out a happy sigh. "I was right."

When I take my seat again, I notice, dimly, that my laptop seems to be in a different position. I pause, frowning. I could have sworn I'd lowered the screen almost all the way down, not just halfway. But then Ms. Rachel returns with important information for our upcoming test, and I forget everything else. I'm too focused on planning out my next move to beat Julius.

CHAPTER THREE

Sometimes your body knows before your mind does.

My skin tingles all the way to the school café at lunch, even though I can't place a finger on *why*. On the surface, everything is the same: the crisp chill in the air, the students lining up outside for warm bagels and hot chocolate, blowing into their hands and wrapping their blue-and-white scarves tighter around their necks while they wait.

But something's different. Something's changed.

"Do you feel that?" I ask Abigail as we join the back of the line. The sun has climbed higher in the sky, throwing wide swaths of golden light over the courtyard.

"Feel what?"

"I don't know," I murmur, glancing around me. My eyes lock with some girl from a lower year level. Her gaze lingers on my face a beat, as if in confirmation, before she twists her head away and whispers something to her friend, her hand covering her mouth. *It's not about you*, I tell myself. *There's literally no reason why they'd be talking about you.* But a sick feeling spreads over my rib cage. "I just . . . feel like people are staring."

"Maybe it's because of how gorgeous we are." Abigail tosses her glossy hair over her shoulder. "I would stare at us too."

"Your confidence is inspiring," I say, "but somehow, I doubt that's it . . ."

We shuffle forward, and it happens again. Another girl catches my eye, then pointedly looks in the other direction.

"Well, darling, you *are* school captain," Abigail says. "People are going to notice you, right? I thought you'd be used to it by now."

And people do notice me. It's why I campaigned so hard to be elected school captain in the first place, why I've thrown myself into delivering speeches at assembly and sending out mass reminders about fundraising events and conducting student surveys the principal only pretends to read. Well, that, and because I knew it would look great on my Berkeley application, and because I'd heard that Julius was running for captain, and anything he did I had to do as well. But right now people are doing more than *noticing*. In my peripheral vision, I see someone I've never spoken to before point straight at me.

"Okay," I say, my uneasiness growing. "Maybe I'm being paranoid, but I seriously think—"

"What the *hell*?"

I whip around to find Rosie, of all people, storming up to us. No, to *me*. Her eyes are narrowed, her phone gripped in one hand. She's only five foot one, so tiny that our classmates sometimes like to lift her up for fun, but there's nothing small or delicate about her as she plants herself firmly to the ground in front of me.

My mind goes blank. All I can think is: *What is happening?*

"Is there, like, something you want to say to my face?" she asks, her voice hard, accusing. "Do you have a problem with me, Sadie?"

"What?" I stare at her. The gears in my head are still turning frantically, trying to produce a single reason why Rosie would go from calling me a saint to acting like I've just run over her dog within the span of two classes. Is this about the notes? Had she wanted them earlier? But it can't just be that. Up close, her lips are quivering, all the muscles in her jaw clenched. "I don't— Of course not. I don't have any problem with you—"

"I thought you were nice." She's speaking louder and louder, her features animated with rage. "And even if you did have beef with me, you should've told me *in private* before blasting it out to everyone."

A hush has fallen over the courtyard, heads turning to watch.

"I don't know what's going on," I tell her, half pleading. Acid churns in my stomach. I hate it when people are mad at me. I hate it, I hate it, I can't stand it. "I swear, it's probably a misunderstanding—"

"Yeah, sure."

"I'm not—"

"Are you really going to pretend it wasn't you?"

"*Hey,*" Abigail snaps, stepping before me, her arm raised to block my body. But even then, I'm shaking, my teeth chattering so loudly I can feel the echo reverberating in my skull. I want to fold in on myself, disappear into the ground. *Don't be mad*, I want to say, as pathetic as it sounds. *I don't know what's going on, but please just don't be mad.* Because it might be Rosie standing here now, but in my head it's someone else. Footsteps storming out the living room and the slam of the door, like a thunderclap, the rumble of the engine, then the horrible, crushing quiet. That's what happens when people get angry. They leave, permanently, and they forget you, and there's no going back.

"Did you or did you not," Rosie says, holding her phone up close to my face, "write this?"

With difficulty, I take in the email loaded onto the screen, and the world falls away from me.

I can hear my own ragged breathing, my blood pounding in my ears.

I recognize every word, because I did write it. I can even remember where I was, slumped against my bedroom wall and fuming. Rosie had sent out a mass email to everyone in the year about throwing a party to celebrate winning the science fair. *Guess you can all call me a nerd now*, she'd joked. And next thing I knew I was typing out a reply faster than my fingers could keep up. *This* reply:

> *If you're going to steal someone's project and take all the credit, you could at least have the decency to not flaunt it around like you actually had anything to do with it. Since when did you even care about science? Since when did you*

care about any of your subjects at all? You spend most of class texting people and online shopping and watching videos of cats and then when the assignment actually comes around, you decide you can just leech off my work? Just because I didn't say anything at the time doesn't mean I didn't know—

"Well?" Rosie demands.

"It shouldn't be there," I whisper, my fingers tingling. My whole body feels numb. It shouldn't be there. It shouldn't. It *can't be*. The email was meant to be in my drafts, for my eyes only. But the truth is staring me in the face. For god knows what reason, my draft was sent out, and not just to her. It was sent via Reply All, which means everyone included in her original email—everyone in the year level—would have received it.

And then a new, terrifying possibility dawns on me.

It's so terrible that my heart shuts down. My blood runs cold.

Oh god—

The crowd shifts, and the last person I want to see right now appears. He doesn't even have to push his way through; he simply walks forward, his head lifted, and everyone parts for him, offering up all the space he needs.

Julius brushes past Rosie and Abigail like they're not even there and stops before me. His eyes blaze black, but the rest of his features are pure ice. And all at once, my worst fears are confirmed.

"Sadie," he says, his voice more a rasp than its normal drawl.

He says my name like it's poison, like it costs him something. "Come with me."

Then he stalks off, without even glancing back to check if I'm following.

I do follow.

I don't want to, but it's either that or stay behind and let Rosie yell at me while everyone stares.

My face feels raw when Julius finally slows down in the school gardens. We're a good distance away from the café and the basketball courts, and there's nobody else around. It's pretty here, I observe through my panic, with ivy crawling over the fences and winter roses blooming in the background. There's even a small pond, glittering amid the greenery. When the school first built the gardens, they'd brought in a duck as well, but then a fox snuck in at night and killed it, and people were so upset that we held a funeral. Everyone attended, and one of the boys in my year level wept, and the duck ended up being buried in the grass.

Actually, I think the duck might have been laid to rest right under the spot I'm standing.

"I'll have you know," Julius begins, low and furious, "that I was *not* named after a Roman dictator."

I'm so disoriented, so shaken still, that I can only say: "You weren't?"

"Absolutely not."

"What . . . were you named after, then?"

"A printing company," he says, then pauses, like he regrets volunteering this information. "But that's beside the point."

It takes me a moment to realize what he's referring to. *A Roman dictator.* My emails. In one of the many angry emails I'd written to him, I had mocked his name. *Your parents must be so proud*, I'd said. *You're really living up to your namesake.*

"No," I whisper, my stomach swooping low. "No, no, no, no. No. No—"

"How long have you been planning this?" he asks, pressing in with both his voice and his body. He leans forward. I shift back, the bristles of a low thornbush scraping my spine. But I would gladly let the thorns pierce my skin if it could hide me from this mess. None of this should be happening. "There were forty-two emails addressed to me. The earliest dated back to *nine years ago.*"

"You read all of them?" Suddenly, I would like to trade positions with the dead duck. "I— How? When?"

"You're asking *me*?" he demands. "You were the one who sent them. Imagine my surprise when I open my laptop at the start of physics class and my inbox is *flooded* with emails from you. If I missed out on crucial content because I was preoccupied with your many insults to my character, I hope you know that you're entirely to blame."

"No," I'm still trying to say, repeating myself over and over as if I can somehow change reality through the sheer force of my denial. *"No."*

"Were you saving them up this entire time? Waiting for the right moment to strike?"

"I wasn't."

"You weren't what?" And unlike Rosie, he actually waits for me to answer.

"I—I didn't mean to send those emails," I tell him. I'm afraid I'm going to faint, or throw up, or both. "I just— A lot is going on right now. But I don't know how they got to you. I really . . . I swear, you have to believe me. You were never supposed to get them."

His dark eyes roam over my face, and the air in my lungs stills. The way he's looking at me—it's like he can see everything, every terrible, ugly thought that's ever flickered through my mind, every impulse and fantasy, every lie and insecurity. "I believe you," he says at last, evenly.

I'm so surprised I almost can't speak. "You . . . do?"

"I believe that you'd never want anyone else to read those emails," he says, folding his arms across his chest, the angles of his face sharp and hostile. "That would go against your *good student* reputation, right? You would never be that brave," he adds with a scoff. "You're too fake."

It feels like someone's held a torch to my cheeks. Everything in me burns. "You think I'm fake?"

"You don't think you are?" He cocks his head. "You go around smiling and charming the teachers and agreeing to anything anyone asks of you like you're some kind of angel, and then you go back and write your secret little emails about how much you hate my guts and wish to strangle me—"

"It's called being nice," I cut in.

"Yes, strangulation is very nice. Practically a peace offering."

"That's not what I'm saying."

He laughs, a cold, hard sound. "You never say what you mean anyway."

There's a dangerous pressure building behind my eyes. I blink furiously, squeeze my hands into fists, ignore the odd knot of pain in my throat. "You can't accuse me of being fake for *having basic manners*." If this were any other day, I would stop here. Just short of getting into a real confrontation, of speaking my mind. But then I realize, with a burst of hysteria, that Julius already knows what I think. There's no point pretending anymore when he's seen the worst of me. It's almost liberating. "I know you don't care about anyone except yourself, and I know you can get away with it because you're *you*, but not all of us are built like that."

Something flashes over his face, and I falter.

Maybe I went too far. Maybe I was too harsh. As much as I hate him, the emails are still my fault. "I am sorry," I make myself say, my tone softening just a little. "I was really, really annoyed when I drafted those emails, so if they hurt your feelings—"

And as if I've hit a switch, his expression hardens. His mouth tugs up in a mocking smile, his black eyes glittering. When he exhales, I can see the ghost of his breath in the air between us. "Hurt my feelings?" He says it like a joke. "You have far too high an opinion of yourself, Sadie. You aren't capable of hurting me. On the contrary . . . don't you remember what you wrote?"

An alarm goes off in my brain.

Danger.

Retreat.

But I'm frozen to the ground, only my heart galloping faster and faster.

"From what I recall, you wrote two whole paragraphs protesting the color of my eyes," he drawls, and I feel myself pale with horror. "They're too dark, like those of a monster from the fairy tales. Like a lake you could drown in on the coldest day of winter. My lashes are too long, more fitting for a girl's. I don't deserve to be so pretty. My gaze is too sharp, too intense; you can't hold it for long without being overwhelmed." He stares right at me as he speaks, like he wants to see if it's true, to witness his effect on me in real time. "You said it makes it difficult for you to concentrate in class."

I've always resented Julius's perfect memory, but I've never resented it as much as I do in this instant.

"That's enough," I try to say.

But of course he won't listen to me. If anything, he only seems more determined to continue. "You then wrote three hundred words ranting about my hands." He flexes his long fingers, examining them carefully. "I had no idea you paid such close attention to the way I held my pen or gripped the violin bow or how I looked when I was answering something on the board."

I unclench my jaw to defend myself, but I can't think of a single solid defense. It really is every bit as mortifying as it sounds.

"You know what I think?" he murmurs, drawing so close his mouth skims my ear, his cruel face blurring in my vision. My breath catches. Goose bumps rise over my bare skin. "I think you're obsessed with me, Sadie Wen."

Heat lashes through me. I move to shove him away, but my hands only hit hard, lean muscle, the flat planes of his chest. He laughs at me, and I want to kill him. I mean it with every cell in my body. I've never wanted to kill him so badly. I hate him so much that I could cry.

"Go away," I hiss.

"You don't have to be embarrassed—"

I hardly ever raise my voice, but I do now. "*God*, just leave me alone. I'm so sick of you." It comes out even louder than I intended, cracking the serenity of the gardens, sounding over the treetops. My throat feels scraped open with the words.

He finally steps away then, his face impassive. "Oh, don't worry, I was already planning on leaving." Because it has to be his choice, not my command. Because he won't even give me this one small satisfaction.

I don't watch him go. Instead I fumble for my phone in my skirt pocket and load up my emails. *Maybe they're not all as terrible as I think*, I attempt to reassure myself, though it sounds delusional, the voice of a girl insisting the fire isn't that big when her house is burning down before her. *Maybe you're overreacting. Maybe the situation is still salvageable.*

But then I open my first email to Julius from nine years ago, and a few sentences in, my insides turn to stone.

> *your a lier, Julius Gong.*
>
> *when the Chinese teacher asked us for the idiom for "water and fire don't mix," I answered at the same time you did!!!!!! How DARE you tell the teacher you were the one who got it right and not me??!!! How DARE YOU take MY gold stickre???? Who gave you the right, huh? you don't deserv any stickers. your a very, very bad person, I don't care how good other poeple think you are. I'm gonna make you regret this so much you'll cry, just you wait.*

My awful spelling at eight years old is almost as embarrassing as the content itself.

Desperate, I pull up another one. A Reply All response to an email Julius had sent to the year level below, offering to sell his study material for an offensive sum only a day after I'd offered up *my* notes for sale. My spelling here is better. The content is, objectively, worse.

> *Sometimes I dream about throttling you. I would do it slowly. I would do it when you weren't ready, when you were relaxed. I*

imagine wrapping my hands around your long, pale throat and watching the fear bloom in your eyes. I imagine your skin turning red, your breathing quickening as you struggle. I want to watch you in pain, up close. I want you to beg me. I want you to admit you were wrong, that I've won. Maybe you would even sink to your knees for me. Plead for mercy. That would be fun, but even then, that wouldn't be enough—

It takes all my self-restraint not to hurl my phone into the pond.

I squeeze my eyes shut so tight I see stars. I like to consider myself a smart person. I take great pride in knowing things, like whether a graph is wonky, or when an answer is accurate, or which essay topic is going to work best.

But it doesn't require much intelligence to know that I'm completely, utterly screwed.

CHAPTER FOUR

When the school bell rings for next class, I'm busy calculating how long it'll take to permanently relocate to another city.

I could go home now. Grab my passport and call up a taxi and book the earliest flight out of here. I have enough red pocket money saved up in my bank account from every Spring Festival to sustain myself for at least a month. And in the meantime I could find a part-time job, support myself by tutoring kids or waitressing at a hot pot restaurant—I've heard that they're always looking for bilingual employees. Maybe I'll dye my hair blonde, get a spray tan and contacts, change my name and fake my whole identity. Nobody from Woodvale would be able to find me . . .

But even as I play out this fantasy, my feet are already dragging themselves across campus to the English classroom.

I can't help it.

It's too deeply ingrained in me, the need to obey the rules, to show up on time, to keep up my perfect attendance. I'm like one of Pavlov's dogs, except every time I hear the bell, my instinct is to find my desk and whip out my notebooks.

I feel physically sick as I stop outside the door. I'm shaking all over, my teeth knocking against themselves so hard I'm scared they'll crack. The scent of disinfectant and shoe polish is overwhelming, the crescendo of voices grating my ears like shrieks. I can't make out what they're saying, but I know, with a sick, solid pang in my gut, that they're talking about me.

My fingers tremble over the knob. I try to take deep breaths, but I suck in too much air too fast, until I'm lightheaded from it.

The bell chimes again.

Just go in.

Get it over with.

The second I step inside, there's a brief but noticeable lag in the conversation. Eyes swivel away from me, landing on random spots on the whiteboard or the cracked-open windows or the outdated poster that reads *Keep calm and Shakespeare on*, which doesn't even make any sense.

As I take my seat in the front row, my neck prickles with the sensation of being watched. I'm aware of my every sound and movement: my laptop opening, my chair creaking, my blazer sleeves creasing when I push them up.

Then Ms. Johnson walks in, and the expression on her face makes me freeze. Her mouth is pinched, her thin brows practically twisted into a double knot. She's been teaching here for six years, and on maternity leave for three; in all the time I've known her, she's never looked this livid before. Then she locks eyes with me—not in her usual *there's my favorite student who always leads the group discussions* way, but in a *there's the brat who ruined my day* way. And all at once, my confusion clarifies into pure, nauseating dread.

Those cursed emails.

I'd been so fixated on what I'd written to Julius that I'd forgotten about the other recipients. Recipients like my English teacher.

"Before we begin diving into the wonderful world of literature today," she says, setting her briefcase down on the desk with a somewhat violent thump, "I would like to make a general announcement that *if*, for some reason, you take issue with a grade that I have given you in the past, you can discuss it with me in a *civil manner*." Her gaze snaps back to me, and I wish more than anything that a sinkhole would open up and swallow me whole.

"I would also like to emphasize that I have been in this teaching business far longer than you have been students," she continues. "While English may be more subjective an area of study than others, we nonetheless grade you based on a strict rubric. The score that you receive in the end is far from random; if you believe that you deserve better, then perform better. Do I make myself clear?"

Slow nods from around the classroom. Behind me, I hear someone whisper, "Damn, who pissed *her* off this morning?"

"Probably the same person who's been pissing everyone off."

There's a pause, and my mind automatically fills up the silence with a vivid mental image of them gesturing at me. All the blood in my body seems to be concentrated in my ears and cheeks.

I press my hands to my burning face, lower the brightness

of my screen as far down as it'll go, and pull up the sent folder in my emails. Then I force myself to read through the entire chain between me and Ms. Johnson, starting with my original email. I remember spending an hour composing it, switching synonyms around to sound as friendly as possible, and proofreading it so many times my eyes began to water.

> *Dear Ms. Johnson,*
> *I hope this finds you well! I was just curious when our scores for our text analysis paper will be released? I recall you saying that they would be marked by last Thursday, but it's been a week and I don't seem to have received anything yet. Of course, I totally understand if they aren't ready because of how busy you are, and I definitely don't mean to rush you—I only wanted to double-check in case I might have missed them!*
>
> *Thank you so much for all your time, and sorry for any inconvenience!*
> *Kind regards,*
> *Sadie Wen*

I'd then held my breath and waited. Her reply had come two days later:

> *your score is 89.5%*
> *Sent from my iPhone*

With each new line I read, I can feel the past rushing back to me, my frustration made fresh again, the scab picked open. It was a terrible score by my standards, just barely above mediocre. Worse, I'd known that Julius had received a 95 percent, because *his* English teacher was a more lenient marker, and the difference between us was significant. Inexcusable. Unbearable. We didn't even have the same letter grade. So I had done my best to bargain.

Dear Ms. Johnson,
Thank you so very much for letting me know—I truly appreciate it! Would it be possible in any way to round my score up to a 90 percent, given that right now it's only off by 0.5 percent? Or perhaps there's a chance for me to do a make-up paper or extra credit? Please let me know, as this grade—and your class—is incredibly important to me. I would be happy to do anything to change this.
Kind regards,
Sadie Wen

To which she'd said only:

No. All grades are final.

And really, it should've stopped there. That should have been the last of our exchange. I'd poured out my humiliation and anger into a late-night draft and moved on.

Until now.

I wince my way through the latest email, the heat in my face expanding.

Ms. Johnson,

I've gone back and read through the essay I submitted, and I must say I disagree with the final mark. Even if it's not worth full marks, it should at least be worth the 90 percent. It doesn't cost you anything to round the score up, but it costs me everything to leave it the way it currently is. Just 0.5 percent. Zero. Point. Five. Percent. How unreasonable do you have to be to deny a student even that? It's basic math. As you might know, I'm currently applying to Berkeley, which has literally been my dream school since I was a child. My grades are more important than ever, and that letter grade could change my entire average, which could be the difference between an acceptance and a rejection.

This isn't the first time I haven't been able to completely make sense of your marking guidelines either. The model essay you showed us in class wasn't even that good—every time it referenced a quote, it quite literally said, "This is a quote from the text." It also began every second sentence with the word "significantly," which, in my opinion, really detracts from the actual significance of the statement . . .

Two weeks ago, months after I drafted that response, I found out Ms. Johnson was the one who wrote all the model essays she handed out to us.

Forget a sinkhole, I think grimly as I snap my laptop shut again, turning my eyes to the high ceiling. *Just let the building collapse on top of me instead.*

Most unfortunately, the building does not collapse within the last three hours of school—but my life does.

Everywhere I go, whispers follow. From the way people are acting, you'd think I was caught murdering a man with my bare hands or something, but I guess this is a kind of murder. As of today, Sadie the Model Student, the Perfect School Captain, is effectively dead.

"It's really not *that* bad," Abigail says as we head down the corridors together. We have math in five minutes, but for once, I'm not worried about the prospect of a pop quiz. A girl elbows her friend and nods in my direction when we pass. They both dissolve into loud, hysterical giggles.

The queasy feeling that's taken up permanent residence in my stomach burrows even deeper.

"What's so funny?" Abigail yells after them, because *she's* never been afraid of confrontation. "Your new bangs?"

"Her bangs actually looked pretty cute," I say through my fingers.

"Yeah, no, they really suit her," Abigail agrees in a lower voice.

"And okay, look, the situation isn't *great*, but I've had a chance to read through some of those emails you sent out—"

"You and everyone else in this school," I mutter, raising my hands higher to hide my face. Another group of friends have stopped outside the bathroom just to stare at me, snippets of their conversation floating after us.

". . . that's her . . ."

"I heard Rosie completely flipped her shit this morning . . ."

"Yeah, figures. Did you see what she wrote?"

"Forget Rosie—I'd be *so* pissed if I were Julius Gong. Like, damn, she really *went there*—"

Abigail continues, louder, clearly in an effort to drown them out. "Of course the tone was a tad harsh in places, and I feel like we really need to set aside some time and dissect your hatred toward Julius—"

My eyes close briefly with horror. "Please, I beg of you, don't mention him." I don't want to ever hear his name again or see him or be reminded in any way of his existence. I don't want to remember the heat of his lips near my skin, the glint in his eyes, the malice dripping from his voice.

"Fine, but what I'm saying is, you didn't do anything illegal. You were just being honest. If I were you, darling, I would own it. Let them fear you a little. Let them know that you have your own thoughts and feelings too."

"I just don't understand how it happened," I tell her, walking faster. If I slow down, if I think too hard, I'll fall apart. "I would never, *ever* send those emails out. It must have been some kind of computer virus. God, I knew I shouldn't have downloaded those mock papers from that dodgy website. I only did it because they weren't available anywhere else."

Abigail chews her lip. "Well, I . . ." But whatever she's about to say dies on her tongue as she comes to an abrupt halt at the end of the hall.

It doesn't take long to figure out why.

Next to our shiny awards display cabinet, filled with countless trophies and medals for everything from the rowing club to the chess team to interstate debating, there's a framed photo of Julius and me. We had taken it in a professional photo shoot not long after we were announced as cocaptains. We're both wearing the full school uniform, his tie fastened, my black hair pulled into a tight bun, our badges pinned to the center of our pockets. He has his arms crossed loosely over his chest, his air of superiority palpable even through the glass frame. I'm smiling more than he is, the freckles scattered over my full cheeks obvious in the light of the camera flash, my thick lashes successfully curled to look even longer.

The photographer had requested that we stand closer together until we were touching, but neither of us was willing to budge any farther, so there's still a good inch of distance between us.

And now, in that gap, someone's drawn a red, jagged line all the way down the middle.

They've also added a spear in my hand, and a sword in his. Instead of cocaptains, we look like we're going to war against each other. Like we belong on the poster of some low-budget superhero movie.

"Oh my god," I breathe.

Abigail purses her lips. "Don't panic—"

I panic.

"This is awful," I hiss under my breath, pressing two hands to the glass like I can somehow reach through and scrub the photo clean. "This looks so bad. This makes *us* look so bad."

"I know what you mean, but if it helps, you both actually look pretty hot—"

"*Abigail.*" It's a half cry of protest, half yell of distress. I hate that I even need to be comforted; *I'm* always the one who comforts other people. I hate needing anything from anyone.

"Okay, okay, got it." She grabs my arms and gently steers me away from the cabinet, speaking in the same soothing tone I've heard meditation instructors adopt. "Look, my darling, it isn't the end of the world. People are only reacting this way because they're surprised. Like, everyone was under the assumption that you two were getting along just fine, especially since you're cocaptains and all, and now that there's drama, they're going to latch on to it. But it'll blow over on its own in a couple days or so."

"Are you sure?" I ask her, scanning the area. In the sea of schoolbags and binders and blue-and-white blazers, more curious gazes catch on mine, then slide over to the vandalized photo. My throat fills with humiliation.

"I'm very confident," Abigail reassures me. But she blinks rapidly when she says it, the way she does when she's lying.

CHAPTER FIVE

The bakery is usually crowded after school.

I push through the doors and let the familiar scent of coconut and butter and sweet milk envelop me. It smells like home. Feels like it too. Our bakery is nestled right in the middle of town, next to the Korean barbecue place everyone goes to in the winter and the Asian grocery with its never-ending supply of Wang Wang gummy candies and fish sauce and braised beef instant noodles. A little farther out is the theater, where you can find the latest wuxia films and Chinese rom-coms and sci-fi films, and the dim sum restaurant that gives out free newspapers to the elderly, and the nail salon that'll do your manicure for free if you're suffering through a breakup.

All of it is as intimate to me as the path to my own house.

I drop my bag down by the counter and squeeze past the customers lined up with their trays of bread. Custard swirls, tuna buns, green tea mochi, jam doughnuts. Tiny cakes layered with diced strawberries and kiwi fruit and fresh-whipped cream. Normally I would wait until everyone was gone to sneak one of the leftover cupcakes from the shelves, but today I feel too sick to even contemplate eating.

"Catch!"

I spin around just in time to see the bright blur of color streaking toward me. By instinct, my hands shoot up and grab the basketball seconds before it can smash my nose.

"A warning would have been nice," I grumble as Max walks up to me.

"Yeah, that's why I said *catch*," Max says, grabbing the basketball back only to spin it on one finger. His black, bristly hair is so shiny that at first I think he's just showered but, upon closer inspection, is the result of a disgusting amount of hair gel.

"Aren't you meant to be on campus right now?" I ask. Max has never shown much interest in our bakery, but he's been visiting even less ever since he moved into his college dorm. Whenever he does choose to pop in, it's because he claims to be too lazy to cook for himself. "Surely even you sports students have actual classes to attend."

He shrugs. "Skipped them. The lectures were boring."

"You can't just— You can't *skip* your classes." *Not when your tuition costs almost as much as what the bakery makes in a year*, I'm tempted to add, but don't. My brother's life is a simple, happy one, comprising just four things: breakfast, lunch, dinner, and basketball. It's the life I want for him, the life I swore to myself I'd let him keep, even with our dad gone.

"Sure I can," he says with an easy smile. "Everyone does it. And it's enough having one perfect student in the family, yeah?"

My expression threatens to waver, my stomach coiling around

itself. Here, in the warmth of the bakery, the email disaster doesn't even seem totally real. I try to swallow, but it feels like swallowing a hard pill without water.

"Where's Mom?" I ask him, sidestepping the subject. It's a miracle my voice holds strong.

"She's in the back."

He bounds after me, humming some sort of video game soundtrack as I slip through the kitchen and find her inside. She's leaning against the wall by the bins, using a broom to support herself like she doesn't have the energy to carry her own weight, her complexion pale beneath the flickering fluorescent bulbs, the hollows under her eyes dark. My heart pinches. She looks exhausted, but that's nothing new.

"Here, I can sweep this place up for you," I tell her in the cheeriest voice I can muster.

She blinks. Shakes her head. "No, no. I'm okay. You focus on your schoolwork."

"I don't have much schoolwork," I lie, even as my mind flips through all my tasks for tonight, my assignments due tomorrow, the articles I still need to write.

Mom hesitates, her bony hands tightening over the broom.

"Give it to me," I say firmly, yanking the broom away from her. "I've got it."

But Max elbows me. "Hold up. Didn't you say you were going to help me practice my passes?"

He's right. I did promise him that.

"I can practice with you while I clean up," I say. "Just don't knock anything over."

"Are you certain you can handle it?" Mom asks, frowning at me. Neither of us even entertains the possibility of Max helping with the cleaning. The last time he did, he managed to knock over all the bins and spent hours picking pieces of eggshell off the ground. "Don't you want to rest first or—"

"Mom, I promise, it's no problem." I laugh at her with such ease I almost believe myself and push her lightly toward the door. I can feel the ridges of her spine underneath my fingertips. There's no meat, only bone and muscle, the results of labor.

As soon as she's out of sight, I start sweeping on autopilot. Half the blisters on my palms and fingers are from gripping the pen too long. The other half are from this.

Beside me, Max starts dribbling the ball. "Ready?" he asks.

I take my left hand off the broom. "Okay. Go." The basketball shoots across the space and lands perfectly in my palm. I bounce it a few times before tossing it over to him, which he catches just as easily.

"Damn, not bad. Not bad *at all*," he says. "You should join the team."

I roll my eyes. "No need to flatter me."

The basketball comes flying back. "For real," he insists, then pauses. "Well, you might need to build some muscle—"

This time, I aim the basketball at his face. "I'm stronger than you are."

"No, *I'm* clearly the strongest in the family," he protests. "Remember, even Dad said—"

We both falter. The ball thuds to the floor and rolls off toward the shelves as we both do our best to act like nothing's happened, like he doesn't exist. But it's impossible, like attempting to cover up a murder scene with napkins. It's easier to remember how things used to be, those hazy, long-gone afternoons when my dad and Max and I would hang around in our small backyard and race one another and play basketball until dinnertime—

No. I stop myself before the nostalgia can sneak up on me. I refuse to miss him, to want him back in our lives.

"You do need more practice," I say mildly.

Max scrambles to retrieve the ball, and when we start passing it back and forth again, we're both careful not to bring him up. Still, the topic nags at my mind. Not for the first time I wonder if he blames me for what happened too. If that's the reason for the faint but always noticeable friction between us, why he only comes back once every week or so, why half our conversations seem to lapse into silence.

By the time we finish, the sun has already disappeared. I save all the leftover bread in a massive container for our neighbors: the Duongs, who both work two jobs to feed their five children; the old nainai who's been living alone since her partner passed away three winters ago, and only speaks a few sentences of English; the Henan-born divorcée who always brings us fresh lemons plucked from the tree in her own yard. I make sure to add a few extra slices of strawberries to the cakes before we close the store.

Then the three of us squeeze onto the late bus home, the bread balanced on my lap, my bulky schoolbag crammed under my arm, Max's basketball cradled in his. The air inside smells like plastic and perfume, and there's a kid sitting behind me who has decided to play kickball with the back of my seat.

Thud.

Thud. Thud.

Irritation flares up in my throat.

Ignore it, I tell myself. *It's not worth making a fuss over, and it'll be your stop soon anyway.* I turn my attention to the scenery as it unfolds outside the window. The streetlights are slowly replaced by old oaks, gray turning to green, the space between houses growing wider and wider until we're fully in the suburbs—

Thud. Thud. Thud.

I take a deep breath. Squeeze my fists again, try to relax each muscle in my fingers one by one. But my fists stay clenched, and without anything better to distract me, the images I've been trying to keep at bay all evening flash through my head. Julius greeting the aunties with his fake smile and false charm. Georgina backing away from our group project. Julius laughing with the girl next to him. Rosie storming up to me, her eyes narrowed in accusation. Julius leaning forward in the gardens, the scratch of his voice against my ear: *I think you're obsessed with me, Sadie Wen.* His twisted smirk, his cold, cutting gaze.

Thud. Thud—

"Can you stop that?" I snap, whipping my head around.

The kid freezes. My mother freezes too; she looks stunned.

I'm shocked myself. The words don't feel like they could have come out of my own mouth. It's like somebody has removed every filter I've fixed in place, cleared out a direct path from my brain to my lips.

Then, to my absolute horror, the kid bursts into noisy tears.

Oh god.

Oh my god. I just made a teeny-tiny human cry. What is *wrong* with me today?

"S-sorry," I mumble, heat rushing up my neck. The passengers around us are all staring at me, probably wondering what kind of monster I am. I couldn't be more relieved when the bus rolls to a stop on our street. I grab my container of bread and hop off with record speed. The child is still wailing as the automatic doors fold shut.

In the following quiet, Max makes a low whistling sound. "Damn, I really thought you were going to punch the kid for a second there. Kind of scary, not going to lie."

Mom peers over at me. "Is everything okay, Sadie?"

I push down the lump in my throat. "Yeah, of course," I say brightly. "I'm sorry. I was just . . . annoyed. And I *wasn't* going to punch anyone," I add, shooting Max a look.

She studies me a moment longer, then sniffs. I wait for her to tell me off. "Well, I know I'm not supposed to admit this because

I'm an adult, but I wanted to yell at that young boy too. Come on," she adds, lifting the container from my arms and turning toward our house. It's recognizable even in the darkness, with its jade-green roof and the fairy lights strung up over the front porch. "You should shower and sleep early. You still have school tomorrow."

School tomorrow.

The reminder hits me like a mallet to the stomach. I don't know how I'm going to survive it.

CHAPTER SIX

Nothing good has ever happened in the Main Hall before.

It's where we take our final exams and where we were forced to sit through unbearable lectures on *our changing bodies* and where Ray once dropped a banana behind the podium and the rats managed to find it before the teachers could.

So I'm instantly apprehensive when we're directed to the hall right after lunch.

"What's going on?" I ask Abigail as we find seats at the very back. The entire room is basically designed to be depressing, with its drab, windowless walls and uncomfortable plastic chairs. A whole year after the incident, the stench of the rotten banana still lurks around like the villain from a major movie franchise—impossible to track down and never fully killed.

"I was hoping you'd know," Abigail says between loud bites of her kaya toast. The sticky note on her lunch box today reads KEEP SHINING! "Don't school captains get advance notice of this stuff?"

"Not this," I say, scanning the room for clues. There's a laptop set up near the projector, and a thermos sitting on the hardwood floor, which means we're getting a presentation of some sort. Then, without meaning to, my gaze slides to Julius in the second row—just as he lifts his head and glowers at me.

A shock goes through my body at the venomous look on his face. I'd hoped his anger would dissipate after yesterday, but it seems to have only fermented.

It's not just him. Word about my emails must have spread to everyone in our class by now. When I sit down, the girl next to me scowls and scoots her chair away as if I'm the source of the banana smell.

My stomach burns.

The sound of clacking heels distracts me briefly from my misery. A serious-looking woman around my mom's age strides up to the front, her blonde hair pulled into a bun so tight I pity her scalp, a school visitor badge pinned to her tweed jacket. SAMANTHA HOWARD, it says, underneath a blurry photo of her. She doesn't say anything, just surveys us like we've collectively committed a crime against her family pet, and presses a button. The projector flickers on, casting a slideshow onto the giant white screen behind her.

I take one glance at the title—"The Digital Student: Online Etiquette and Cybersafety"—before my stomach plummets, my misery returning with full intensity.

"Your school called me in light of . . . recent events," she begins, confirming my very worst suspicions. "They've asked that I give you a refresher on how we should conduct ourselves through digital communication channels."

Thirty pairs of eyes instantly flicker to me.

I've done it, I think to myself. *I've discovered hell on earth, and it's right here.*

"Now, you might be under the impression that since you're the younger generation and you grew up with your little tablets and laptops and iPads and gadgets, you don't need any advice, right? You know exactly what you're doing, right? *Wrong*," she says, so loudly a few people jump. "Before we dive in, let's have a quick show of hands: How many of you in this room have a social media account of some kind?"

There's a brief moment's hesitation. Then every single hand in the room goes into the air.

"That's very disappointing," Samantha Howard says on a heavy sigh. "Not surprising, but disappointing. And tell me: How many of you post frequently on these accounts? Videos and photos and the like?"

A few hands are lowered, but most of them stay up.

"This is your first mistake," Samantha tells us. "Everything you post will leave a permanent mark on the internet. Every comment, every interaction, every *selfie*." She spits out the word like it's the name of someone who once poisoned her morning tea. "After today's session, I hope you all go back and private your posts. Better yet, delete all your accounts completely. Keep your content to yourself—" She pauses midsentence and blinks at Abigail. "Yes? Do you have a question?"

Abigail stands up, her expression almost as grave as Samantha's, her platinum hair swinging over her shoulder. "Yes, just one." She clears her throat. "What do we do if we're really feeling ourselves?"

Snorts of laughter travel around the room.

Samantha frowns. "This is not a joke. This is a matter of security—"

"I don't think you're understanding," Abigail says innocently. "I'm talking about, like, *really* feeling ourselves. Have you never drawn the perfect cat wing and felt the utmost need to share it online, for it to be saved in perpetuity, to become your lasting legacy? Don't you think it's a crime *not* to show the world the new black dress I bought and how good it makes my figure look?" She finishes her little speech by falling back in her seat and grinning at me.

And though I really should disapprove, I have to bite my lip to stop from laughing as well. Partly because I know why she's doing this. Abigail has never minded being disruptive in class, but she's always more disruptive when she senses that I'm in a bad mood. It's her way of simultaneously raising my blood pressure and my spirits.

"I assure you, young lady, that's not the kind of legacy you want to leave," Samantha says, her nostrils flaring. "This is exactly what I'm talking about. I know your prefrontal cortexes haven't fully developed yet, but you have to start thinking *beyond* your impulses in the moment. Your digital footprint could affect your school records, your future colleges, your future *jobs*. Let's all take a look at examples of what you should be avoiding, shall we?"

She moves on to the next slide, which is a mock-up of an email.

Dear Brady,

Your personality sucks, your face sucks, and your existence sucks. I don't like you very much at all. You should run out in front of a train.

The room's attention swivels back to me.

I duck my head, my whole face red-hot with humiliation. Even though it's not *my* email, the reference is clear—and, evidently, deliberate.

"Can somebody tell me what's wrong with this?" Samantha asks. Nobody volunteers, and for a few incredibly naive, foolish seconds, I think I might be safe. We can get back to that nice lecture on how posting selfies will result in our inevitable murder. But then Samantha looks out at the room. "Participation is important. If we're feeling shy, I'll pick someone at random. How about . . ."

So long as it's not Julius, I pray in my head, my fingernails digging into my skirt. *Just don't let it be Julius—*

"You," Samantha says, and points right at Julius.

Maybe I should run out in front of a train.

"Me?" Julius repeats as our class dissolves into furious whispers. When he rises from his seat, his back straight, hands in his pockets, I'm offered an unwanted view of his side profile. For once, he doesn't look smug about being called on to answer a question.

"Yes. What's the problem with this example?" Samantha

prompts. "Should someone—no matter how they're feeling—send out an email like this?"

Julius's eyes cut to me, quick as lightning, cold as ice. "Well, I don't think anyone should ever *write* an email like this to begin with. It's remarkably immature, and a sign of the sender's unresolved anger issues—not to mention low self-esteem."

"But what if the recipient deserved it?"

I don't realize I've stood up and spoken until everyone whirls around to stare at me, the concentrated weight of their attention like a hammer to the stomach. But I'm only staring back at one person. Julius. The tightness of his jaw, the darkness of his eyes.

"So you're saying it's the recipient's fault," Julius says with a laugh. "Wow. Sure."

Okay, stop talking, the logical part of my brain tells me. *Shut up and sit down right now.*

But my mouth seems to have cut ties with my brain. "I'm just saying that maybe if the recipient were a *little* less infuriating and wasn't *quite* so adamant on tormenting the sender for years on end—"

"Maybe if someone weren't so sensitive—"

"It's called having a normal human reaction. Emotions, you understand. I know that may be a foreign concept—"

"Excuse me, you two," Samantha calls tersely from the podium. "This isn't the point of the activity."

We both do something we would never dare with a teacher—not even an art teacher—we ignore her.

"You didn't seem to care so much about anyone else's reaction when you were writing the emails," Julius says, his voice rising.

"Again, I didn't mean for them to *get out*," I snap. I'm very distantly aware that the hall has gone dead quiet, that everyone's watching, listening, witnessing this. Someone's holding up their phone. But nothing registers except the anger pumping thick through my blood, the desire to destroy the boy standing across from me. "I was just venting—"

"Have you ever heard of a diary, Sadie? It might be a worthy investment."

"Don't disgust me. I would never write diary entries about you—"

He cocks his head. Smiles with his lips but not his eyes. "And yet it's clear I'm all you ever think about."

"Think about *killing*," I amend, grinding my teeth together. I could kill him right now.

"See?" Julius gestures to me, as if delivering a speech. "This is what I mean about the unresolved anger issues."

"You mean that you're the source of them? Because yeah, you'd be correct—"

"*Silence!*" Samantha yells.

I snap my mouth shut and pull my attention away from Julius.

It could just be the unflattering artificial lights in the hall, but Samantha's face has turned an awful shade of gray. The veins in her forehead are on open display, so visible they could be used as a diagram for first-year premed students. "*Never*," she seethes, "in all my years of visiting schools have I come across students so—so *rude* and undisciplined. This behavior is absolutely unacceptable." She stabs a finger toward our badges. "And you're meant to be the school captains? This is the kind of example you choose to set for your peers?"

I hadn't thought it possible to taste any new flavors of humiliation, but apparently I can. The skin on my cheeks and the back of my neck is so hot it itches.

"Before coming here, all I'd heard about Woodvale was how it's one of the top academic institutions in the state. Selective. *Prestigious*." She yanks out the cord from her laptop as she speaks. "But this is—well, it's just beyond disappointing." Picks up her thermos from the floor. "I'm afraid I simply cannot go on." Lifts a dramatic hand to her chest like an actress in a tragic play. "I'll have to end this early."

With that, she marches out the door, a few seconds of silence following close behind her.

Then Georgina says, hopefully, "Does this mean we get a free period?"

Before anyone can celebrate, the door swings open once more, and Samantha comes marching in again. Her complexion has changed from gray to crimson. "I just remembered that I won't be paid the speaker's fee if I don't stay for the full session." She sniffs and plugs her laptop back into the projector, continuing to the next slide as though that brief episode never happened. "Now, where were we? Ah, yes, your digital footprint . . ."

CHAPTER SEVEN

Two years ago, our final assignment for English was a class debate.

Julius had been placed on the affirmative team, and I'd been placed on the negative, the battle lines drawn early. In the lead-up to it, I'd spent weeks preparing, diving into academic articles, researching everything on our topic: whether human cloning should be legalized. On the day, my head was on fire. I was ready. Most of the time it seemed to me that I was only pretending to be smart, like an actor who has to play a neurosurgeon. What mattered was convincing other people I was intelligent.

But as I stood up to make my points, I felt it too. My mind whirred, as smooth and fast as a machine, and my hands remained perfectly steady over the cue cards. I didn't even need to look at them. I was so familiar with Julius's logic that I could predict his arguments and counterarguments in advance, could spot the gaps in his reasoning, prod at the inconsistencies in his evidence. I remember the uncommon quiet of the classroom as I spoke clearly and calmly, keeping my eyes on him the whole time. Nothing could faze me. When I finished, there was a beat of stunned silence, and I'd heard someone whisper *whoa* in a tone of genuine awe. Then the applause had come, building into a crescendo, cheers rising over the claps. It was one of the most satisfying moments of my life.

I'd ended up winning not only the debate, but Best Speaker. When the final results were announced, Julius had glared at me, his jaw locked, his eyes blazing with an intensity that almost startled me. I'd always been confident that I hated him a little more than he hated me—but in that moment, I wasn't so sure.

It's the same resentful expression he's wearing the next morning when I bump into him outside the math classroom.

Literally.

I'm about to head inside the exact second he steps out. My face crashes straight into his shoulder.

I lurch backward, rubbing my nose, certain he's going to make a jibe about my poor coordination or demand an apology or mock me for the emails again, but instead he fixes me with that awful, sharp look and says: "We've been asked to see the principal."

My heart stops beating.

"What?" I choke out. My first half hope, half instinct is that he's pulling a prank on me, messing with my head, that this is his perverse means of revenge. He should know this is my worst fear.

But then he moves past me, down the hall in the direction of the principal's office, and my heartbeat starts up again at twice its normal speed.

"Wait," I call, running after him. He slows down slightly

without turning back. "Wait, you're being serious? We have to go right now?"

"No, Sadie, we are expected to see him twenty-three years down the line," he says, his voice so dry and scathing it could cut open bone. "I am only telling you now so that you have sufficient time to prepare."

I'm too panicked to think of a comeback. "But—did he say why?"

"You are awfully perceptive today. Why do you think? What event has occurred in the past forty-eight hours that is so terrible it warrants an in-person meeting with the principal himself?"

Yet even as he's talking, the answer has already come to me. The emails. Of course it can only be that. I choke down a hysterical laugh. The last time I'd visited the principal, it had been with Julius as well, but it was because we had both broken the record for having the highest grade-point average in the history of the school. A *remarkable achievement*, according to the principal, and something I ought to have celebrated, except our averages were *exactly* the same, all the way to the second decimal. I'd left that meeting promising myself I would boost my average so it was higher than his.

Maybe Julius is remembering the same thing, because his upper lip curls. "This is a first for me, you realize. I've never been called to the principal for anything other than good news."

"A first for *you*?" I hiss. Class should have officially started by now, so the hallways are all empty, save for us. It feels strange to walk past the rows and rows of closed classrooms. Through the narrow glass panes in the doors, I can see the teachers marking off the roll, students shuffling through their notes. "I've literally never been in trouble before—"

"Before two days ago," he cuts in, "in which you managed to offend half the faculty and student body in one go. Oh, and yesterday, when you decided to start a petty argument with me in front of the entire class. It's a pretty impressive feat, if you think about it. You always like to outdo yourself, don't you?"

"*You* were the one who was arguing with me."

"Well, we wouldn't have been in that position in the first place if not for your emails. Thanks to you, the entire school's talking about us. It's anarchy. And did you see what they drew over our captains' photo? There was red marker." He pauses for emphasis. "On my *face*."

I doubt he would look this incensed if someone had vandalized the *Mona Lisa*.

"If I were you," he continues, "I'd be thinking up a very good explanation right now. Even if you didn't send the emails, you're the one who *wrote* them and dragged both of us into this mess—"

"Oh my god, shut up."

He falters briefly, then gives me an odd sort of smile, like he's caught me doing something I shouldn't, like he knows me better than I want him to. My skin tingles from the unwelcome attention. "Your language turns cruder by the day. Decided to drop the model student act for good?"

"Seriously, Julius," I say through clenched teeth, lifting my hand, "if you don't stop talking, I'll—"

"Hit me?" His smile sharpens, as though in challenge. It's a smile that says *you wouldn't dare*. "Choke me, the way you fantasized about in your email?"

Immediately, my skin goes so hot I wouldn't be surprised if you could see steam rising from my body. "Are you ever going to let it go?"

"No," he says, decisive. "Not until we're even."

"What do I have to do, then?" I demand. "For us to be even?"

He stops, his black eyes raking my face. I force myself to meet his gaze, even though everything in me wants to run away. "I'll let you know how you can make it up to me," he says, letting the words simmer in the space between us, stretching out the threat. "But first, I have to see how bad the damage is."

A spike of pure, cold dread runs through me when I realize we've reached the principal's office. Even though it's in the same building, it feels like a completely separate space. The paint on the walls is newer, the windows wider, the plaque that reads PRINCIPAL MILLER polished gold. The single door to his office is made of tinted glass, the kind that serves as a one-sided mirror. I imagine Principal Miller staring at us from his desk, watching me as I wipe my sweaty hands on my skirt. The thought only makes my palms clammier.

Julius stares down at the doorknob, but makes no movement.

"Why aren't you going in?" I ask.

"Why can't you go in first?" He says it coolly, as if I'm the one who's being ridiculous, but there's a wariness to his expression. His eyes keep sliding to the door like it might open up the gates of hell.

He's nervous, I realize. I would take much greater delight in this discovery if I didn't feel like throwing up my breakfast all over the white rug at my feet.

"Just go in," I urge him.

He doesn't budge. "You go."

"What are you so scared of?"

"I'm not scared," he says, actively backing away from the door now. "I just don't want to be the first to step inside."

I make a sound halfway between a snort and a sigh. "This is so childish—"

"*You're* being childish. I'm being chivalrous."

"Right," I say, rolling my eyes so far I can almost see the back of my skull. "Because you're such a gentleman."

"I am."

"Open the door, Julius."

"No, *you*—"

"Come in," a gravelly voice calls from inside.

I startle, my pulse skyrocketing. It takes me a moment to recover, another moment to shove the door open on my own, cursing Julius silently in my head.

Principal Miller is reclining back in his leather seat, spinning a ballpoint pen with one hand, holding a takeaway coffee cup in the other. The whole office smells like coffee. The reading lamp beside him is a pale, clinical white that reminds me of hospital waiting rooms, the light glancing off his bald head.

"Hi, Principal Miller," I manage, trying to read his expression. It's pointless, like trying to find a pattern in a blank wall. His dark eyes are devoid of emotion, the space between his thick brows smooth. "You . . . You asked for us?"

In response, he merely gestures to the two seats across the desk from him.

The chair is still warm when I sit down, and I can't help thinking about the last person who was in here. Maybe they were expelled, or given detention, or maybe they were being congratulated on coming in first place in a national equestrian competition or finding a cure for eczema. That's the thing about being called by the principal—you know it's either really good news or really bad news.

Julius takes his place on my left, his spine rigid.

"I know you're both meant to be in class right now, so I'll cut to the chase," Principal Miller begins, setting his pen down. "It has come to my attention that a series of rather . . . aggressively worded emails have been circulating around the school. Is that correct?"

My mouth is too dry for me to speak. I can only nod.

"Ah," he says. It's just one syllable, yet it sounds horribly ominous. "And is it also correct that you addressed many of these emails to your cocaptain and called him, among other things . . ." He glances at his computer monitor and clears his throat. "A *spoiled brat*, an *insufferable thorn*, a *cold-hearted deceiver*, and a certain word that refers to the . . . downward region of the human anatomy?"

I blink. "Sorry?"

Principal Miller shoots me a pointed look.

"Oh, right—you mean *assho*—" I clamp my mouth shut, but not before I catch Julius laughing into his fist. It's nice that he can still find it in himself to make fun of me under our present circumstances. Very heartening.

"Now, normally, we do not like to interfere with personal disputes between our students," the principal says. "But in this specific scenario, I'm afraid I have to. After yesterday's session, Samantha Howard has expressed her grievances to me regarding your shocking behavior. Disrupting the class, fighting with each other, making *open threats*. Needless to say, she has a terrible impression of our school, and she won't be coming back here again."

"I'm sorry, Principal Miller, but she's exaggerating," Julius says. I have to admire the fact that he can even find the courage to speak. I'm just about ready to curl into the fetal position. "Yes, Sadie and I were having a somewhat . . . lively conversation, and perhaps we got carried away, but it's really not as bad as—"

"As this?" Principal Miller holds up his phone.

We both lean in with confusion.

A video is playing on loop over the screen. A fan-edit, to be exact, of Caz Song—that popular actor all my cousins in China have a major crush on. We watch about five seconds of him running his hand through his hair to special flash effects before Principal Miller abruptly retracts the phone and scrolls down.

"Sorry," he says, turning the screen around again. "Not that one. *This.*"

The new video is less confusing, but infinitely more concerning. It must have been taken by one of our classmates during the cybersecurity session yesterday. Julius and I are both standing up and—even in the bad lighting of the hall—very clearly arguing. My hands are clenched tighter than they are now, and his chin is lifted at a defiant angle, his jaw taut.

"It seems you learned absolutely nothing from the session, because this is a blatant breach of the school's IT policy." Principal Miller shakes his head. "We've asked the student to take the video down, of course, but it had already gained fifty-three views."

Julius lets out a sound that could very well be a scoff. Privately, I agree with the sentiment. "Only? That's barely anything—"

"Fifty-three is fifty-three too many," Principal Miller cuts in with a stern look. "As it stands, the video was seen by one of the mothers who attended the tour. She had been planning on sending her daughter to our school, but she's since changed her mind, and the other mothers are reconsidering too. This has already reached the school board, and needless to say, they're most displeased. Do you understand the severity of the situation?"

I nod, fast, clenching my teeth to stop them from knocking together. I'm still not entirely sure which direction this is going, but I can already predict it's going to end with a crash. All I can do is brace myself for the impact.

"Right now, our chief concern is making sure we prevent any further negative impacts to the school's image and culture." His eyes land first on Julius, then on me. "As a solution, we ask that you work closely together over the coming month to bridge your differences, until your tensions have dissolved. I don't just mean in your regular captain duties, but across the school, throughout various activities. Consider it a show of comradery."

My stomach drops.

I'm already around Julius Gong way too often—I can't imagine spending even *more* time with him. I don't think I'll be able to without losing my sanity or leaving his body in a ditch.

When I glance over at him, he looks equally horrified, as if the principal has just proposed that he snuggle up with a feral cat. And though the feeling is very much mutual, it still drives a small, blunt nail into my gut. Turns out I always want to be wanted, even by the boy I loathe.

"With all due respect, I didn't do anything," Julius says. His voice is level, almost convincingly calm, yet there's a breathless edge to his sentence. His hands flex over the wooden armrests, like he's trying to steady himself against them. "*I* wasn't the one who wrote the emails. Why do I—"

"It may seem unfair, but the reality is you're both involved. If you are unhappy with my proposal or unwilling to take the necessary steps to resolve your conflict, I will have to reconsider your suitability for the role and contact your parents—"

"No," Julius says sharply, with such force the principal flinches. "Apologies," he adds, quieter, recomposing himself, though I can still see the muscle working in his jaw. "I only mean . . . I only mean that I agree with your solution."

"I'm glad you're being reasonable," Principal Miller says. Then he turns to me. "And you, Sadie? Are you happy to cooperate?"

Happy is hardly the right word for it. *Disgusted* would be more fitting. Or *appalled*. Or *incensed*. I've never resented anything more. But it's not like I have much of a choice in this. Without my captaincy on my final transcript, Berkeley could cancel my admission. Forget Julius. I would force myself to work with the devil if it meant I could keep my future plans intact. I'm supposed to be the reliable child in the family, the person most likely to succeed and turn our lives around. My mom and my brother are counting on me.

"Yes," I get out. "I am."

"Excellent." The principal claps his hands together, smiling at both of us. He's the only one. "In that case, you can start by cleaning the bike shed together after school."

CHAPTER EIGHT

The bike sheds at Woodvale Academy are a more reliable source of information than the school newsletter.

Instead of vague updates about the rowing regatta or the new netball court or the teacher who's leaving because of "unforeseen circumstances," you can find the real news scribbled in bright markers over the walls. Breakups, betrayals, scandals; who's popular this week and who's dating someone new. It's almost artistic in an avant-garde way, the blend of cute, curly fonts with sharp, angry letters and doodled hearts and struck-out names and half poems. By now there's more writing than blank space on the gray bricks.

And we're supposed to clean it all up.

I let the bucket and brush I'm carrying thunk to the ground. For a moment, I can only stare with horror, processing the sheer scale of our job. This will take us hours at the very least if we're quick—and judging from the way Julius is holding the hose like it's a dead snake, we probably won't be.

In fact, I doubt Julius has scrubbed a single thing in his life.

"This is ridiculous," he says, shaking his head. "This is just the school's excuse to make us do manual labor."

"Well, we better get started." I tug my hair free from its usual high bun, flipping it over my head and smoothing it with my fingers before retying it into a ponytail. I straighten in time to catch Julius staring at me, a strange, faintly confused look on his face. "What?"

"Nothing. I've just . . . never seen you with your hair down before."

I feel myself bristle. "And?"

"What do you mean, *and*?" His mouth puckers. "It was only an observation."

"With you, there's always an *and*," I tell him, fighting the sudden urge to touch my hair, to flatten it, to check it in a mirror. It's true that I never wear my hair down at school, partly because the rules don't allow you to if your hair's any longer than shoulder-length—though the younger, nicer teachers don't really care—and partly because it gets in the way when I'm jogging or taking notes. "Your entire existence is basically a run-on sentence."

At this, his expression readjusts itself into a familiar sneer. "And here I'd thought you'd already used up every possible insult in your emails."

"Don't worry, I can always think of more." I pick up the brush again and step forward before he can respond. "Okay, for simplicity's sake, let's split this between us. You can hose down the walls, and I'll scrub."

"Why me?" he demands. "Why can't you use the hose?"

I breathe in deeply through my nostrils. I can't believe the principal thinks this plan will help us *bridge* our differences. If anything, my desire to throttle Julius has only tripled since this morning. "Because," I say, keeping my tone as neutral as possible, "to be honest with you, I don't think you know how to scrub."

The corner of his lip twists farther down. "Of course I know how."

"Right," I tell him, unconvinced.

"I'll prove it to you." As he speaks, he pulls out a pair of black gloves from his pockets and starts snapping them on.

"What is that?" I frown at him. "Why on earth are you wearing gloves? We're not here to rob a building."

"Protecting my skin. I have very nice hands—as you have already observed in the past. It would be a shame to ruin them."

My face flushes despite myself.

"Here." He throws the hose to me and takes the brush in his perfectly gloved fingers. "Watch."

I do. I turn the hose on and spray a small patch of the wall and watch, incredulous, as he moves the brush around in a pathetic circular motion. The bricks are darker, the surface shining with water, but none of the marker comes off. Actually, I think he's managed to smudge it further.

"Why are you massaging the wall?" I ask him.

He stops. Spins around with a scowl. "Forgive me for not attacking it like some *animal*—"

"You're wasting time." I tip my head up, scan the sky. The light has already started to fade from a brilliant cerulean to a heavy indigo, and most of the cars have pulled out of the parking lot across the oval. Panic pinches my stomach. My mom will be waiting for me to get home and make dinner. I still have to defrost the pork ribs and turn the rice cooker on and stew the soup—

"I can still do it better than you," Julius insists, moving the brush over a pair of initials that reads AJ + BH FOREVER. It's since been crossed out and replaced by the words AJ + LE FOREVER.

My frustration boils fast inside me. "Oh my god, you're so stubborn."

"You're so bossy," he shoots back.

"Difficult," I seethe.

"Demanding."

"Arrogant."

"Impatient."

"Cynical." I speak over him, my fists clenching around the hose as more water spews out. "Snobby—"

"Overcritical," he jeers at me.

"Manipulative—"

"Judgmental— *Hey, watch it.*"

I jerk back and lower the hose, but it's too late. The water's sprayed everywhere, soaking through half his shirt and his hair. By some stroke of luck or dark magic, the black strand hanging over his forehead remains unmoved. But everything else about him is disheveled. His sleeves are wrinkled from the damp, his tie unraveling from his collar. As he stands there, dripping wet, blinking fast against the water in his eyes, and wipes a gloved hand over his face, a bubble of laughter lurches to my throat.

"Sadie." He says my name like it's in itself a curse, his features tight with shock and disdain. And maybe all the recent drama has messed with my brain, because rather than tripping over myself with apologies or fretting over lost time, I double over, cackling.

"I'm—sorry," I squeeze out through my giggles. "I didn't—mean—"

His eyes narrow, but it's hard to take him seriously when the front of his shirt is plastered to his skin. "If I didn't know better, I'd think you did that on purpose."

"I swear—it wasn't—" I clutch my stomach, breathless with laughter, and it hits me out of nowhere that this is the first time I've really laughed in almost two days. It's like my body is a rubber band, stretched too tight in every direction—and now it's finally snapped, the tension released. I gulp down the cold, sweet air, filling my lungs with it.

Then he grabs the hose faster than I can react and turns it on me.

I yelp.

The violent blast of water is so cold it almost burns. It's in my nose, my half-opened mouth, the inside of my shirt. I can feel it running down my spine, pooling into my shoes. And the only clear thing in my blurred vision is Julius's face. He's smiling now, evidently pleased with himself.

"I'll kill you," I decide on the spot. "I'm literally going to kill you."

I lunge for the hose again, but he holds it up high over his head, out of reach. Taunting me.

"Give it," I snap.

"No way."

"I said, *give it*—" I jump and manage to wrap one hand around the end. He doesn't let go, though, just pulls it back as if we're playing tug-of-war, and next thing I know we're wrestling with it, and the water's still pumping out, drenching us both. I'm choking and shivering and yelling at him but somehow I'm laughing too, because of how ridiculous this is. Because I haven't had the chance to do something so ridiculous in a while, to behave like a child.

It's only when we're both soaked from head to toe and breathing hard that he steps back. Takes one look at me. Then abruptly twists away.

"What?" I say, confused.

"Our school shirts are made from polyester" comes his bizarre reply. He appears to be staring at the trimmed grass beneath his feet with extreme focus.

"Since when were you interested in textiles?"

He ignores my question. "And white polyester," he says, his voice strained, "once wet, becomes transparent."

I'm pretty sure some small part of me dies right there and then. Simply implodes. Disintegrates into ash. My skin is so hot I don't even register the ice-cold water anymore. I wrap my arms around myself in a futile attempt to cover up and make a frantic dive for my schoolbag before remembering that, *of course*, my blazer isn't there. I left it inside my locker, all the way on the other side of campus. Because that's my life now, apparently.

Just when I'm contemplating whether I should dig myself a ditch, Julius says, "My bag. My blazer's inside."

I pause. On their own, the words make perfect sense. But strung together, and coming from him, they might as well be an alien language. There's no way he's making an offer—

Except he continues, with some impatience, "The front compartment. Just don't rifle through any of my stuff."

I don't move. Surely, this is a trap.

He sighs. "If you won't get it yourself, I'm going to have to turn around—"

"No—don't you dare," I say hurriedly, even though his head remains bowed, his eyes fixed on the grass. "I-I'll grab it."

My hair is still dripping water as I unzip his bag, leaving dark splotches in the fabric. His blazer is folded neatly at the top, ironed smooth. On him, it's a perfect fit, practically tailored to his frame, the lines straight and sharp at the shoulders. But when I drape it over myself, it falls around me like a cape. I don't mind it though. It's warm and dry and it smells like him: like mint and cedar and the beginnings of something sweet, familiar, something that reminds me of summer when we were fourteen years old. Then I catch myself inhaling, hugging the soft fabric closer to my shivering body, and freeze.

There must be water lodged in my brain for me to be acting this way.

"Thanks," I say, willing my voice to sound normal. "You can turn around now."

He turns slowly. His gaze catches on the blazer where it ends just above the knee, covering up my skirt. A slight movement in his throat, like he's swallowing something sharp. "You better not lose it," he says at last. "All my badges are pinned on there, and many of them are limited editions. You couldn't replace them if you tried."

Whatever spark of gratitude I felt toward him flickers out. "I'll give it back to you tomorrow morning, all washed and dried. Happy?"

"You don't have to wash it," he says carelessly. Then, as if sensing my surprise, his eyes narrow. "I don't trust you to. You'll probably end up shrinking it anyway."

I would come up with a retort, but it occurs to me that what he said about polyester applies to him too. Now that he's fully facing me, I realize just how thin the school shirt is. The silvery-white material clings to the narrow curve of his waist, the lean cords of muscle in his arms.

When I speak again, I speak to the wall. "Do you . . . need to change?"

"Oh, good point," he says. "Let me just find the spare uniform

I always keep on hand in the event that my cocaptain attacks me with a hose."

"Suit yourself," I grumble, reaching for the brush. "Neither of us is allowed to leave until the job is done."

This time, he doesn't protest. He turns the water back on without another word and hoses down the wall to my left. It's probably less that he concedes I'll do a better job and more that he's concerned I'll spray him again, but at least we're being efficient. We work in silence, falling into a steady rhythm. He sprays one area, and I scrub it right after, scraping away secrets, names, curses, wishes. My hair has started to stiffen, hanging in thick, heavy clumps over my shoulders, and my shoes squelch unpleasantly every time I shift position. But Julius makes no complaints, so I don't either.

We're close to finished when I notice the message scrawled on the corner of a brick.

It's new, the black marker bold and fresh. Just five words, and my stomach drops out.

Sadie Wen is a bitch.

My ears ring. I blink at it, and the cold seems to congeal over my skin. My clothes are too itchy, my throat too tight; an awful, sick sensation builds inside me, swelling up to my chest, squeezing the breath out of me. I feel nauseous.

"What is it?" Julius asks, coming over.

Dread churns through me. He can't see. I can't bear the thought of him reading it, of him laughing at me or agreeing or rubbing it in. It's too humiliating. I'll die from it.

"Nothing," I say. I block it with my hand, but his eyes fall on my face first, and he glimpses something there that changes his demeanor at once. His gaze sharpens. His shoulders tense.

"What is it, Sadie?" he asks again, but in a different way. Lower, more serious. Urgent.

I just shake my head, my fingers splayed over the words. But even with them concealed, I can see them as if they've been etched into my own skin. *Sadie Wen is a bitch.* How long has the message been here? How many people have walked past it already? Did someone write it right after my emails were sent?

"Show me," Julius says.

"No—" My voice comes out small, shaky. "Don't—"

His long fingers wrap around my wrist, pulling it down, and then the words are there, exposed, starkly visible to the both of us. Shame stings my skin like acid, roils deep inside my gut.

For a long time, he doesn't say anything.

The quiet is maddening. I'm too scared to glimpse his face, to see any signs of contempt or glee. "I guess you're not the only one who hates me now," I comment, just to fill the silence with *something*, to try and pass it off as a joke. He can't know how much it hurts me. How easy it is to hurt me.

"That handwriting is hideous," Julius says finally. His tone is indecipherable. "It must be Danny's."

"Who?"

"Danny Yao, from history."

The name settles in the back of my mind like silt. Danny. I'd written him an angry email as well, even though it was three years ago. He had borrowed my protractor right before a big math test and lost it. He'd only thought to email me and let me know after the test was over, after I'd panicked and begged anyone I could find for a spare protractor. Funnily enough, it was Julius who'd handed one to me in the end—or, more like, he'd thrown it at me. *It's giving me a headache, watching you run up and down the school*, he had drawled, barely even looking in my direction. *And this way, you won't be able to make any weak excuses about being unprepared when I beat you.*

I wonder if he even remembers. I wonder if he keeps as clear a record of our every exchange as I do.

"Doesn't matter who did it," I mumble. "It's what everyone's thinking."

I can sense him watching me. My eyes burn, and I stare up at the violet sky, forcing the tears to recede before they can spill. I haven't cried since I was seven, since the day my dad left and I found my mom weeping quietly into her hands, curled up on the couch in the empty living room. The air in the house was so heavy it threatened to crush me. I had sworn then that I wouldn't cry, ever. I wouldn't add to her sadness, wouldn't drag her even further down. I would be the good daughter, the strong one, the one who kept everyone afloat.

"Well," Julius says from behind me, "it's a very uninspired choice of words. Such a basic pejorative denotes low intelligence."

This, of all things, jolts a weak laugh out of me. But I can't stop myself from glancing at the message again. It's a masochistic thing to do, foolish, like stretching out a broken leg to test how bad the damage is. My breath lodges in my throat as a fresh wave of pain washes over me.

Sadie Wen is a bitch.

It looks so ugly. Like a bloodstain.

As I stare, my stomach sinking lower and lower, Julius moves closer and loosens the brush from my stiff fingers. Then he brings it down hard over the brick and begins scrubbing, using so much force the muscles in his shoulders flex beneath his damp shirt. Unlike his previous attempt, he erases all the marker in one go.

"Done," he says, letting his arm fall back to his side. "Simple as that."

But nothing about this moment feels simple. I open my mouth, though I'm not sure what I plan to tell him. *Thanks? Please forget this ever happened? Do you think I'm a bitch too?* Before I can make up my mind, he's walking away. Not with his usual slow leopard's stride, as if it's a gift to mankind to simply see him in motion, but with purpose, like there's somewhere he needs to be. Someone he needs to find.

CHAPTER NINE

All throughout the next day, I feel like I'm walking around the school with a huge neon sign on my forehead: SADIE WEN IS A BITCH.

It doesn't help that other people are acting like it too. When I spot Rosie before history class and catch up to her in the corridors, she whirls around with such a frosty look in her eyes that my insides shrivel.

"What do you want, Sadie?" she asks, her voice tight. I remember how she smiled at me only three days ago, her straight white teeth gleaming. It's hard to believe she's the same person.

"I just—" I falter. I had come here prepared. I had a whole script memorized, starting with an elaborate, heartfelt apology and ending with a plea for forgiveness. But the words taste brittle on my tongue, and the longer the silence stretches, the more my courage buckles. "I only wanted— I know you're still mad— I mean, I would be mad too—" Everything comes out scrambled, in the wrong order.

"Yeah, I'm really pissed at you," she says, crossing her arms over her chest.

I hadn't expected her to say it outright. "I'm sorry," I try. "I really—"

She cuts me off. "Instead of apologizing, why don't you figure out a way to fix all this, hm? Once everyone's forgotten about the emails and stopped calling me a cheater, then we can talk." She doesn't wait for a response. She simply tidies her books, shoots me another glare that cuts all the way down to the pit of my stomach, and heads into the classroom without me.

Her words clang inside my head. *Fix this.*

It's what I've always done, or tried to do. Fix the back door in the bakery. Fix the error in the math worksheet. Fix the seating arrangement for student council. Fix the gap in my family, the holes in my life, patch everything up, smooth everything over. She's right. I just need to fix this too, and it'll all work out.

But how?

I'm so absorbed in my own thoughts that I'm almost late for history. I'm not the last one through the door, though—Danny Yao is.

My blood freezes as he brushes past me. The image of the bike shed presses against my mind. I imagine him cursing my name, scribbling the words over the wall, laughing about it with his friends. But then my attention goes to his face, and I stifle a gasp. His entire left eye is swollen shut, the skin around it a vivid purplish-blue. The bruise wasn't there yesterday afternoon.

"What happened to him?" I whisper to Abigail when I sit down.

Everyone else is whispering as well, gazes sliding to and away from him.

"He's been saying he got it from a motorcycle accident," Abigail murmurs, her voice thick with disbelief.

I frown. "A motorcycle accident?"

"Yeah. Last time I checked, he doesn't even know how to ride a bicycle."

I watch Danny make his way to the front of the classroom. He usually sits right behind Julius, but today he hesitates, then pulls up a chair two rows away. As he dumps his stuff out onto the table, his hair falls over his injured eye, and his features twist into a pronounced wince.

It would be far too arrogant to believe this is some sort of karma, that the universe has kindly overlooked all my mistakes and taken pity on me and stepped in on my behalf. But the timing also seems a little too perfect to be a pure coincidence . . .

"How's the email thing going?" Abigail asks, breaking through my confused jumble of thoughts.

I scan the seats around us. Most people are too busy filling in yesterday's worksheet—which I've already turned in—to be listening. Still, just to be safe, I tear out a fresh page from my notebook and scribble: *Everyone still hates my guts, if that's what you mean. But I'm planning on changing that. I just need to win them all over.*

Abigail reads it, then writes underneath my last sentence in pink gel pen: *Win them over?*

Yeah. I was thinking cupcakes, but that's probably insufficient?

Don't undersell yourself. You make some pretty incredible cupcakes, Abigail writes back.

I snort under my breath. *Are they so incredible they'd make you forget someone writing six hundred words about all the ways you'd wronged them in the past?*

Okay, fair point, she concedes. She pauses, tapping her pen against the paper the way she always does in tests when she's stuck on a question. Then the pen stills in her fingers, and her eyes light up. *What if you threw a party?*

A party? I stare at the words in her fun, loopy cursive, then in my own sharp, tidy letters. I've never hosted a party before. I've never even held a birthday party. My mom's offered multiple times in the past, but it always felt too frivolous, too inconvenient.

Abigail smiles. *There's no quicker way to bond than over cheap beer and good music. I'll make a playlist.*

But who would even come?

It's a party. People will want to come, no matter who's hosting. Trust me.

Our friendship has always been like that—her leading the way with the big ideas, and me following reluctantly, coaxed into buying that bold red lipstick or cutting my hair or going on a spontaneous road trip or dressing up as girl group members for Halloween. *Trust me, I know what I'm doing*, she'll say every time, and she's never been wrong before. I *did* get compliments on the red lipstick the few times I wore it, and our trip to the coast was the most fun I've had in years, picnicking on the sand with the salt breeze in my hair and the sun on my skin. I owe some of my best and brightest memories to her.

Still, I'm shocked to find myself actually considering the party. It's not impossible. My mom and brother are always invited to stay over at our aunt's house every two weeks or so. Sometimes I tag along, but most of the time I stay behind to focus on my schoolwork. I could host it when they're gone, clean up before they're back.

Because beneath my apprehension is the stronger, deeply ingrained need to be liked. To be accepted. To be forgiven. To be recognized as *good*. I'll do anything to redeem myself. The words on the bike shed flash through my mind again, and my chest contracts, like all the air has been sucked out of the room.

"Okay," I say out loud, suppressing a grimace. "Let's give it a shot."

I don't even have a chance to change my mind.

Abigail jumps into action straight away, spending the next several periods scrolling through all her contacts to pick out who we should invite. There's some kind of unspoken rule here about who you need to tell first to spread the word, who will go only if this other person is going, who *won't* go if this other person is going. She tries to explain it to me as her nails click over the screen, tapping out the details, but it just makes my head fuzzy. I wonder if this is how she feels when I'm teaching her stoichiometry.

She's already placing orders for alcoholic beverages when the lunch bell rings.

"I'll handle this," she says, sliding down from the desk and waving me off. "Go to your book club thing."

"It's the yearbook committee," I correct her.

She looks at me blankly. "We still have one of those?"

"Who do you think assembled all the photos and wrote the articles and produced the physical yearbooks that everyone went around signing at the end of the year—" I stop myself. "Never mind. Just—just don't organize anything too wild."

Her lips purse. "Define *too wild*."

"Abigail."

"Fine, I'll park the fireworks display for now. And the mini petting zoo."

I'm worried she isn't joking, but my thoughts are soon occupied by other concerns. The yearbook committee's fortnightly meetings are always held in the English classroom during lunchtimes, which means they're run by Ms. Johnson.

Ms. Johnson, who evidently hasn't forgiven me for the email yet.

"Sadie." She sniffs when I walk in. The committee is small enough that you could count all its members on two hands. Most of them are already inside, leaning over to correct a document on someone's laptop, spreading out flyers over a desk, pulling the cling wrap from their sandwiches as they wait for the printer to load.

Julius is here too. He's reclining in one of the old plastic chairs like it's a throne, his long legs stretched in front of him. And he's wearing his blazer. I'd folded it neatly inside an old shopping bag and dropped it off at his locker early this morning to avoid the awkwardness of handing it directly to him. At the sound of my name, his black eyes flicker up to me.

My pulse skips.

Yesterday afternoon still feels too fresh, too raw, like an open flame between us. The memories smolder inside my head. Him with his damp hair falling into his eyes, the weight of his blazer around me, his slender hand around my wrist.

And it's irrational, because I've seen him almost every day for the past ten years. I should be used to it by now—to *him*. He's as permanent a fixture as the clock hanging on the walls, the view of the emerald school oval from the windows, the dull circular patterns in the carpet. But something feels different. Slightly askew.

". . . listening to me, Sadie?"

"Huh?" I startle, and hastily turn my gaze back to Ms. Johnson's disapproving face. "I'm so sorry, could you . . . say that again?"

Before Emailgate, she would have smiled at me, or peered at me with concern. Now she just heaves an irritable sigh and beckons for Julius to come over. "Since I'm going to have to repeat myself, I might as well tell you both at once."

Julius positions himself to my far right, leaving four wide feet of distance between us. It feels particularly pointed today, like he's trying to prove something to me, or to himself.

"Principal Miller has asked me to assign a task to you two," Ms. Johnson says. "We have a four-page spread for the notable alumni section of the yearbook, but not enough content to go in there . . ."

"Why don't you name another one of the curtains in the cafeteria after a notable alumnus and hold a grand naming ceremony again?" Julius asks innocently.

I have to stifle a snort.

Ms. Johnson misses the sarcasm. "That's a good idea, Julius, but as of now all our curtains are already named. We thought it would be a better idea for you to conduct an interview with one of our very own alumni. See what they've been up to since they left Woodvale. Celebrate their successes. What do you think?"

I open my mouth. "I—"

"I'm glad we all agree," Ms. Johnson says, and whips out a long list of names. "You can find the contact details here. I'd suggest you call them instead of email—you're much more likely to get responses that way. The final draft for the interview is due the Friday after next. Any questions?"

I try again. "Just one—"

"Great," she says briskly, smiling at only Julius, then struts back to her desk.

A silence falls over us. We both stand there, rigid, listening to the low whirring of the printer in the background, the muted tapping of the keyboard. Neither of us wants to do this.

"Wow, she *really* doesn't like you," Julius says after a beat. He can't even hide the surprise in his voice.

"I know," I grumble. It's the obvious truth, but my skin still stings from it. I grab the list to hide my burning face and flip through the pages. "Let's aim to finish this before the end of lunch," I tell him, making my way to the empty table at the back of the classroom. My fingers itch with the need to *do* something, to prove myself to Ms. Johnson, to get into her good graces again. Maybe if we handle the interview well, she'll like me again. Or at least stop hating me.

Julius takes the seat next to me. But again, he makes sure to leave a significant amount of space between us so there's zero chance of him touching me by accident.

For some reason, I'm more irritated than glad.

"You're not going to be able to see like that," I point out.

"What?"

"The contact information."

"I can see it just fine from here," he insists.

"Really?" I hold the list up. "What does the first name say?"

He squints at it, which really goes to show how far away he is. My irritation thickens. "Sarah . . . Newman?"

"It's Clare Davis," I say flatly as I punch her number into my phone. I'm praying she'll pick up on the first ring, say she's available for the interview, and then we'll be done. "None of those letters were accurate. The *number* of letters wasn't even accurate. Why are you all the way over there if you can't see? Are you afraid I'll bite you or something?"

He rolls his eyes with what feels like exaggerated disdain. "In what world am *I* afraid of you?"

"Then come closer."

"Fine." He drags his chair forward until he's right next to me, his shoulder almost pressed to mine, the heat of his skin seeping through my shirt. Until I'm aware of nothing except him, his nearness, his physical presence. And suddenly I find myself regretting my own request. It's hard to think straight like this. I can't even move without brushing against him. But asking him to go back would be admitting defeat—worse, it would be admitting he affects me. So I pretend to ignore him and focus on the call.

My phone heats up in my hand as the dial tone sounds through the speaker. Once, twice, three times . . .

On the fifth ring, Clare picks up. "Hello?" Her voice is curt, skeptical, like she's 90 percent certain I'm a scammer about to sell her insurance for solar panels she doesn't own.

I try not to fidget in my seat. I wish I wasn't the kind of person who is always so sensitive to other people's shifting moods and tones, who startles when someone raises their voice even a little, who cowers when someone else gets annoyed. "Hi," I say, with as much warmth as I can project into the line. "This is

Sadie Wen. I'm, um, calling on behalf of the yearbook committee at Woodvale—"

"*Woodvale?*" She lets out a snort so loud I almost drop the phone. "Nah, I graduated that flaming garbage dump ages ago—"

I quickly take her off loudspeaker and bring the phone up to my ear, but everybody's already heard. Ms. Johnson is staring my way, her lips disappearing into a fine line. The students sitting at the other desk dissolve into giggles.

". . . I'm, like, so over high school," Clare says. I hear honking on her end, the white rush of movement, then a muffled curse. "*Stop cutting in front of me, you asshat*—I'm driving, by the way."

"Oh," I say. Then, as if I've been possessed by the spirit of a driving instructor, I add, "It's not safe for you to be calling, then. Eyes on the road."

"You called *me*," she says.

"Right. Sorry. Um—" I can feel myself growing flustered. It doesn't help that Julius hasn't lifted his eyes from me this whole time. "We were only wondering if you would be interested in doing an interview for—"

"Nope."

I have no idea how to respond. "Um, that's fine, then. Thanks for your time and—"

The line clicks.

"Bye," I mutter to nobody, setting the phone back down.

"That's it?" Julius says. He shifts forward, his left shoulder bumping against mine with the rising motion. "That was terrible. You weren't even trying to be persuasive."

I glare at him. "You heard her. She wasn't interested."

"All I heard was you telling her to drive safely, then apologizing for no good reason, as per usual," he drawls. "*She* should have apologized; she was the one with an attitude."

"You act as if you could produce better results."

"I can." He holds his hand out for the phone, but as I pass it over, my gaze falls on his knuckles. They're split open and raw red. My first impression is that it must be from scrubbing the shed yesterday, but that can't be right. He'd been wearing those ridiculous gloves for the very purpose of protecting his skin.

And this looks more unnatural, more deliberate, as if he'd slammed his fist into something hard . . .

Like Danny's face.

He's dialing the next number when he glances up. Catches me staring.

"Your hand," I begin, because there's no point hiding it. "Did you—"

"Did I what?"

What I'd been meaning to say was, *Did you hit Danny yesterday? Was that where you went after we cleaned the shed?* But before the words can leave my tongue, I note the coldness in his eyes, the closed-off way he's holding himself, and I realize how utterly ridiculous that question is. It must have been a strange coincidence, that's all. Julius Gong is far more likely to high-five Danny than hit him.

"What happened?" I ask instead.

"None of your business." His voice is aloof.

Okay, it definitely couldn't have been him. I'm mortified I had even considered the idea. "I was just asking out of politeness—"

"Well, then, you don't have to pretend to care."

I bristle, certain I'm about to start breathing fire. Why does everything have to be so difficult when it comes to him? But it's not just anger twisting its way around my stomach like a serpent. Embarrassingly enough, it's hurt too. There had been the briefest moment yesterday afternoon, when he offered me his blazer, where I thought . . . I don't know. Maybe he didn't *detest* me. Maybe he had the capacity to be nice, like a normal human being. Another absurd, impossible idea.

"Yes?" A male voice floats up from the phone. "Who is this?"

"Hello, I'm Julius Gong. Is this Logan?" He's firm but polite, each word clear and crisp but not too loud. He makes me want to kick something. "We have a great media opportunity here and as the most accomplished Woodvale alumnus, you were the very first person we thought of . . ."

"Liar," I mouth at him.

He doesn't even blink before continuing, "Your list of athletic accomplishments is truly impressive—"

But the man cuts him off midsentence. "Yeah, listen, I'm

flattered, but this *really* isn't a good time right now. I'm, um, with company."

Just then, a girl chimes in the background, *"Lo-gan."* She stretches the name out into a long whine. "Aren't you coming back?"

Julius stares down at the phone like it might grow teeth and bite him. For the first time, he looks wildly uncomfortable, a flush spreading up the smooth skin of his neck. "I can . . . call back," he offers.

"I'm probably going to be, ah, preoccupied for the rest of today," Logan says. "Sorry, man, I don't think I'm the right person to ask. Better luck with someone else."

Then he hangs up.

Julius appears to be frozen with shock. At last, he thaws enough to force out the words "Did he just *hang up* on me?" Like it's a supernatural phenomenon, a violation of the laws that govern our universe.

I would be laughing if we weren't tied down to the same task. Still, I can't help getting a jibe in while I can. "That was—what was the word you used? Oh, yes. Terrible."

He scoffs, but I can tell he's affronted. "That was an exception."

It quickly becomes apparent though that Clare and Logan aren't the exception, but the norm. While the other students munch on their toasted sandwiches and relax by the sunlit windows, we run through the rest of the list, crossing off one name after another with increasing frustration. My fingers become stiff from dialing. Some of the phone numbers are no longer active. Some are switched off. Many people simply don't pick up. The few who do are busy, or foresee that they will soon be very busy, or just can't be bothered to make any commitments. One person *would* be available, except they're about to embark on a thirty-day trek through a jungle and won't have any signal. One woman cusses me out for bothering her, and I'm so horrified that Julius has to pull the phone from me and end the call.

But before he does, he says pleasantly into the speaker, "Have a horrible rest of your day. Oh, and also . . ." Then he gestures for me to say something.

"I don't know what to say," I hiss, panicking.

He lifts a dark brow. "You didn't have any trouble finding the words when you were insulting me. Go on. You're not going to let her curse at you for nothing, are you?"

It could be a trick, or a trap. But I have to admit: I'm tempted. And I'm tired of being called names, of absorbing other people's anger. So I lean closer and clear my throat. "I hope, um, you miss the train home and . . ."

Julius looks at me, expectant. It's a look that says *Is that the best you can do?*

I can't help rising to the challenge. "I hope you find that you have no clean plates left for dinner," I continue, my voice strengthening with every word, even as my heartbeat accelerates. "And your neighbors start partying at ten p.m. but their music taste is solely advertising background tracks, and the shower runs out of hot water right after you've applied shampoo."

"I think it's fairly safe to say we won't be interviewing her," Julius remarks as he sets the phone down.

I laugh, which seems to please him, which in turn makes me feel like I've done something wrong. Missed something important. And yet—it *had* been satisfying, speaking aloud the things I would normally reserve for my drafts.

The downside is that we now only have one name left.

"We've gone through everything," Julius says, flipping the paper around. "Maybe we should just interview me instead. I'll join the list of notable alumni shortly after graduating—might as well do it in advance."

My brows furrow. "Hang on. There was still one—"

"I don't think so," he says. His fingers splay over the list, the movement subtle but deliberate.

"Why are you acting so weird?"

"I'm not." His chin juts out.

I glance at the clock over Ms. Johnson's desk. Three minutes left of lunch. Around us, the other committee members are already starting to unplug their chargers, snap their lunch boxes shut, throw away scrap paper and grease-stained wrappers. I have no idea what's going on with Julius, but I don't have the time to sit around and argue over nothing. "Whatever," I say. "I've got the name and number memorized. It's James Luo."

The line of his shoulders tightens, and for a split second, faster than I can blink, some dark emotion clouds his features. "How did you . . ."

"You're not the only one with a good memory," I remind him as I stab in the numbers. I'm bragging a little, but I'm not exaggerating. I've never had much trouble recalling dates, facts, names, the places on a map. But sometimes my own memory backfires on me. Because besides cold, hard statistics, I remember every single time I've lost to Julius in a test, every time someone's yelled at me, every embarrassment and failure and disappointment. Everything leaves an indelible mark on me, buries a permanent blade under my skin.

When the line connects, the voice that speaks up sounds oddly familiar. Something about the tone, the inflection of the words, the faint rasp at the edges. "Hello? This is James speaking."

"Hi," I say, my mind spinning, struggling to place it. "I'm Sadie Wen, calling from Woodvale—"

To my surprise, he laughs. "Oh, I know you. You're the other captain, right? My little brother talks about you all the time."

I falter. Beside me, Julius has gone very still, his complexion pale. "Your . . . little brother?"

"Yeah," James says breezily. "My brother, Julius Gong."

CHAPTER TEN

"I can't believe I didn't know you had a brother," I tell Julius.

He makes the same face he's been making all afternoon—a kind of pained grimace, like there's something sharp stuck to the sole of his leather shoes. "Yeah, well, most people don't." With one hand, he pulls open the glass door to the bookstore and follows me inside. "We don't share the same family name, and he graduated six years ago. So."

"Right," I say, lowering my voice.

It's very quiet inside the store; you can hear the blaze of the fireplace, the sound of rustling paper, the soft thud of a book being placed back onto a shelf. The displays at the front are lined with the most recent bestsellers—a mix of politicians' memoirs, brick-sized fantasy novels, and self-help books that contain expletives in the title—and handwritten notes from the staff, gushing over their favorite picks for the season. The cream-colored walls are decorated with recommendations too, as well as posters advertising a debut author's launch tomorrow.

At the back of the bookstore, past the Mystery and Thrillers section, the aisles open up to a mini café. The aroma of fresh-ground coffee seeps through the air, layered over the distinct, smoky book scent I'm used to smelling in our school library.

There are only two tables available, and an elderly woman has already taken the one closest to the window, a plate of half-eaten raspberry cheesecake set down before her.

I sling my schoolbag over the chair by the other table and tug out my phone and laptop to take notes for the interview. Then I sit and cross my legs. And uncross them again.

"What?" Julius asks as he sits down across from me.

I stare back at him. "I literally didn't say anything."

"I know you want to say something though," he presses. "You've been all weird and fidgety since lunch. Just get it out already."

My lips purse. The truth is that I am a little, kind of, just somewhat extremely curious—or maybe *bewildered* is the better word for it. I've always conceived of Julius as a singular, self-sufficient entity, a lone force. I wouldn't expect him to be a *brother* to someone else, the same way I wouldn't expect the mahogany table to have a sibling. Because that cracks open the door to thousands of other bizarre possibilities: of Julius as a young child, of Julius as a boy who goes on summer vacations and has movie nights and family dinners, who wrestles his brother for the remote control or sulks in his room after a fight or goes on a hunt around the house for his favorite shirt. It makes him feel too real, too human.

But that's not the only strange thing about this discovery.

"Why . . . are your surnames different?" I ask, then wonder if this is a sensitive topic. Maybe their parents are divorced. Maybe he comes from an incredibly complicated background, where his mom isn't really his mom or his dad is his brother's dad but not actually his dad or something. That would explain why *he's* been moody ever since his brother agreed to do the interview with us after school.

"My mother didn't think it was fair for us to both take my father's last name," he says with a shrug. "So when I was born, she gave me hers."

"I kind of love that, actually."

He gives me a long, almost defensive look. "Are you being sarcastic?"

"No," I say, annoyed. "Not all of us are incapable of expressing sincerely positive sentiments, Julius."

"It can be hard to tell, with your usual tone."

"What's wrong with my tone?"

He raises his brows. "Most of the time when you're talking to people—teachers, especially—you sound like you're in an advertisement for organic fruit juice. It's overly cheery."

"You're accusing me of being *too happy*?" I forget to lower my voice this time, and the elderly woman shoots me a glare over the top of her historical romance novel. I mouth an apology and continue in a fierce whisper, "That's ridiculous. There's no such thing."

"Acting too happy," he corrects me, his gaze piercing. "When I don't really think you are."

My chest burns, like the words have squeezed their way inside and peeled the flesh from my heart. But I can't let it show. "You don't know me that well," I mutter.

I expect a sharp retort, a kick to follow the punch, but he sits back. Clears his throat. "Sorry," he says, looking uncomfortable. "I . . . That was unnecessary. I'm just—" A sigh drags out between his teeth. "Not particularly looking forward to this."

And that makes two things I didn't know Julius had before: an older brother and the ability to apologize. The bitter emotion clenched inside me loosens slightly. "The interview, you mean?" I ask. "Why? He's your own brother."

"I know."

"And he sounds really accomplished. Like, *really*," I say, opening up my phone to my research notes.

James Luo is so accomplished that he has his own Wikipedia page. It goes through all his major milestones and achievements so far, including how he graduated from Woodvale as valedictorian at the age of sixteen and received a full scholarship to study at Harvard, where he wrote his literary debut within a month "on a whim" and sold it for seven figures before he'd even turned twenty. Or how he won some kind of huge international debating tournament three years in a row but then made the unprecedented move of quitting last minute, because he didn't find it "intellectually stimulating in a way that was meaningful" anymore.

The most recent update was about his sophomore novel, *Blue Crescent Blade*. It doesn't even come out for another three months, but it's already received countless glowing reviews, an exclusive profile in *O, The Oprah Magazine*, and is being hailed as a "tour de force," an "utter triumph," and a "reckoning"—with what, I'm not sure. Some big celebrity called it one of their two favorite books ever, the other being the Bible.

"Look." I pull up another article, featuring a glossy, professional black-and-white photo of James in a plain turtleneck. He's staring out the window with a pensive expression on his face, and the resemblance to Julius is striking. They have the same sculpted lips, the same thick black hair and fine angles. But James is broader jawed, and he's wearing these square frame glasses that emphasize the hollows in his cheekbones. "It says here his book is the breakout book of the decade."

"Who says that?" Julius asks without glancing at the article.

I scan through the page, but even though a dozen other celebrities are name-dropped, the quote isn't attributed to anyone. "It, um, just does."

"One can only assume it's universally true, then." He says it in a brisk, offhand manner, but his tone is sour.

Then he catches sight of someone over my shoulder, and his grimace twists deeper, as if the sharp thing in his shoe has transformed into a lethal scorpion.

"Hello."

I spin around to find James Luo striding up to us, his palms spread out, his mouth stretched into a wide grin. He looks exactly like he does in his author photo, with his slicked-back dark hair and square glasses; he's even wearing what appears to be the same turtleneck. But he's taller than I expected. When Julius stands up, a few inches of distance remain between them.

"I can't believe you didn't ask me about the interview right away," James is saying as he thumps Julius on the back so hard you'd think Julius was choking. "You know how happy I always am to help you out with your cute school projects, even when my schedule is packed."

Julius's expression darkens. "It's not really a school project. The principal signed us up for this."

"You're right." James nods sagely, his eyes sweeping the room. I swear they light up when they land on a pyramid of his books placed right in the middle of the shelves. "School projects are very important."

Julius scowls but doesn't say anything.

"And you." James suddenly turns his attention to me. "You must be Sadie Wen. You're practically a household name."

I conceal my surprise. I'd thought he was grossly exaggerating when he told me on the phone that his *little brother talks about me all the time*. But then I notice the crimson color creeping up Julius's neck, and the only logical explanation for it is that whatever he's said is either terrible or wonderful. "What has he said about me?"

Julius looks horrified. James, however, looks delighted.

"Oh, you know. When you beat him in that biology test last month he wouldn't shut up about it for *days*—"

"Stop," Julius mutters out of the side of his mouth. He refuses to meet my gaze.

But James continues with good cheer, "And he's always going on about how intimidatingly smart you are. How hard he has to work to keep up with you."

Intimidatingly smart. I hold on to those words, examine them up close. I've never thought of myself as intimidating or scary, yet it feels like the greatest compliment. A confirmation of my wildest hopes. Julius Gong takes me seriously. He isn't just competing because he thinks it'd be embarrassing to lose. He's *afraid* of losing to me.

"You know," James says, "he got really sick last summer, but he wouldn't even rest. He brought all his textbooks back to his bed because he could barely stand and insisted that, like, if he didn't study hard every single day you'd pull ahead—"

"Wait." My gaze swivels to Julius. "You were sick?"

That doesn't make sense—I *remember* last summer. On the very first day, he'd sent me an incredibly difficult equation from some kind of advanced university paper as a challenge. I'd solved it just to spite him, and dug through all the papers available online to find something even trickier, and sent that back. We'd then fallen into the habit of exchanging questions every morning. We never said anything else. Just the screenshot and the answer. One blow traded for another. He would respond each time without fail, and we'd kept it up all the way until school started again.

How could he have been ill?

"It wasn't that serious," Julius says, running a hand through his hair. "And even with a fever, my brain still works better than the average person's."

"That's not how you acted." James raises his brows at me. I've seen Julius make that exact expression so many times it's like looking at a mirror image of him. "When he wasn't studying, he was sulking. Kept asking our mother to make him his favorite soup, luo song tang—"

"I thought you said you only had twenty minutes to do the interview?" Julius interrupts loudly. He sits back down and pulls out the Moleskine notebook he always uses to take notes. "Shouldn't we be getting started?"

"Ah, of course." James beams, and I find myself thinking, *Their smiles are different.* James smiles like he has an infinite number of them, like it costs him nothing. But Julius's smiles are sharp, sudden, sometimes ledged with mockery or laced with poison. His real smiles are so rare that each one feels like a miracle, like you've won something. "What do you want to know?"

I want to know if Julius was afraid of the dark when he was younger. If he ever believed in ghosts or Santa or the Loch Ness monster. I want to know where he studies, whether it's by the light of the living room window or alone in his bedroom, if he keeps the door wide open or closed. I want to know what he would dress up as for Halloween, what song he picks out at karaoke. How early he rises, how late he sleeps. What dishes their mother cooks for the Spring Festival, what he talks about on long car rides. I want to collect these pieces of information like ammunition. Part of me wants to embarrass him, and part of me is simply, overwhelmingly curious.

But we're here to interview James about his career, not his brother, so I restrain myself and ask him instead about where he draws his inspiration, how much time he devotes to writing each day, what the drafting process is like.

"For me, you see, the words are like sparrows," he says, rubbing his eyes. I blink hard, but I'm not imagining it. His glasses are, apparently, frames only; his fingers pass right through them. "I could spend the whole day chasing them, but they'd only startle and fly away from me. It's more important to stay still, and let the sparrows come on their own."

"Mm," I say, hastily tearing my gaze away from his fake glasses to write down his response. "That's very interesting."

"Now, obviously, there are days when you do have to coax the sparrows down with a bit of birdseed," he continues. "Certain types of birdseed work better than others. And sometimes you think you need the premium brand, but it's in fact the organic brands, or not even a particular brand at all—only the berries you pluck in the wild—that are the most effective."

"Um. Sorry." I pause. "I'm sort of getting lost with this analogy. What . . . are the birdseeds meant to be?"

"Nothing," he says.

"Oh, okay—"

"And everything," he goes on. "I will leave that to your interpretation. Interpretation is crucial, you see. It's what this is all about."

Julius either rolls his eyes or finds a very interesting spot in the ceiling to stare at. He hasn't spoken much this whole interview.

"So are you working as a full-time author now?" I ask, moving down the list to the next question I've prepared.

"Oh, no." James throws his head back and laughs so loud the elderly woman glares over at our table again. "No, no, no. God, no. I couldn't do that—for one, it would be such a waste of my Harvard Law degree. I mean, anyone would *kill* just to get into Harvard, you know? I'd be a fool to throw all that aside. And my professors would be crushed too, seeing as I'm the most promising student they've taught in centuries. Their words, obviously, not mine."

"Your professors must be very healthy," I say.

A soft, half-muffled sound draws my attention to Julius. He's pressed a hand to the lower half of his face, his shoulders shaking, then stilling just for a second before he loses it again, shaking his head too, as if he's annoyed he finds it so funny in the first place. At least he's stopped looking like the tortured subject of a Renaissance painting.

"Hm?" James just looks confused.

"Seeing as they've been teaching for centuries and all."

He falters, then recovers. "Well, they're so experienced it certainly feels like they've been teaching that long. Harvard is all about the history, you know."

I note quietly that this is the twenty-fifth time he's brought up the word *Harvard* in the past ten minutes. If Harvard were a ghost, he would have successfully summoned it back to life by now. "So you're not writing full-time. That must be hard to balance, then."

"Well, it's worth the financial stability." He folds his hands together. "The book money is really just a fun little bonus, but I'm definitely not going to rely on it for retirement or anything like that."

In the back of my mind, the words from the article appear in screaming, bold black text: *sold for seven figures*. That's his idea of a fun bonus? The absurd statement also seems to have an instant sobering effect on Julius, who definitely rolls his eyes this time.

"It's really more of a side hustle for me," James says. "The old saying is true: Don't put all your eggs in one basket. Now I've separated my eggs into the law basket, and the author basket, and the investment basket, and also my debating coach basket . . ."

Even though I'm talking to him, I'm watching Julius. He appears to be muttering something to himself—either *kill me* or *cashmere*, which seems less likely.

"Yeah, sure," I say, distracted. "I hear that you've done a lot of debating."

"Absolutely. It really sets you up for success in so many fields, even if you don't end up becoming a professional champion debater like myself. That's why I always encourage Julius to get more involved in debating." He gives Julius a light shove. "Right, Ju-zi?"

I almost choke on my own saliva.

Ju-zi throws me a warning look, then frowns at his brother. "I thought we'd retired that nickname already. It makes no sense. Why would I be called a tangerine in Chinese?"

"Why? Because it's *so* adorable." James grins. "And I really mean it, about the debating thing. You don't have to feel bad just because I'm naturally good at it. If anything, you should be encouraged by the fact that we share the same genes. It's impossible for you to be *terrible*, even if you aren't *quite* as good—"

Julius stands up. "I'm going to get us some drinks. You want any?" He directs the question at me, which is truly a sign of how much he does *not* wish to be around his brother. That, and the fact that he would so eagerly volunteer himself for any sort of task without a gold star or extra credit or compliment attached to it.

But I think I'm starting to get it. The vicious look on his face when I'd beaten him in that class debate. Why he's never mentioned his brother before. Why he's so ruthlessly determined to be first all the time. Why he's scowling now, the lines of his shoulder tight.

We place our orders. He's still scowling when he returns later with a glass of warm water for me, black coffee for himself, and some sort of herbal infusion tea that I thought people only pretended to like in theory to convince everyone else they're on a health kick. But James downs the drink in one go and asks for a refill.

"Get it yourself," Julius grumbles.

James merely looks over at him, expectant.

With a sigh, Julius pushes off his chair again. When he comes back, we're just wrapping up James's final response about his plans for the next year, which include a fully funded trip around Europe, a major film adaptation he's both writing for and producing, and a lecture at some fancy lawyers' convention.

"This has been great," he says, beaming. It's a wonder how he manages to smile so widely and speak at the same time. "Now, I'm going to go sign some stock while I'm here. It'll probably take a while—I have *thousands* of copies to get through." He gives James another loud thump on the back. "You kids have fun though."

We do not have fun.

Mostly, we tidy up our notes and sit in silence until I break it first. "Well. We definitely have enough material for that four-page spread now . . . Actually, just his description of the five-star hotel he stayed at for his debut novel's national tour is enough material for the spread."

Julius nods along, but his eyes follow his brother as he shakes hands with an enthusiastic fan. They take a selfie together,

James's signature winning smile and the cover of his debut on display. The fan appears to be bawling.

"People always act like that around him," Julius remarks under his breath. "Even our own parents."

"Your parents . . . always ask your brother to autograph the collar of their shirt?" I ask as James whips out a gold Sharpie he apparently just keeps in his front pocket.

Julius lets out a surprised scoff of laughter, proving my theory from earlier. His smiles really do feel like miracles. Especially when you're on the receiving end of them.

Warmth spreads through me, but then I give myself a mental kick. Remind myself of who I'm talking to. *Julius Gong.* The boy who's made my life unbearable for the past ten years. He wouldn't even be here right now if he wasn't forced to by the principal.

"I better go home," I say.

His expression flickers. "So soon?"

I pause, caught off guard, and his demeanor changes in response. The smile is gone in a flash, the lines of his face carved into their usual cool, unimpressed mask.

"I mean, aren't you going to transcribe the notes first?" he asks. "Surely you don't intend to leave that work to me?"

This is the Julius Gong I know. The Julius Gong I can comfortably hate. I'm almost relieved. "I'll transcribe them," I tell him, only so we can wrap this up faster. "I'll email the finalized version to you by midnight."

"Okay. Good. You better."

I begin to shove everything in my bag, but he adds, "I hear you're throwing a party this weekend?"

My hands freeze over my notebook. "Is there a problem with that?"

"So you really are. Hosting a party." He stretches the last word out like it's something ridiculous, like I'm planning to house an elephant or organize a Christmas feast in late April. "Why?"

"Because I feel like it," I say, defensive. I'm lying, of course, but I'm more offended by the implication that I can't be the kind of person who'd throw a party for fun. That he thinks he has me all figured out. That I'm an open book to him, and he can read me easily, better than anybody else.

"You never do anything just because you feel like it, Sadie Wen," he says, flattening his palms over the table. "You must have a multistep strategy. A long-term objective. Or else why are you inviting people like Rosie to your house?"

"Does it matter?" Irritation races through me like brush fire. "It's not like I'm inviting *you*."

His black eyes glitter. I watch his throat move slightly before he replies, his voice cold, "I wouldn't have come even if you did."

"Okay," I say flatly. I don't tell him I had considered inviting him this afternoon; we're inviting most of the year level anyway. But now that thought—the very fact that I'd even *entertained* the idea—mortifies me. Why would I ever give Julius a reason to reject me? Rejection is the most humiliating form of defeat.

It's losing the battle before it's even begun. It's lowering your weapon so they can spear you in the chest. "Then don't."

"I won't," he says, his jaw taut.

"You've said that already."

"I want to make it clear."

"Don't worry, it's *very* clear to me."

We glare at each other, breathing hard as if from physical exertion, my nails digging into the metal spiral of my notebook. Nobody else has ever had the power to fill me with such pure, blistering rage. To make me so angry I want to flip over a table, stamp my feet like a screaming toddler, burn holes into the carpet. Before I can do any real damage, I take my things and leave without even bothering to zip up my bag.

But my fingers itch the whole way home, and for the rest of day, as I close up the bakery and do my daily workout routine and finish my homework and brush my teeth, I can't think about anything except him.

CHAPTER ELEVEN

Our school forces us to fill out these career surveys at two separate points in time: one in year five, and one in year eleven. They assure us that the surveys are anonymous, so we *should feel comfortable being honest*, but the results always end up posted on the very public bulletin board with our names attached right below. Well, the majority of the results anyway. The student who'd written *sugar baby* for their answer had theirs taken down within an hour.

A quick glance at the board and you can pretty easily spot the emerging pattern. The kid who wanted to be a playwright now wants to be an accountant. The boy who wanted to be an astronaut now plans on becoming a pharmacist. The one who wanted to be an artist now has their sights set on med school. Hobbies are traded for more stable, lucrative, practical careers. Dreams are shattered once the mechanics of going to the bathroom in outer space are taken into greater consideration.

But for Julius and me, our career goals have stayed consistent throughout the years. In year five, we were already researching the highest-paid jobs and the most in-demand degrees; him, because he craved the prestige, and me, because I just needed the fastest route to the best future for my family. Something that paid the bills on time, that guaranteed stability regardless of what became of my brother's sporting career, that would give my mom something to brag about to the nosy aunties. So on both occasions, he wrote down *lawyer*, and I wrote down *data analyst*.

Abigail's career ambitions, on the other hand, have jumped all over the place. Her results were a list of crossed-off and rewritten answers, covering everything imaginable: professional taster, professional equestrian, ballerina, fashion stylist, online dating ghostwriter (which I didn't even know was a thing), and party planner.

"You know what? I really, truly feel party planning could be, like, a viable career for me," Abigail says as she backs away from the confetti machine and surveys my transformed living room. "What do you think, darling?"

I'm thinking that there's a literal confetti machine in my living room. "It's very, um . . ." It's a *lot*. I have no idea what kind of budget Abigail is working with here. Frankly, I'm not sure Abigail understands the concept of a budget; whenever she wants something, all she has to do is ask her parents and they'll give her two of it. It's not that she's super rich or anything. Abigail and her family are simply devout believers in the value of a Good Experience, of living in the moment. They're the type to spend a month's worth of savings for concert tickets to their favorite artist; to book the trip to Italy *now* and worry about the cost later; to stay in the hotel room with the ocean view even if it's twice as expensive as the regular rooms, because *we're already here, so we might as well enjoy it properly.*

As someone who's a strong advocate of saving up just in case a comet crashes into our house and insurance refuses to cover it, it's a bit harder for me to enjoy the elaborate bouquets of flowers and chocolate fountain Abigail's bought for this one occasion. I barely even recognize my own house. She's dimmed the lights and planted candles around the place so the walls appear to be a shade of pastel pink, obscuring all Max's muddy sneaker marks. There are also giant cartons of alcohol lined up along the couches. I don't know where Abigail procured them from, but I doubt her methods were fully legal.

As if my list of worries weren't already long enough.

"I'm only renting the confetti machine for the night," she reassures me. "It's just to set the mood from the beginning. You want people to come in and be like, *Wow, I can tell right away from the quality of the confetti scattered casually but strategically across the floor that this will be the best party I've ever been to.*"

I let out a snort. "Nobody thinks like that."

"They'll think that when they see your house."

"But . . . will they even come?" I worry, pressing my ear against the front door—because it's a comfortable position, of course. Not because I think this is the most effective way for me to be alerted and prepare myself the instant I hear the sound of footsteps in my driveway. "We said it would start at six on the dot and—" I glance at the clock. "And it's already five forty-three."

"Not everyone is as punctual as you are," Abigail says. "Your idea of ten minutes late is equivalent to the average person's idea of twenty minutes early. And trust me, they're *definitely* going to want to come. They'd rock up to a serial killer's house if there was the promise of free booze."

"That's highly concerning. You realize that's highly concerning, right?"

She shrugs. "Just how it is."

"Also—" I pause. Frown. "I'm sorry, did you just compare me to a serial killer?"

"No," she says, with too much emphasis. "Although, just to put it out there, even if you *were* a serial killer, I would absolutely stick by you and sharpen your knives."

"How sweet."

"I'd also clean the blood off your bathroom floor," she adds brightly. "I was reading this fascinating article the other day about how to use basic laundry detergents to do just that. You wouldn't have to worry about leaving behind any evidence."

"Okay, wait." I hold up a hand. "In this—frankly disturbing, highly unrealistic—scenario you've conjured out of nowhere, why am I murdering people in my *bathroom*?"

"Well, you wouldn't be murdering people in your kitchen. That's just unhygienic."

I grimace. "I fear this conversation has gotten away from us."

"Yeah, sorry, what were we talking about again? Oh right. They'll show up, Sadie, I promise—"

Before she's even finished her sentence, the sound of voices drifts over from the front yard.

"Oh my god, people are actually coming," I say, my throat drying. All of a sudden, it feels like someone's playing kickball with my intestines. The skirt I'm wearing is too tight, the fabric too itchy.

"See? I'm always right." Abigail smiles. She refastens the sash around her shimmery dress, fluffs up her hair, and gently guides me out of the way to open the door. "Hello, hello," she calls out. "Please do come in."

It's Ray.

He's rocked up with four other guys from our history class, and as he steps inside in his oversized varsity jacket and pristine trainers, his eyes sweeping over the party decorations, I experience a moment of pure, heart-stopping panic. What if he isn't here for the party itself? What if they've coordinated some kind of attack on my house? What if they're going to all start egging the place or laughing at me? But then he sees the alcohol, and he breaks into a grin. "Damn, I knew I'd come to the right place."

"Welcome," I say tentatively.

"See, you guys?" Ray calls to his friends as he moves past me. "Told you there'd be free drinks. Let's get the others over here as well."

He shoots off a message on his phone, and in hardly any time at all, dozens of people start pulling up in my driveway. Abigail really was right. I shouldn't have worried about my classmates not showing, even with my current social status. Soon, there's so little room left for parking that the cars are lined up all the way down the street, girls checking their lipstick and giggling as they join the crowds streaming inside.

Nobody eggs my house. Nobody stalks up to me and slaps me. Nobody calls me a bitch. Though I brace myself for the worst every time I open the door, people seem more impressed than anything by the alcohol supply and the decorations. I even manage to get a little smile and a compliment on my outfit from one of Rosie's influencer friends.

Slowly, my muscles relax.

My heart unhooks itself from my rib cage. My breathing evens out.

Then the door swings open again, and I find myself staring at the last person in the world I'd expect to appear.

"What are you here for?" I ask Julius. I'm too surprised to remember to sharpen my words, to hold on to my grudge from the bookstore. To do anything except stare.

He looks just as confused, as if someone else had guided him to my house. He's certainly not dressed for a party; he's wearing a navy blazer that brings out the darkness of his eyes, the natural red tint of his lips. But then his features wrap themselves into a perfect little scowl, and he stuffs his hands into his pockets, straightens his spine. "The same thing as everyone else," he says. "I heard there was free liquor so I thought I'd drop by."

I blink at him. "I didn't know you drank. Actually, I recall you saying last year that *the only beverages worth your time were coffee and mineral water.*"

His skin flushes, though his scowl remains in place. "Perhaps I've changed my mind."

"Or perhaps you're here to make fun of me," I guess.

"This may come as a shock, but not everything is about you, Sadie. I don't care whose party this is; I simply didn't have anywhere better to go," he says, his voice bored.

"How sad. You're not wanted in your own home? You have to come bother me in mine?"

He flinches, then rights himself again with cool poise. The twist of his mouth turns cruel. "Well, if I can make your night a little worse, why not? I'll at least have accomplished something here."

I lean against the doorframe, my heart speeding. Had I imagined it? Struck some invisible nerve? Was it something I said? But when I assess his face, his gaze is cold as stone; it seems impossible he could feel any human emotion at all.

"What are you waiting for?" He glances over his shoulder at my front yard, then back at me, his brows raised. "You're blocking the entrance."

I realize it's true. There's already a line forming behind him, people squeezing past one another to edge closer. I sigh and step back and they spill through the door all at once. A guy I've never spoken to before pauses on his way in, catches Julius's eye, and calls out at the top of his voice so it's audible even over the thudding music, "Cute outfit, Julius Caesar. Are you planning on heading to a job interview soon? Because with that blazer, I'm *sure* they'd hire you."

Laughter bubbles up from around the house.

Julius's face darkens. "Are you satisfied?" he hisses under his breath, the accusation stark in his gaze. "It's all thanks to you."

I swallow. I can't lie, I *do* feel bad. No doubt that comment was inspired by another one of my responses to his emails, which had unfortunately been addressed to our entire class. The new nickname as well. "I'll fix it," I tell him. "I can fix it. I've got it under control already."

"Do you consider yourself a god or something? How are you planning to fix it?" he demands.

"I'm throwing the party—"

"Hang on. Is *that* what this is about?" He shakes his head with disbelief. "See, I *knew* you had some kind of ulterior motive—"

"Don't make it sound so sinister," I snap.

"Don't be so naive about this," he retorts, just as fiercely. "You really think you can just put on some upbeat music, bring a bunch of alcohol, and everyone will have *such* a wonderful time tonight they'll forget you insulted a significant portion of the student body?"

"Well, it's working," I say.

At least, that's what it seems like. People are lounging on my couch, chatting in the corridors, drinks in hands, falling over themselves laughing, their expressions open, relaxed. Happy. The air is warm with the heat of bodies and the flickering candle flames.

Aside from that guy's one remark, the emails might as well not exist in this space.

"If you truly believe that, you're about to be very disappointed," Julius scoffs. "And what's the point of hosting a party if you aren't even having fun?"

I tighten my jaw. "What do you mean? I'm having *plenty* of fun." My eyes snap to the group of boys on the other side of the room. "In fact, I'm just about to go and tell those people to stop dipping raw cabbage into the chocolate fountain."

"Yeah, a real blast," he mutters. But when I turn to go, he stops me. "Wait."

"What?" I say irritably.

He hesitates. Runs a slow, self-conscious hand through his hair. "Do they . . . really look bad? My clothes, I mean."

I'm dumbfounded—as much by the question as the fact that he's asking *me*. "You look how you always look, Julius," I manage.

His eyes are wary. "And how is that?"

"Completely pretentious," I say. I shouldn't elaborate any further, but something about the stiffness of his posture, the rare vulnerability in his face, makes me add: "In a nice way though."

Then I bite down on my tongue and make a quick exit before I can say anything else I'll regret.

I should have prepared myself for this.

I've heard of it happening at other parties. I've seen it play out in movies. I know it's a popular way to pass the time, especially once the novelty of the chocolate fountain and confetti machine starts to wear off. But I still experience a horrible shock when someone suggests, two hours into the party, that we play a game of truth or dare.

"It'll be fun," Georgina says. She arrived about thirty minutes ago, with sparkly butterfly clips in her hair and blue mascara streaked down her cheeks. The word has since spread that she'd been dumped by a girl on her gymnastics team for one of the glamorous equestrians at another school. "I really just want to have fun tonight, 'kay?"

I accepted long ago that my definition of *fun* tends to differ from the general teen demographic. Fun is baking a new batch of egg tarts, or beating my previous record for the two-hundred-meter dash, or adding my grades to my academic spreadsheet. It's not roller coasters or getting wasted on a beach or participating in a game that requires you either embarrass yourself or expose yourself to a number of people.

But I'm clearly the only one with reservations.

"Sounds cool to me," Ray chimes in, and the others are all nodding, sitting themselves down in a circle.

"Hey." Abigail nudges me. She's rarely sheepish, but there's no other way to describe the way she's smiling. "I'm so, so sorry to do this, but I have to leave early. My sister's car just broke down on a freeway and Liam's been ignoring her texts—*yes*, again, I know, don't give me that look—but are you going to be okay on your own? Because I can, like, figure something else out if you need me to."

I do need you here, I want to say. *Don't leave me at this party by myself. Please don't go yet.* But the words stick to my throat; I've never been good at asking people for things. "No, that's completely fine," I tell her. "Go."

"Give me updates later," she says, grabbing her purse.

"I'll message you," I promise. *If I manage to make it through this alive*, I add inside my head, dread dragging its ice-cold fingers over my stomach.

The first few rounds of the game are fairly tame. Somebody dares Rosie to text her ex; she whips out her phone without hesitating and sends them a selfie. Somebody dares Ray to do fifty push-ups, which he performs with such flair, the sleeves of his shirt rolled up to expose his muscles, that I have to wonder if he'd arranged the dare beforehand just to show off. Someone else asks one of the theater kids what her biggest fear is, and she responds with "The realization that life is little more than the slow leak of time until we meet our inevitable demise," which sends everyone into an uncomfortable silence for a while.

Then it's Julius's turn.

Frankly I'm surprised he's still here. Even more surprised that he'd join the game.

"What do you pick?" Rosie's friend asks him.

Julius manages to look indifferent when he replies, "Truth."

Of course he'd pick that, I think scornfully. God forbid anyone force him to do something unseemly, like mess up his hairstyle.

Rosie's friend giggles. Peers at him under her long lashes. "Okay, then . . . Do you like anyone?"

It has nothing to do with me, but my heart seizes as if I've just been electrocuted. I'm blinking too fast, sitting up too straight. I can't control my body, can't control the weird, nervous feeling fluttering through my veins. Can't stop myself from looking at him as if I can find the answer written over his face.

For the briefest second, he looks back at me.

Then he frowns and shakes his head, once. "No." His voice is firm.

The girl's face swiftly crumples in obvious disappointment. Inexplicably I feel a pang of it echo through my own chest.

"How boring," Georgina complains. "You really don't like *anyone?* There are so many pretty girls in our year level."

Julius shrugs. "You asked for the truth."

"Fine. Next person, then. Truth or dare, Sadie?" Georgina asks. Now all eyes are on me, and the air in the living room suddenly seems to have weight. I can feel it pressing down on me, crushing my ribs, sealing my next breath inside my lungs.

My throat dries. If *I* choose truth like Julius did, they'll most definitely ask me about the emails, and I can't afford to upset anyone further. All my work for tonight, this whole party—it'll be for nothing. So I reply, "Dare."

Ray grins. "Dare, huh?"

Too late, I'm hit with the terrible, sinking realization that I've chosen wrong. Walked headfirst into a trap. I can't even imagine what they'll think up. *This* is why I should have been better prepared; I could have thought through my options more carefully, made up for my lack of experience by doing more research.

Ray ducks his head and murmurs something to his friends, and they hoot with laughter.

"Is it too much?" the girl sitting cross-legged next to them asks.

"Nah, it's all for fun, right?" Ray replies, his smile widening. "And Sadie's a good sport."

Dread simmers through my veins like acid. I wring my fingers in my lap, then curl them behind my back. Nothing helps.

"Okay." Ray claps his hands together with the pompous air of a game-show host. "We've decided. We dare you . . . to kiss Julius."

My mind shuts down on itself.

I can only gape at him, unsure if this is their idea of a joke, if I've misheard. I must have. There's absolutely no way they would ask it of me. They *know* our history by now, they've read the emails, they know we've hated each other for the past ten years—

But of course, that's exactly why they're asking.

My gaze cuts to Julius again. I just need to see his reaction. I expect him to look disgusted by the idea, or enraged, or perhaps delighted at my imminent humiliation. But his expression is unreadable. He shows no outward emotion, and somehow that's worse. Maybe that's how little it affects him, how little it means. Maybe that's how little *I* matter.

It's like there's a stone lodged in my chest, blocking the blood from rushing to my heart.

"Well?" Ray challenges.

I swallow. Force myself to mimic Julius's nonchalance. "Sure, why not?"

Surprised murmurs rise from the circle. Even Ray looks stunned, like he'd been waiting for me to protest.

And Julius is staring at me, his brows faintly creased. I've managed to catch him off guard as well. I feel a flush of victory, not so dissimilar to the thrill of finishing ahead of him in a race.

"Come on," I say, standing up and smoothing out my skirt, praying nobody can see my hands quiver. *It's just a kiss*, I tell myself. *It's just a boy.*

Julius hesitates, then pushes onto his feet too. Nobody speaks; they're all watching us, deadly focused, anticipation building like the wind before a storm. The lights seem to dim further, and the space between us feels like nothing, like twenty miles, like ghost flames.

He's waiting. For me to make a fool of myself. For me to make the first move.

I let my anger carve away my nerves and close my eyes and kiss him. It's so fast, so light that I only have time to register the startling softness of his lips before I'm reeling back again.

Oh my god.

I did it.

I actually did it.

The guys are laughing in the background. Someone else is calling my name, but I can't hear them. This isn't about them anymore. This is only about us, about the painful beat of my heart, the heat scorching my face.

Julius touches a finger to his lips like he can't quite believe it either. Then he straightens. Cocks his head, his eyes black with cool amusement. "You call that a kiss?" he says on a scoff. His voice comes out lower than usual, and I can see the effort in the movement of his throat. "That was barely anything."

The heat inside me flares higher, incinerating all logic and reservation. I want to slap that smug look off his face, but then I think of something even better.

"What about this, then?" I challenge, and before he can reply, I grab the collar of his shirt and pull him to me.

This time, when our lips meet, I don't back away. I deepen the kiss, letting my fingers slide up his neck, curl into his hair. For one moment, I can feel his shock, the tension running through his frame like a heated wire, and I think: *I've won*. I've proven him wrong. Then he kisses me back, presses me closer, and something inside me slides off-balance.

It's not meant to be like this. The thought is hazy, distant, lost to the sensation of his mouth on mine.

Because I was lying to myself before. Julius isn't just a boy. He's my enemy. My equal. My point of comparison. He's the one I'm constantly trying to outrun, to outsmart, to impress. He's the ever-moving target in my peripheral vision, the person I've mapped all my plans around, the start and finish line and everything in between. All my dreams and nightmares are about him and only him.

I can't concentrate. The most terrible part of this is that it doesn't feel terrible at all; not the warm flush of his skin against mine or the firmness of his grip or the breathless sound in the back of his throat.

I want to stay like this.

I want to keep going.

As soon as I think it, white-hot panic jolts through me, reviving the little common sense I have left. *No.* No, I shouldn't want this. I shouldn't be doing this at all. I push against his chest and he lets go instantly, eyes wide, hands dropping to his sides as if he's been jerked out of a daze.

Neither of us speaks, and I'm mortified to find myself breathing hard. The harsh, uneven sound fills the room.

"Damn." Someone whistles. "Didn't know she had it in her . . ."

On a regular day, this alone would make me curl into a ball and die on the spot. But my attention is pinned on Julius.

"Excuse me," he murmurs, clearing his throat. He won't meet my eyes. "I'm going to go outside for—" He makes a vague gesture to the door without finishing his sentence, and then he's striding out, his footsteps quick and urgent, his shoulders tensed.

I don't even want to imagine how red my face is right now.

"I'm also, um—I need to grab a drink," I say. My voice sounds odd, choked. "I-I've already done my dare."

Nobody tries to stop me.

The night air wraps around me when I step outside.

It's warmer than it's been for months, and I can find the early hints of spring in our backyard. The budding roses, the sweet scent of fresh green grass, the birds rustling in the trees. A breeze snakes through my hair, ruffles my skirt. The sky is a deep, starless black, but the fairy lights twinkle over the back porch, glowing pink and blue and yellow, as if the stars have fallen down to earth instead.

Julius is looking up at the sky too, the outline of his frame lit with gold. His arms rest over the railing, and when I step closer, I notice him digging his nails into his palms.

My feet slow over the wooden planks. I pull at my sleeves, self-conscious all of a sudden. I don't know how to act, what to say. I don't even know why I followed him out here.

Then Julius spins around, and so many emotions flash over his face that I can't begin to decipher them all before they're wiped clean again, leaving just one: anger. "Why did you have to do that?"

The venom in his voice makes me freeze. "What?" I say, confused. "What do you mean? I— It was a dare. They asked me to."

"You would kiss someone you loathe just because of a childish dare? Just because other people wanted you to?" Contempt laces his tone. Each word is an arrow, and his aim lands true every time. "Do their opinions really mean that much to you?"

This is so unreasonable, so deeply insulting, I'm rendered speechless. I can't believe I'd kissed him bare minutes ago. I can't believe I'd let him pull me close like that—run his fingers over my skin like that—

Something blazes over his face, as though he's remembering it too.

"What's *wrong* with you?" I finally choke out. "If you didn't want to kiss me, you could have just refused."

"You think I had a chance to? You grabbed me—"

"You stood up too," I cut in, my voice trembling with fury. "You kissed me back—"

"It was a natural reflex," he says. "Not that I expect you to know, but—"

"Who's to say I wouldn't know?"

That shuts him up.

He stares at me. Through the brick walls, the noise from the party—the pounding of music, the rattle of bottles, the hum of conversation punctuated by muffled shrieks of laughter—feels a hundred miles away. Like it belongs to another world, another time, another place. "That . . . wasn't your first time kissing someone," he says. A half question.

"Of course not." It was only my second kiss, but I'm enjoying this, proving his assumptions wrong. And I don't want to give him any reason to think that what happened just now was special, that it meant something when it didn't. It shouldn't.

"Who?" he asks. A full question now.

I lean over the railing, my head turned away from him. "Why do you care?"

"I don't," he says heatedly. "But I want to know."

"Well, I don't want to tell you," I say, just to be difficult. Just to deprive him of something too, after he stripped me of my pride.

"Does he go to our school?" he presses, then corrects himself. "No, that isn't possible. I'm sure I would have heard rumors about it."

I stay strategically silent.

"On vacation, then? At camp?"

He's right.

It must show on my face, because he presses in, "It was at camp, wasn't it? One of those outdoor adventure camps?"

The idea that I would attend a camp to learn fun little skills like woodcutting and weaving and marshmallow baking instead of something academically rigorous is too offensive for me to swallow. "Coding camp," I say, then see the satisfied curve of his mouth. He'd been baiting me. Of course. He knows I wouldn't be caught dead wasting my summer on a camp like that when I could be getting ahead of the coursework.

"So a coding camp," he says, turning this information over on his tongue like it's something sour. "What's his name?"

My shoulders hunch in self-defense. "You seem awfully invested in the details for someone who doesn't care."

"I already told you, I don't." He pauses, his lips sculpted into a sarcastic smile. "I'm curious to know who would have such— peculiar taste—to have dated you. Unless, of course, you're making it up—"

"I'm not," I snap, pushing off from the railing and whipping my head around. A misstep. He looks dangerous in the darkness, the scattered lights sharpening the hollows of his cheekbones, the bladed look in his eyes. "His name was Ben. He asked me out after our second seminar together. You can look him up, if you want. He was a swimmer, and he tutored kids during spring break. Everyone said he was attractive."

I leave out the part where he broke up with me only two weeks after our first date. The night before that, there'd been a game of trivia, and my team had beaten his. I'd gone to him when it was over, holding up the plastic trophy and beaming, expecting him to be impressed, but he hadn't even congratulated me. When he dumped me outside the lecture room, he'd said it was because I was too intense. *Everything's a competition with you, Sadie*, he'd accused, rubbing a hand over his face. *You only care about winning. It just gets really exhausting being around you all the time, you know what I'm saying? I want someone who can, like, chill out.*

It's funny, thinking about it now. Because Julius has also accused me of plenty of things in the past, but he's never faulted me for being intense. For being too much of anything. For wanting to win. He's part of the reason why winning is worth it.

"Did you . . . think he was attractive?" Julius asks. The words sound forced out.

I consider this. Yes, I could understand on a general, biological level why others found Ben attractive. He had a swimmer's body, thick lashes, a smile like the sun. Every time I think about him I associate him with summer: salt air and warm sand and open waves. Nothing like Julius, with his cold glances and sharp edges. Julius is the dead of winter, ice on your tongue and white frost and the ghost of your breath in a dark hall.

But I don't tell him that. "Yeah," I say, lifting my chin. "Of course. And he was a great kisser too."

He's silent.

It makes me nervous. "What? Are you jealous?" I say it only to provoke a response out of him, to annoy him.

What I don't expect is for his cheeks to flush. For his hands to bunch into fists. "Why would I be jealous?" he demands with a sneer, distaste written all over his face. "I would rather die than kiss you again."

Shame burns my skin. It feels like my whole body has caught fire. The flames shoot through my bloodstream, fill my throat, scald the inside of my lungs. It hurts. It hurts so much that the only way to distract myself from it is with rage. The need for revenge, to hurt him back, hurt him more. I lurch forward and do the first thing I can think of: I kick him. Hard, right in the knee. The sound of impact is even louder than I anticipated, a terribly satisfying thud that vibrates through my own bones.

He lets out a hiss, part pain and part surprise. "Have you completely *lost your mind*, Sadie?"

"You deserve it," I say hotly, my blood pounding in my ears. My head is buzzing. Nothing about this night feels real.

"Sadie—"

But I've wasted enough time. It was an awful idea to follow him out here in the first place. What had I been looking for? What had I expected from Julius Gong? So when he calls me again—maybe to demand an explanation, maybe just to throw out another insult—I ignore him. I toss my hair over my shoulder and march back into the house, slamming the door behind me so hard the glass panes rattle.

CHAPTER TWELVE

The house has descended into complete anarchy.

For a few moments, I can only stand there and take the scene in, my mouth agape with horror. Someone's pouring liquor into one of my mom's favorite porcelain vases and using it as a giant wineglass, the citrus scent of alcohol wafting into the air so strong I can almost taste it. *Three* couples are making out on the couch in one row, as if they're in a competition to see who can make the most disturbing sounds or flash the most skin. The dining table has been pushed back to make room for a noisy game of beer pong; all the chairs are stacked up, the fruit bowl set down on the floor. Every now and then, a yell of frustration or delight is followed by a chorus of cheers. There are wrappers everywhere, half-empty plastic cups, glitter from god knows where. Even worse, I'm now noticing that people are wearing their outdoor shoes indoors, leaving muddy marks all over the beige carpet.

I try to take a deep breath, but I end up choking on it.

This is a nightmare.

And this is entirely my fault.

I've never felt so foolish, so helpless. I shouldn't have hosted this party. Ben was right about me. I'm not the kind of girl who can *chill out*, the kind of person who invites the whole year level to their house and sits back to let the destruction happen. I need to get everything under control. "Can you please set those down?" I ask the boy closest to me. He's on the baseball team, and he's currently juggling five apples at once.

But the music has been turned up to full volume, the heavy bass shaking the walls. My voice is all but drowned out.

"Hello?" I try again, louder, straining my vocal cords. When that doesn't work, I tap his shoulder.

"What?" The boy glances at me without pausing. "What do you want?"

"The apples—you're going to hit something—"

The words have barely left my mouth when his hand slips and one of the apples goes flying. It knocks over the potted plant on the bookshelf. The clay shatters at once, all the dirt spilling out onto the floor.

"Oops," he says faintly. "Maybe I can—"

"No—no, it's okay." I eye the remaining apples, terrified they're going to end up hurtling across the room too. "You just . . . stay there. I can handle this myself."

I push past the sweaty dancing bodies and giggling clusters of friends and head straight for the cleaning cabinet in the laundry room, but one of the football team stars comes staggering out. Jonathan Sok: tall, tan, handsome, and famously terrible at holding down his liquor. He's swinging an empty beer bottle and straddling our only broom like it's a horse.

"Look at my horse," he calls out with glee, galloping around the cramped space in a circle. He's so drunk that his words are barely coherent. But he keeps talking. "Look at my horse—look at my horse—look at my horse—"

"Yes, I can see," I say, to humor him. Mostly, I just want my broom back. "If you could please give it back to me—"

"It's a *horse*," he protests, pouting. "Her name is Wendy."

I'm too tired to sit around and debate the name of an inanimate object. "Sure, whatever. I really need to clean this mess up . . ."

He prances out of the way. Up until this very moment, I didn't think people could actually prance. "You'll have to catch me first," he says.

"No, this isn't a game—" I reach for the broom at the same moment he twirls around on the spot, promptly smacking me in the face with the handle.

It doesn't hurt that much. Not enough to leave a bruise. But the sheer physical shock of it sends me reeling backward, clutching my cheek. It feels like it's knocked something askew inside me. Or maybe I'm already off-balance; maybe I have been since I grabbed Julius and kissed him, or since I kicked him outside. Maybe this is one of those Jenga block scenarios, where the whole structure is shaking, unsteady, and all it takes is a single wrong move—or in this case, an unfortunate collision with the end of a broomstick—for everything to come crashing down.

"Okay, you know what?" I drop my hand from my sore face.

Jonathan Sok gapes up at me with bleary eyes, too dazed to be fully apologetic. "This party's over."

"Huh?"

"I said, *it's over*." My voice comes out louder and harsher than I meant, and the conversations around me die down. The air seems to congeal. "I need to clean everything up and there are way too many people so if you could please all just . . . I don't know."

There's a terrible pause. The music's turned off, and the immediate silence is deafening by contrast. I can hear my own ears ringing.

"Well, fine. Jesus," somebody mutters. They toss their bottle into a bin, grab their jacket, and turn to go. It's not long before the others follow in a staggered line, collecting their bags and fumbling around for their phones, the sober ones jangling their car keys. A few stop by to thank me for hosting the party, or apologize for making a mess, but most of them don't even look at me.

So much for fixing things.

My face and eyes burn. Slowly the house empties out, leaving me with the dirt on the floor, the overturned vases and chairs. It feels like someone's scraped my insides raw. It's a feeling worse than crying, because there's no escape, nowhere for the disappointment and shame to go.

At what point, I wonder, staring at the front door as it swings shut one last time, *does something become unfixable?* At what point is a tapestry riddled with so many holes and loose threads that it's impossible to patch it up again? That it deserves to be thrown away instead?

"Wow. This place is a mess."

I jump at the voice, my heartbeat pounding in my throat.

I'd thought that everyone had left, but when I spin around, Julius is there. He's stayed. There's an unfamiliar expression on his face, something conflicted, something almost soft, like there's an ache in him. In the orange glow of the living room lights, he looks far more vulnerable than he had outside, against the shadows and sky.

I wonder if he's going to make me apologize for kicking him. I'm not sure I'd be able to, even if I do feel a faint pinch of guilt.

But he doesn't say anything else. He simply rolls up his sleeves and starts smoothing out the cushions on the couch.

I stare at him. "What are you doing?"

He doesn't glance back up. "What does it look like?"

"I . . ." No words come out. I half expect it to be a trick, but then he crouches down to clean up the confetti on the floor, his eyes dark and clear, his face serious.

Tentatively, I join him. Neither of us speaks, but the silence no longer feels like a death blow. If anything, it feels peaceful. I focus on the repetitive motions, the easy rhythm of the task, the hushed swish of the broom. Maybe it's because we've already worked together before on the bike shed, but we seem to understand each other. He grabs the trash can without me even having to ask; I pass him the water when I notice him reaching up.

In one psychology class, the teacher had explained to us how memories are formed. What kind of memories stick with us over the years. It's not always the ones you think matter the most, the typical milestones. Like, I can't really remember what we did for my thirteenth birthday, or the Spring Festival that year we flew to China, or the day I received the prestigious All Rounder Award.

But I do remember coming home from school one afternoon and smelling lemon cake in the kitchen and sharing it with my mother on these new pretty porcelain plates she'd bought on discount. I remember a random Saturday from nine years ago, when Max and I tried to lure the ducks home with little bites of bread. I remember the face of an old woman I'd passed on the street, the precise floral patterns of her shirt, the dandelion sewn into her handbag, even though we never spoke and I never saw her again.

And I know, even as the present is unfolding, that I'll always remember this. The gleam of confetti on the hardwood floor. The night falling around us. The dark strand of hair falling over Julius's eyes. The quiet that feels like a truce, a reprieve from the war, something more.

"So," Julius says as he carefully removes a party hat from one of Mom's wood statues. "I think it's safe to say you won't be throwing another party anytime soon?"

I manage a snort, as if the idea itself doesn't make me nauseous. "No. No, I probably shouldn't have thrown this one. I just wanted . . . I just thought . . ."

"You thought it'd make up for the emails."

It's so embarrassing to hear it spoken aloud, by Julius no less. It sounds so pathetic.

"But why?" he presses.

I sweep the remaining confetti up into a small pile. "What do you mean, *why*? I didn't have many other choices. It's not like I could have afforded to send each person a personalized apology letter and expensive gift box for emotional damage."

"I mean, why do you think you have to make everyone forgive you? What is there to forgive? Not saying that you were right to write those emails," he adds hastily, catching the look on my face. "But I read the one you sent Rosie. She stole your science fair idea. If we're really talking about forgiveness, shouldn't she also be asking you to forgive her?"

I don't know what to make of this. I haven't given any thought to what others might owe me, only what I owe them. "That's . . . different," I say eventually. "She's more upset."

"You're upset too."

"Yeah, but she doesn't seem to care, and I do. I really—" My breath catches in my throat. I bow my head, dump the confetti into a plastic bag, watching the artificial colors catch the light as they swirl through the air. "I really can't stand it when people are angry at me. Like, I know it might be simple for others, but

I can't focus on anything else. I can't just forget about it and go on with my own life. It's like there's something hard wedged inside my chest. I'll always feel guilty. I'll always want to make amends."

He doesn't reply, and I realize I've said way too much.

"Forget it," I mumble. "You won't understand."

"I'm trying to."

My head jerks up, and when I meet his eyes, I experience a roaring rush of heat. "Why?" I fling the question back at him.

He holds my gaze for a second. Two. Three. I count each one as it passes, the way I count my own staggered breaths. The silence stretches out like a string—then he sets down the half-filled plastic bag in his hand, the crushed cans and containers rattling inside, and the silence snaps. "I don't know." He clears his throat. Motions toward the sitting room. "I'll . . . I should go clean up in there. I believe someone was trying to re-create the Eiffel Tower with your textbooks."

I nod, once. Like I couldn't care less where he goes. "Okay. Thanks."

I make a conscious effort not to stare after him as he leaves. An even more concentrated effort to stay in the living room, to keep the distance between us, to not dwell too hard on our conversation. But thanks to him, there's not much left for me to clean. Once I've mopped and vacuumed up the last of the dirt and pushed the couches back to their original positions, I pause at the doorway.

Everything has already been tidied. He's standing at my desk, his gaze drawn down to the photo in his hand. He's so focused that he doesn't hear me walk over until I'm right behind him.

"I didn't mean to—" He spins around. Flushes. "I swear I wasn't snooping. Someone pulled out this album from the cabinet and a few of the photos fell out and . . ."

My eyes find the photo too, and my heart twists.

It's an old family photo, taken ten years ago. We're at a hot pot restaurant, the four of us squeezed around the round table, the plates spread out in front of us. Max is little more than a kid, his hair spiky and his cheeks round. He's wearing that basketball jersey he loved so much he'd refuse to take it off even to wash the toothpaste stains on the front. My mom's dressed up in her favorite cardigan and turtleneck, her raven hair curled and styled in a way it hasn't been since that night. And my dad's gazing over at me with such pride that it hurts to inhale. We look . . . happy. It must be the world's greatest magic show; it's so convincing, even if it's false. Made up. Make-believe. Because less than a month after the photo was taken, he had left.

"I've never seen your father before." He says it carefully, because I'm sure he knows by now. They all know, to some extent, no matter how hard we've tried to hide it, to smooth out the visible lump in the carpet. When your dad doesn't show up to a single Father's Day breakfast ten years in a row, people are bound to suspect something's off.

"He probably doesn't look like that anymore," I say, taking

the photo from him. I resist the urge to rip it into shreds. To hug it to my chest. "I mean, I wouldn't really know. Maybe he's grown a beard." It was one of those things we always laughed about. *I prefer clean-shaven men*, my mom had insisted whenever he raised the idea. *The day you get a beard will be the day we get a divorce.* It used to be a running joke in the family.

Julius peers over at me, still in that careful, attentive way, like the floor is made of glass. *You won't understand. I'm trying to.* "Is it hard? Not having him around?"

"No," I say instinctively. Force of habit. I've repeated it so many times to myself that most days I believe it. I slide the photo back into the faded album, snap it closed, but for some reason, I keep talking. "I mean, I don't . . . Maybe it's not that I miss him. But there are times when—when I wonder what it'd be like if he were still here. Like when my mom and I got into a fight last summer over who had lost the phone charger and, as she was yelling at me, I just found myself wishing . . . he was there to step in. To tell me it was okay. To comfort me and take my mom outside until we'd both calmed down.

"Or, as ridiculous as it sounds, when we go to my favorite restaurant. My mom and my brother both have the same tastes, you know—they hate spicy and sour foods. But my dad and I would always get this sour stir-fried chicken dish. They only make it in servings of two, so now . . . now I never order it. Because I don't have anyone to share it with."

Because having one parent is enough.

Until it isn't.

"So where was your brother in all of this?" he asks.

I blink, confused. "My brother?"

He nods toward the album, seemingly confused by my confusion. "He's the eldest in the family, right? Shouldn't he have . . . I don't know, stepped in?"

"No. No, but it's not his fault," I add quickly, catching the faint furrow between his brows. *Of course not. It's all* your *fault*, a cool, familiar voice whispers in my head. *You were the one who ruined everything.* "He took it harder than I did. I remember that he used to be pretty well-behaved, but after our dad left, he kind of just . . . gave up. He started ditching his classes and handing in his homework late and getting into trouble at school. Honestly the only thing he still seemed interested in was basketball—without that, I'm not sure if he'd have gotten into college."

Julius absorbs this without any outward emotion, but he hasn't looked away the entire time.

"Sorry," I mumble, stepping past him and shoving the album into the cabinet. I don't know what's gotten into me, why I'm suddenly spilling out my guts to *Julius*.

"What are you apologizing for?" he asks.

"Sorry, I didn't mean to," I say, then catch myself. A snort lurches out of me, and the ice inside my chest thaws slightly. "Okay, no, actually, I take it back—I'm not sorry. At all. About anything."

"You certainly didn't seem sorry about kicking me."

I tense, but when I look up, the corner of his mouth is curved up. Like we're sharing an inside joke. Before I can relax, he slides one foot closer, and the air between us suddenly turns molten.

"You also didn't seem too sorry about . . ." He trails off on purpose, but his eyes flicker down to my lips. Linger there, for a beat too long.

This is something else I know I'll always remember, no matter how hard I try to scrub it from my memory, to pretend otherwise.

That I had kissed Julius Gong.

That I'd kissed him, and wanted it.

The heat in the air spreads through my veins, and I twist away, searching for a distraction. From him. From this whole night. From the stuffy feeling in my chest, the crushing weight of everyone's disapproval, the consequences of the party. Easily—almost too easily—I find it. There's a bottle of beer left on the desk. Unopened. Untouched. My fingers twitch toward it.

Could I?

It's astonishing that I'm even contemplating it. It would be impulsive, foolish, completely unlike me. But how many impulsive things have I done tonight? Would another really make any difference?

There's a false assumption people tend to make about me: They believe that all I care about is being the best. That the closer I am to the top, the happier I am. That if it comes down to it, a 30 percent is better than a zero; that being mediocre is at least better than being *bad*. But I swing between extremes. If I can't be the best, I would rather be the best at being the worst. If I'm going to fail, I would rather fail at it thoroughly than do a job halfway.

And if I'm going to self-destruct, then why stop at kissing the enemy?

"You don't want to drink that," Julius says, his voice slicing through my thoughts. He's studying me, his head tilted to the side like a bird of prey. He sounds so confident. Like he knows better. Like he always knows better.

It's infuriating—and it's exactly what helps me make up my mind.

I uncap the bottle, holding his gaze the whole time in challenge, and take a long, deliberate swig. The liquid burns my mouth, so much stronger than I'd been prepared for. It tastes like fire. Rushes straight to my head.

I cough, spluttering, but I keep going.

The first few mouthfuls are disgusting. Bitter and biting, like medicine but heavier, with an unpleasant aftertaste. I can't believe this is what adults make a big fuss about. I can't believe people pay real money just to endure this. But then my body starts to warm up from within, and my head starts to spin. Normally I would hate it: the loss of control, the disorientation. But tonight it smooths out the sharp edges, dials down the background noise to a lovely hum, numbs the pang in my chest.

The next few mouthfuls are much easier to swallow. It still doesn't taste very good, but I kind of like the way it scorches my throat.

I drink quickly, encouraged by Julius's muted surprise. *That should shut him up*, I think to myself. I've almost finished the entire bottle when I twirl it around to check the label, and realize that it isn't beer after all. It's bourbon.

"Oh," I say, setting the bottle down. "Oh. Crap."

No wonder I'm so dizzy.

It occurs to me that I should be more concerned. That this is very, very, *very* bad. But the panic stays on the sidelines, like a spider in a neighboring room: not so close as to necessitate a response just yet. If anything, I feel perfectly fine.

"This would be a very inconvenient time to find out you're a lightweight," Julius mutters.

I squint at him. Search his face. And maybe it's because of this new warmth, this dreamy sensation—both like falling and like floating—that I find myself marveling at how well-defined his features are. Not *handsome*, like the princes in fairy tales. But beautiful and cold and deadly, like the villains we're taught to fear. "I'm not a lightweight," I inform him, pronouncing each word loudly and carefully, as proof. "I was kind of worried just now—like, literally, a second ago—that I would be drunk, but now I think . . ." I close my eyes. Scan my body. Open them again. "I'm actually okay. I don't think it's made any noticeable difference? Wow, yeah. It's so wild. I can't believe I'm just, like, absorbing this alcohol into my bloodstream. It hasn't impeded my speech one bit. I could go to school like this. I could *take a test* like this. Granted that it's in a subject I've studied before."

Amusement touches his mouth. "Right," he says. "Of course."

"Do you want some?" I ask him, offering up the little remaining liquor to him, since it's only polite. "It doesn't taste that disgusting once you get used to it."

He gently pushes the bottle back down. "No, thanks."

"What do you want, then? I can give it to you."

This should be a simple enough question. Multiple choice at most. But he falters as if he's received a three-thousand-word essay prompt. Swallows. Looks away. "Nothing," he says at last. "I don't—want anything."

"Are you sure? You're, like, turning red." Maybe I shouldn't be pointing this out. A small voice in the back of my head tells me that I'm not supposed to. But why? Why *not*? It's not like I'm lying. I shift forward, just to get a closer look. And I'm right. His neck is flushed, the color seeping through his cheeks. "It's really obvious here," I say, tracing out the line of his collarbone with one fingertip. Even his skin is unnaturally hot.

Something flashes over his face. He wets his lower lip and steps back.

"Is it sunburn? Oh wait, that makes no sense." I laugh at myself, laugh like it's the funniest thing in the world. Everything strikes me as hilarious now. "You can't get sunburnt at *night*. Or . . . no. Can you? Is that, like, a possibility? Is this something that could come up in our next science quiz?" I have the overwhelming urge to find out, right this second. I must know. I hate not knowing things. "Alex?" I call.

No response.

"Alex?" I call again, louder, spinning around. "Hello? Are you there?"

Julius stares at me. "Is there a random man named Alex hiding inside your house? Or did you mean Alexa?"

"Isn't that what I just said?" I demand, annoyed. "Alexis? *Alexis*, can you hear me? Answer me. I really, really need to know if you can get sunburnt after dark. This is incredibly important."

"Again, it's Alexa," Julius says.

"Be quiet." I clamp both my hands over his mouth. "You're prettier when you don't talk."

He makes a faint, incredulous sound that's muffled by my palm, his breath tickling my skin. His expression doesn't change much, but I can sense his surprise, how it flickers beneath the surface. "Did you just call me pretty?"

"When you don't talk," I emphasize. "Which you're doing at present."

"So you admit it."

"What?" I've already lost track of our conversation. Maybe I am drunk. Or maybe my memory is declining. That's a terrifying thought. But then my attention shifts to the stray strand of hair tumbling over his forehead. I want to reach for him, brush it back. *Don't do it*, that same voice whispers, but it sounds more and more distant by the second. Inconsequential. So I give in to the impulse and lean forward, smoothing his hair. "It's so soft. Even softer than it looks," I murmur, playing with a dark lock of it between two fingers. He's gone very still before me, his pupils black and dilated. I can feel the air ripple with his next expelled breath, almost a pained sigh. "I always did like your hair."

"I thought you hated it," he says. His voice is scratchy, like he's swallowed sand.

I frown. Tug absently at the strand. "Did I say that?"

"You did. In your email." And then with his eyes on me, without having to pause or think twice, he recites, *"From the bottom of my heart, I really hope your comb breaks and you run out of whatever expensive hair products you've been using to make your hair appear deceptively soft when I'm sure it's not, because there's nothing soft about you, anywhere at all."*

They're my words, but on his lips they sound different. Intimate. Confessional. "How do you . . . remember all that?" I ask.

"I have all your emails memorized word for word," he says, then instantly looks like he regrets having spoken.

"You do?" My mouth falls open.

"No." He scowls. "No, forget I said—"

"You do," I say, an accusation this time. "Oh my god, you totally do." I start laughing again, laughing so hard I stumble back and land on the floor and clutch at my stomach. I laugh until I'm breathless, until I can't feel any pain in my chest, until nothing else matters except this. When my mirth finally dies down, I grin up at him. "Well, Julius Gong. It sounds like *you're* the one obsessed with me."

He rolls his eyes, but the skin of his neck turns a deeper shade of crimson.

"Can I ask you a question, then?" I say.

He regards me warily. "Depends."

"Sit down first," I command, patting the floor next to me.

"I would prefer not to—"

"*Sit,*" I say, grabbing his wrist and tugging him down.

"The floor's cold," he protests, though he remains sitting, his long legs sprawled out in front of him, his hands supporting his weight.

"Not as cold as you," I say. My head swims, and it feels like I'm moving in slow motion when I shuffle around to face him. "So. Tell me. Why is it always me?"

His brows crease. "What kind of question is that?"

"Why is it *me*?" The words come out slurred, swollen on my tongue. I wave my hands around with growing frustration. "Why do you . . . Why do you put all your energy into making *my* life difficult? What did I ever do to you to make you . . . hate me so much? It's been happening since the day we met each other. With dodgeball. With the spelling quiz in year six. With our history project. With *everything*. Why do you always single me out?"

"Because," he says quietly, a curious expression on his face.

I've never seen him so serious. So sincere. "You're the only person worth paying attention to."

And the pain comes crashing back through my chest, but it's transformed. Warm at the edges, burning hot within. I close my eyes, swallow, unable to speak. I want him to say it again. I wish he'd never said it.

"Are you satisfied now?" Julius asks. He sounds almost angry about it, spiteful, like he's been forced to prove a point against himself.

My eyes flutter open, and I'm alarmed by how close he is. Was he that close before? I can see the dark blue shadows under his collarbones, the flecks of gold in his irises, the soft curve of his lips, the pulse beating at his neck. *What if we kissed again?* The foolish notion floats to my brain, and I can't shake it away.

But before the idea can expand into something dangerous, I hear the unmistakable rumble of a car engine. Headlights flash through the windows, briefly bathing the front entrance in bright orange light, the silhouette of trees outlined against the glass. Then voices drift through the front yard. Max's voice, loud no matter the hour. ". . . can't blame me for *winning*, can you? You're always telling me to learn from my sister and set higher goals for myself. Shouldn't you be glad I'm so good at—"

"At mahjong?" comes my mom's shrill reply. "You think I should be proud of you? Where did you even learn to play, huh? Have you been gambling when you're supposed to be at school?"

"No! Bro, I swear—"

"I'm not your *bro*. Ni bu xiang huo le shi ba—"

"Okay, then, dearest mother, maybe it's just natural talent. Maybe this is my calling— *Ow*, stop hitting me—"

Oh my god.

They've come back early.

"Crap." I stand up too fast, and for a second the room is nothing but a blur of color. My head pounds harder. *"Crap."*

Julius jumps to his feet too. "What—"

"My parents," I babble. "I mean—my parent. My mom. She's back. She didn't— She doesn't know I was throwing a party. She's literally going to kill me and throw my corpse into a dumpster when she finds out."

"I think you're misusing the word *literal*—"

I cut him off. "You have to get out of here before she sees you."

"I— Okay." He steps left, then right again. Hesitates.

"The back door." I sweep the bottle into the bin—god, I could *slap* myself, I should never have let myself drink—and push Julius out of the room with both hands. The footsteps outside are drawing closer. The automatic lights on the front porch switch on. I can feel my heart pounding in my throat. The metaphorical panic-spider is no longer locked in the other room; it's now scuttling up my leg, and I want to scream.

"Here," I hiss at Julius, motioning toward the door. But then I see the top of Max's spiky hair through the bushes. He's coming in this way. I grab a fistful of Julius's shirt and yank him back.

"What the hell?" Julius demands.

"Front door," I amend, shoving him in the other direction. "Use the front door instead."

No sooner than I've spoken, the lights on the front porch flick on as well.

My stomach drops. We're surrounded on both sides.

It's an ambush.

"Okay, *think, Sadie*," I instruct myself out loud, massaging my head. "Stop being drunk and *think*. Get it together. You don't have any time left."

"This is a very fascinating look into your thought process," Julius remarks.

"Shush," I snap. "I'm *thinking*—"

And then a solution comes to me.

"The window." It's the only way.

His eyes widen a fraction. "You're joking. I'm not climbing out your window, Sadie. It's undignified."

"I'll owe you."

"You already owe me. How do you plan on returning all these favors?"

I ignore that and start dragging him toward the window in the laundry room. It's wide enough to fit his whole body, and it drops down to the narrow side path nobody ever uses. Most of it is concealed by overgrown shrubbery. "Here," I say, lifting the window for him. Faintly, through the door, I can hear the rattle of keys. *"Hurry."*

He glares at me but complies, swinging his leg over the white-painted frame and landing softly, gracefully on the wild grass below—

Right as the front door creaks open.

CHAPTER THIRTEEN

I'm trying to tiptoe my way down the hall when my mom calls my name.

"Sadie? What are you still doing up?"

I spin around, and the room spins too. The alcohol is still sloshing around in my stomach, my bloodstream, rendering everything blurry and surreal. I have to squint hard to focus. My mom's removing her coat, setting her car keys down on the counter; they're easily recognizable because she refuses to throw out the bright ribbons from chocolate boxes and insists instead on wrapping them around the key ring. There should be five ribbons in total, but when I blink, they duplicate into a mess of squiggly pink and blue lines.

God, I'm so drunk.

"I'm not drunk," I announce loudly. This seems like the normal, not-guilty thing to say, but I can tell from the way Mom stares at me that I've slipped up somehow. *It's okay*, I attempt to calm myself, biting my tongue so hard I taste the sharp tang of blood. *At least she hasn't found out about the party. You've cleaned up most of the evidence. There's absolutely no way—*

"Did you . . . host a party while we were gone?" Mom asks, frowning. Before I can reply, she strides into the living room and starts inspecting all the furniture. I want to disappear. "The dining table is askew. The books on the shelf aren't in alphabetical order. The left cabinet drawer is open. And is that—" She wipes a finger over something on the wall so minuscule that I can't even see what it is until she holds it right up to my face, under the lights. "That's a piece of *glitter*, isn't it?"

She's being very accurate. It is, indeed, a singular, dust-sized speck of glitter.

"We don't own anything with glitter in this house," she says, switching to Mandarin now. She always speaks in rapid Mandarin when she's agitated, as if all the words in the English language aren't enough to contain her rage. "Glitter is, without a doubt, the worst thing humanity has ever invented."

For reasons that escape me, I decide that the best response to this is: "What about weapons of war?"

"Excuse me?"

"Nothing," I backpedal. I'm having trouble standing up and talking at the same time. Or maybe just standing up without support. Or maybe being a human in general.

"What's going on with you?" she asks, her gaze heavy on me.

Everything is too heavy: the air around me, the clothes on my body, the skin on my bones, the invisible force pressing against my chest. The effort of a single, shaky breath. I can feel my palms sweating, the truth rising up like bile. "I—"

"Did you miss us?" Max comes strolling into the room from the other side of the house, grinning wide. He's holding up a packet of Wang Wang soft gummy candies—the lychee-flavored ones I love the most—which he waves around before me like a victory flag before dropping it into my palms. "Dude, you should have been there. Da Ma invited a bunch of her friends over and I absolutely thrashed them at mahjong. They ran out of money and had to start paying up in candy—you like this flavor, right? Anyway, it was hilarious. Mom forced us to leave before I could take everything, but I swear, if given the chance—"

"I'm talking to your sister," Mom says irritably. "Go wash up."

"Wait. Whoa, whoa, whoa. Wait a second." My brother stares at me. "Are you—*drunk*? Dude, I can't believe this. What the hell happened?"

I open my mouth to deny it—

And break down into tears instead.

I'm completely, utterly horrified. I never act this way. I'm only meant to absorb what others feel, present the best side of myself, sit still and swallow my own emotions. But it's like I've lost control over my own body, like I'm watching myself from the ceiling as I stand here in the middle of the living room, crying and clutching the gummy candy. I'm inconsolable. Hysterical. I'm sobbing ten years' worth of tears, choking as if there's something sick and poisonous inside me, something painful, and I need to force it out of my system. But it's stuck. It's festered beneath my flesh for so long now that it's a part of me, the deep ache like a thumb on a tender bruise.

"Hold up." Alarm flashes over Max's face. I've witnessed him having a mental breakdown over an ad about a lost squirrel before, but he hasn't seen me cry in years. "Bro, you're scaring me—"

"Max," Mom says quietly. "Go."

He doesn't protest this time, but he keeps shooting me worried glances over his shoulder as he hurries down the corridor.

Then my mom gently grabs my arm. Sits me down on the couch next to her.

"What's wrong?" she asks. If Mandarin is her language for anger, it's also her language for softness. It's her voice coaxing us to sleep when we were younger, her humming under her breath as she sewed the buttons back into our jackets so they were good as new again, her telling us it was time for dinner, her whispering goodnight as she turned off the big lights, her calling to let us know she would be there soon, just wait.

"I regret it," I manage to say on a stuttering breath. I weep like I haven't in ages, not since I was an infant.

"Regret what?"

Everything.

I regret writing the emails, I regret throwing the party, I regret kissing Julius in a moment of impulsivity and giving him the power to humiliate me. I regret it so much it feels like my liver is bleeding dry. I regret it so much it feels more like hatred, a knife turned inward, nails squeezing into flesh. I hate myself for everything that's happened, because every mistake is my own to bear. And it feels like fear too. Like pure, animal terror, the stomach-curdling moment in the horror film when you realize you made the wrong move, you unlocked the doors too soon, and the masked man with the chain saw is standing right behind you.

There's nothing I want more than for time to be a physical thing, something I can split into two with my own hands, so I can turn it around, shatter it, undo all the consequences.

"Is this about the party?" Mom asks. "Because I'm not mad. I wish you had *told* me, and I don't condone the alcohol, but I'm actually quite happy. It's about time you did things like a normal teenager."

This is so shocking my tears freeze in my eyes. "You're—not?"

She smiles at my surprise. *Smiles.* I wonder if I've been transported into an alternate universe. In the correct version, she would be lecturing me or chasing me around the house with her plastic slippers. She would be mad that I keep ruining everything, and she would have every right to be. I don't deserve to be forgiven so easily. "Of course. When I was a teenager, I threw parties every few weeks. They were very popular."

"I— What?" A dull throbbing sensation has started behind my eyes, but I can't tell if it's from the liquor or the crying or the strain of fitting this bizarre information into my brain. "Since when? I thought you said . . . I thought you said you herded the goats around the mountains when you were a teenager."

"Just because we had goats doesn't mean we didn't have parties."

I blink. The room is spinning again, faster than before. "But . . . I'm not allowed to. I shouldn't be having fun and throwing parties and—and doing the wrong things. I'm not supposed to cause any trouble."

"Who told you that?" she asks. "Who said you weren't allowed?"

Nobody, I realize. But nobody ever *had* to tell me. It was enough for me to cower behind the wall as my parents fought, enough to watch my father leave, to feel the doors trembling in his wake. It wouldn't have happened if it weren't for me. That's the truth I always crawl back to, the bone that set wrong in my body all those years ago. My dad had been at work, Max had been out playing basketball with his friends, and my mom needed to go buy groceries, so she'd asked me to steam the pork buns for dinner. I'd been so eager to prove that I was reliable, but then I'd gotten distracted by the show I was watching. I only remembered the boiling pot again when I smelled the smoke. The sharp, bitter odor of something burning.

I had slammed my laptop down and sprinted into the kitchen to check, but it was too late: The fire had burned a hole straight through the bottom, the metal scorched so severely it was coal black. It had been my mom's favorite pot, the one she had bought with her savings and shipped all the way from a store in Shanghai. I didn't try to hide it when she walked in an hour later. I just stood there guiltily, my head bowed, the damage on open display behind me.

"How can you be so irresponsible?" she'd demanded, rubbing her face like she hoped to scrub away her exhaustion. "I only asked you to do this *one* thing while I was gone. You're not a baby anymore, Sadie; I expect more from you."

I'd apologized, over and over and over. "I know. I'm sorry. I'm really sorry, Mom. Please don't be angry with me. I'm so sorry."

But then my father had come home, and he'd been angry too—not at me, but at my mom. "She's still a child," he'd insisted, dumping his briefcase on the couch. "Why do you always do this? Why do you always make a big deal out of nothing? It's just a pot."

My mom had whirled on him with alarming speed, her eyes flashing. "You say that because you *never* cook. You go to work and come back and expect dinner to be all ready and waiting on the table for you. You're no better than a child yourself."

"It's my fault," I'd put in. My parents so rarely argued that I didn't know what to do, only that I hated it and needed to make it stop. "I'll fix it, I promise. I-I'll find a new pot, the same brand as the old one. I won't do it again—"

But they were no longer even looking at me.

"I never cook because you don't let me," my father was saying. "You lose patience within minutes; look at you, you're losing patience now—"

"Don't be such a hundan," Mom had snapped, and that's how I knew she was really furious: She was swearing in Mandarin.

And just like that, my father had exploded. He'd slammed

his hand down on the table so hard I expected him to break something, his features twisted with rage. The melted pot lay forgotten on the stove. They glared at each other from opposite ends of the room, and then it was like some kind of invisible barrier had broken, and they were flinging accusations at each other, complaints, curse words.

"Do you *enjoy* making other people miserable?" my dad had accused, and I couldn't help it anymore. I was caught between two sides of a war, and by pure protective instinct, I stepped out in front of my mom. Chose my alliances without thinking.

"Don't talk to my mom like that," I'd said. Quietly, at first, then louder. "You're upsetting her. Just—*just go away*." I hadn't meant it. I was only sick and scared of their fighting. I only wanted the argument to stop.

Hurt had flickered over his face, and I got the sense I'd committed some terrible act of betrayal, before his thick brows drew together, his hands balled into fists. "You all want me to go? Fine," he spat. "I will."

Then he was leaving because I'd all but asked him to, and my mom was right there, watching him, witnessing our lives collapse in on themselves. "Don't come back," she yelled, and he never did.

Once the dust had settled, she told me it had nothing to do with me. It had been her choice. They were grown adults; they made decisions for themselves. All the expected, hollow excuses. But I didn't believe her. *Couldn't.* Every time I played the scene back, I saw myself poised at both the starting and end point. I had been the trigger, and all that came after had happened for what? Because I hadn't listened to her. Because I hadn't been well-behaved. Because I'd been impulsive.

Because some mistakes were irreversible, like glitter in the carpet, a wine stain on a favorite dress.

"What's really going on, Sadie?" my mom asks, peering at my face.

I can't bring myself to tell her about the emails, so I settle for the closest answer I can find. "Everyone hates me," I whisper. "I did something to make them all hate me, and I thought . . . I thought I could change their minds."

She absorbs this for a moment. "Well, I doubt that's true. And even if it is, it's not the end of the world."

I let out a shaky laugh. Adults are always saying that. Other than *If someone asked you to jump off a cliff, would you do it?* (which simply doesn't strike me as a realistic scenario; who would benefit from making somebody else hurl themselves off a cliff?) and *You'll understand when you have children of your own* (even though I don't plan on ever having children), this seems to be their favorite line. *It's not the end of the world.* And maybe there's some tiny grain of truth in it. Maybe I'll grow up and change my mind a decade later. Except for now, this *is* my whole world. The people I sit next to in class, the faces I have to see at school every single day, the teachers who determine the grades that get sent to the university that determines the trajectory of the rest of my life.

"Why don't you just give it some time?" she suggests. "The more you force something, the less it works. Haven't you heard the saying? A melon picked too soon is seldom sweet."

I stare. "You mean . . . do nothing?" It's an absurd notion. It's the route people who turn their essays in two days late would choose. But all of a sudden I'm aware of how exhausted I am.

"Yes, do nothing," she says firmly. "Live your life and see what happens. Of course, I don't mean around the house," she adds. "I expect you to clean up all the rooms and return everything to its original place."

"I— Okay." I start to stand up but she yanks me back down onto the couch.

"Tomorrow," she says. "Tonight, all you need to do is drink the chicken soup I'm about to make you and go to bed, okay?"

"Okay," I repeat again, stunned. I must still be very drunk, because I can't help the next words that tumble out of my mouth: "I'm really sorry."

She shakes her head. "You don't have to apologize for the party—"

"Not about the party," I say. "About—about my father."

Silence.

It's the one topic in the house we never bring up. It's like a rash you're told not to scratch, even when it pains you, for fear of making it worse. I already regret it, already want to take the words back, but my mom's gaze is calm.

"Sadie. It's not your fault."

"But—"

"It happened," she says, "and it was inevitable, and now we have the rest of our lives to live."

"*Inevitable?* How? You never fought. You were both so happy up until that night," I whisper.

"Oh, no, we weren't happy. We weren't in love with each other. We were simply *polite*," she says, looking over my shoulder now, as if she can see her past projected onto the bare walls. "I almost wish that we had fought more, that we'd cared enough to challenge each other and bicker over the little things. Better that than just swallowing our resentment and staying quiet until we couldn't take it anymore."

I feel like somebody has knocked me upside down. Like I might throw up at any moment. "That's not possible," I tell her. "I should have sensed it. I would have known—"

"You were so young," she says. "You're *still* so young. And we didn't want you to know." She squeezes my wrist lightly.

"But then . . . you're not happy now," I say, scanning her face, noting the familiar signs of fatigue in the faint purple around her eyes, the downward turn of her lips. "It's because he's gone, isn't it?"

She shakes her head. "If there's any reason why I'd be unhappy, it's because *you're* not happy."

I am. I'm fine, I try to say, except the lie won't even make its way past my lips.

"All you do is work and study and live for other people," she goes on, gesturing to the stacks of textbooks on the floor, the shiny awards and sports trophies on the bookshelf. "Yes, you help out a lot, and I'm very grateful for it; the bakery wouldn't be running without you. But I'd much rather see you enjoying your teen years while you can. I worry that you're going to look back when you're twenty or forty and all you'll remember is your desk and the dishes. Really, it would ease my guilt if you did." Her smile is sad. "I never wanted you to have to grow up this fast."

My head buzzes. I can't believe it. It's like spending years of your life training for a game only to realize you understood the rules all wrong.

"I'm going to make that soup now." Mom stands up. "Stay here."

And then she heads into the kitchen, leaving me to reassemble all the pieces of my life I was once so certain of.

CHAPTER FOURTEEN

Everyone hates the Athletics Carnival.

Everyone. The nonathletic kids hate it because it's one whole day spent sweating in the open and stumbling after your classmates. The athletic kids hate it because there's an incredible amount of pressure to perform, and someone always ends up with a sprained ankle or torn ligament.

Though I fall into the latter category, I don't usually mind the event as much as the others. But after spending the weekend hungover and miserable, it's difficult to drum up any enthusiasm.

"I have a solution," Abigail says as we walk into the rented stadium, our duffel bags bumping against our knees. The sun is unreasonably bright today, and the temperature rises anywhere the light touches, so that soon most students are shrugging out of their thick sweaters and tracksuits. Better this, I guess, than the year the school insisted we run in a literal thunderstorm. More than one person sprained their ankle that time. "What if you ran me over gently with a car? They'd have to cancel the carnival, right? I'm willing to take one for the team."

A small snort escapes my lips. The stadium is so vast that it takes us ten minutes just to reach the stands and plop our water bottles down on the plastic seats. Every year, we come here, and every year, I still find myself intimidated by the sheer size of the running track.

"If you want to take one for the team, you could join the relay," I tell Abigail while I slather multiple layers of sunscreen all over my body. Those year-round UV radiation infographics they shoved down our throats in primary school have really stuck with me. "We still have an opening left."

She makes a face. "Listen, we both know I'm multitalented, but running is one of the only things I'm *not* great at."

"Doesn't matter. I'll run fast enough to make up for it."

"Could we please at least consider the idea of hitting me with a car?" she whines.

"Abigail."

"Fine." She throws her hands up. "Only because I still feel guilty about leaving the party early."

My gut squirms at the reminder, but I force myself to smile. "I told you, it's fine. It went well."

"That's not what everyone else is saying."

I make an effort not to react. *I don't care.* I squeeze more sunscreen into my palms and smear it thick over my neck, the strong, artificial smell burning my nostrils. *I don't want to know. It's better if I don't know.* "What . . . What is everyone else saying?"

She hesitates. "That you kind of, like, flipped out."

They're not wrong, but it feels like a slap in the face anyway. A hundred protests and explanations and apologies make their way to my lips. I swallow them all down. After my little breakdown,

I'd promised myself I would listen to my mom. I would give it time. Resist picking any unripe watermelons, or whatever the metaphor is meant to be.

"Also," she says, frowning, "I heard that something . . . happened with Julius?"

My stomach contracts. "Hang on. First tell me what happened with *you*," I say, wiping the excess sunscreen on my arms. I'm mostly changing the subject to buy myself time, to figure out how I'm supposed to tell her I kissed the boy I've been ranting about for the past decade. "Did you manage to help your sister?"

A shadow crosses her face. "I did. Well, kind of. I helped her with the car, but . . ." She chews her lower lip, then heaves a sigh. "The reason she and Liam were fighting was because she found out he's been cheating on her. Not just with one person, but *multiple people*."

I wince, sympathetic but unsurprised.

"I can't believe I didn't know," she says, kicking at the artificial grass. "I even encouraged her to stay with him the last time they fought. I should have been able to sense something was off."

This is the thing about Abigail: She might not have the best grades or the most reliable career plans, but I know she prides herself on having good instinct, whether it's about shoes or boys or if the teachers will actually be collecting the homework on Monday. She makes all the calls, gives out the advice. She's always right—and that's a direct quote from one of the sticky notes on her lunch box.

"I just— I thought I was doing what was best for her," she continues in a small voice.

And I realize that I absolutely can't tell her what happened between me and Julius. The party had been her idea too. The last thing she needs to hear right now is how much I regretted the whole night, how it's made my weird relationship with Julius a thousand times more complicated. "You couldn't have known," I reassure her. "It's an unfortunate feature of douchebags that they're good at hiding their douchebag tendencies. And by the way, you were totally right about the party."

"Really?"

The fact that she's even asking is proof she's just suffered a terrible blow to her self-esteem. "Yeah, seriously. Like, yes, I kind of lost it at the end because things got a little out of control, but before that, I had so much fun. I haven't felt that enthusiastic about life since I finished color-coding all my history notes." It's a miracle I don't choke on the words. Before she can detect my lie, I spin around. "Now, if you'll excuse me, I have to go get a bunch of people to sign up for races they would rather die than run."

It's a legitimate reason. Ms. Hedge cornered me outside the bus before we left this morning and forced the task on me. Julius and I each have twenty spots to fill, which is why I spend the next half hour running around the stadium—not in races, but in search of potential participants. By the end, ten spots are still left empty. Nothing works, even when I use every strategy I can think of:

Pleading.

"It's really important," I beg one of the sportier boys in our year. He's lounging in the front row of the stands, shamelessly scrolling through some pretty girl's account on his phone. He doesn't glance up at me. "Please. Everyone should sign up for at least one race—"

"Is it compulsory though?" he asks.

"I . . . It's *expected*—"

"Will the principal expel me if I don't run this race?"

"No, but—"

"Yeah, I'm good, thanks." I watch him send the girl's recent post to a friend, alongside a disturbing number of heart-eye emojis. "Good luck finding someone else."

"Good luck getting her attention with your current profile picture," I can't help muttering. I wouldn't under normal circumstances, but after the party, I figure I can't be any *less* popular than I already am.

Now he jerks his head up. Looks alarmed. "What? Hey, wait, what's wrong with my current—"

But I'm already moving on to my next target with another strategy.

Negotiating.

"Just one race," I tell Georgina when I find her by the water fountains. "I can run the fifteen hundred meters for you if you run the five hundred meters."

She shoots me an apologetic smile. "Sorry, Sadie. I twisted my ankle on the bus just now. It's probably best that I don't."

"On the—on the *bus*?" I repeat, blinking. "How did you . . . How is that even . . ."

"I think I was sitting down," she says.

"And?"

"And then I stood up," she says somberly.

"You twisted your ankle," I say, in case I'm misunderstanding. "From the very act of standing."

"Yep. That did it," she agrees, and turns away. Which leads me to my last resort—

Guilt tripping.

"We need you," I say, cornering Ray outside the bathrooms. "If you don't run at least one of the races, then Georgina Wilkins will have to, and she's twisted her ankle. You're not going to let her go instead of you, are you?"

Ray dries his hands on his shirt and raises his brows. "Twisted her ankle? How?"

"You don't need to know," I say hastily. "Can you run? Or will you sit on the sidelines, in the shade, and watch all your classmates struggle out there on the track, sweating and gasping for breath?"

"Sit in the shade," he says without hesitation. "I have a fear of running, you see."

I almost throw up blood. "You're not serious."

"It's a very real fear. Google it."

"I'm sorry, but how does that even work?"

"As soon as my feet start moving very fast," he says, "my heart just starts beating wildly, and my vision goes all blurry. It's like being on a roller coaster. Or in a race car. The speed at which the world rushes past me is terrifying."

"How poetic," I remark under my breath.

"You're welcome, by the way," he adds.

I stare. "For *what*?"

"The dare at your party." He grins. "Never imagined you and Julius would be so into it."

"I wasn't—" My voice comes out ten octaves too high, and I forcefully lower it back down as Ray's grin widens. "I was *not*. And he most definitely wasn't either." Just the memory makes my face burn like it's being pressed to a stove. *I would rather die than kiss you again.* "Forget it," I decide, shaking my head free of all unwelcome thoughts. "I'll just—I'll run the races by myself."

"Well, you better go soon," he says, stepping right into the shade. "I think the relay's starting now."

I'm cursing the world when I take my place beside Julius.

He looks unreasonably relaxed. Prepared. The sun dances over his hair as he stretches his limbs out and surveys the running track. Of course, if I had *his* team, I would probably be relaxed too. He's got Rosie, Jonathan, and a national athlete as his first three runners for the relay. They're all known for being fast. I have Abigail, one of Rosie's friends, and the guy who came in dead last in the one-hundred-meter sprint last year because he got tired halfway.

"How did you go with the sign-ups?" he asks, glancing over at me.

"Fine," I say briskly, flexing my right leg, then my left. The race will be starting in two minutes.

"Well, I've filled up all the positions for my races," he says. "It was hardly any trouble getting people to enter."

"How nice that it worked out for you."

He pretends to miss my sarcasm. "Aren't you going to wish me good luck?" he asks. "Since we're racing against each other and all."

I bounce slightly on the balls of my feet to warm up, waiting for my nerves to morph into adrenaline. Since it's the first race of the day, the relay is always the one everybody pays the most attention to. I need to focus. I need to win this. I need to beat him. "Are you going to wish *me* good luck?"

He laughs. Literally, laughs in my face. "Now, why would I do that?"

In the distance, the teacher lifts the starting pistol. All the muscles in my body tense.

"In that case," I say, staring straight ahead, "I hope you break your leg."

"You're very prickly today," he comments, unfazed. "Is it because you couldn't find anyone willing to run? Or is it because of your massive hangover?"

I stiffen, my focus breaking, and whirl around to face him. Luckily all the other runners are already in position, so there's no one around to overhear.

"Don't tell me you've forgotten how drunk you were," he says, his gaze sharper, assessing.

"I—I don't know what you're talking about."

"Really?" He cocks his head. "Nothing?"

"No." I'm lying, sort of. The details from Saturday are fuzzy, but I remember the feeling growing inside me when it was just the two of us. Like there was a burning torch in my chest, heat buzzing through my veins, more potent than the liquor itself. I remember the wanting, the dangerous knife point of desire, the need to do something foolish and reckless with him. Now that I'm completely sober, it's easy to dismiss it all as pure, physical attraction. It makes scientific sense. The alcohol would have helped me ignore the many defects of his personality, until all that was left was his geometrically pleasing features, his eyes and his lips and his hands. And from an evolutionary standpoint, isn't it normal to want someone pretty, who happens to be your age, and who also just happens to be in your house? Isn't it coded in our biology?

"Then why are you blushing?" Julius asks.

I twist my head away. "Stop it. I know what you're doing."

"What am I doing?"

The pistol goes off with a loud bang, and cheers rise from the stands.

It's starting.

"Distracting me," I reply through my teeth, willing myself to focus on the race. On Abigail. A few seconds in and she's already falling behind Rosie.

"You wouldn't think that if it wasn't working," Julius says, and I can hear the poisonous smile in his voice. "But do you really not recall any details?"

The second runner on their team has picked up the baton. Jonathan is so fast I swear I can see the wind at his heels. Abigail, meanwhile, is panting hard, holding out the baton with one shaking arm—and the next runner fumbles it.

A mixture of screams and frustrated cries sound through the stadium.

It's okay, I reassure myself. Repeat it like a chant inside my head. It's okay. It's fine. I'm the last runner for a reason. I can make up for all the lost time.

"You don't remember what you asked me to do?" Julius presses.

I can't help it. I swivel toward him again, my heart thudding, even though I'm aware I'm rising to the bait. "What?"

But *now* he chooses to shut up. Their team has completed their second exchange, and I can only watch, choking on my own frustration, as Julius smoothly accepts the baton and takes off.

"Come on," I hiss, tapping my feet. Our runner is still five feet away.

Four feet.

Julius is racing far ahead, only the back of his head visible from where I stand.

Three feet.

I tense my muscles, stretch my hand out.

Two feet.

"Hurry," I urge under my breath, even though I want to scream it. Julius can't win. He can't. I won't give him that satisfaction.

One foot—

My fingers close over the baton, and I'm running.

It takes a moment for me to find my rhythm, but once I do, all the built-up adrenaline floods through my limbs. I run faster than I ever have in my life, my eyes pinned on only one person: Julius. My target, my goal. This is what we do, what we have always done. We chase each other and circle each other and catch up to each other.

I have to catch up to him now.

I force my feet onward, relishing the hard push of the ground beneath me, the blood burning inside me, my hair flying back in the wind. Colors blur past my vision. Noise rushes down to me in waves. I'm running so fast I feel weightless. I feel like I'm falling, my body moving ahead of me. There's no gravity, no friction, nothing except the frantic beat of my heart and the person in my vision. I'm only a few steps behind him now, and I can sense his awareness of me from the way he speeds up. He's breathing hard, his forehead covered in a sheen of sweat. His eyes dart to me.

The distance between us widens, then narrows, like a game of tug-of-war.

A muscle in my side starts to cramp, but I ignore the pain. Lengthen my strides. Cut my hands through the air. It's not only a physical competition but a mental one, a test of willpower, of who wants to win more badly. And I'm *so close*. We're neck and neck by this point, and the end is just ahead of us.

I need to keep going.

Keep running.

He pulls ahead again by an inch and my vision flashes red.

With one final burst of pure, unrestrained energy, I leap forward, the air whipping my face as I break the finish line—a split second before he does.

I'm beaming, laughing between great gulps of air. *I've won.* Victory is always delicious, but it tastes even better when it's Julius I'm beating. We both slow down. The crowd applauds wildly in the background, the claps indistinguishable from the sound of my heartbeat in my ears. *Seven points to me*, I gloat inside my head, though I realize I can't remember what our scores were before. I haven't been properly keeping count.

Most runners double over as soon as the race ends, or collapse dramatically on the ground, the way Abigail is doing now. But of course Julius is too dignified for that. He merely stands, wipes the sweat from his brow, and turns to me, his lips pursed.

"Aren't you going to congratulate me?" I ask, mimicking his smug tone from before.

He rolls his eyes. "Shameless."

"I must have learned it from you," I tell him, my grin widening.

He pauses then. His irritation melts away, replaced briefly by a confused, dazed sort of look, like he's just been presented with something unexpected. He stares long enough for me to feel self-conscious.

"What?" I try to sound casual. "Are you too stunned by your own defeat?"

A scowl quickly reappears on his face. "That was only a warm-up for me."

"We'll see if that's true in the next race," I tell him before I walk away to fetch my medal. I can feel him glaring after me.

Regrettably I don't have time to savor his defeat. I don't even have time to sit down or grab a drink of water. There are too many races to run, too many people demanding my attention. I manage to win the next race, but Julius wins the sprint after that, as well as the long jump, which I bitterly attribute to the unfair advantage he has in height.

The sun rises higher in the sky, throwing off blinding beams of light.

I start to lose count of how far I've run, how far I still have left to go. I just push my body harder—and it's *working*. I'm invincible. I'm doing so well I even manage to come first in the eight hundred meters. Another medal collected, another tick next to my name, another number added to my winning streak.

But as I stagger off to the sidelines, a sudden wave of exhaustion crashes over me, and—

I can't breathe.

The realization sends me into a panic. I try to suck in more air, but it's like there's an invisible hand wrapped around my throat, squeezing tighter and tighter. The oxygen gets stuck halfway down, and my lungs are empty. I double over, trembling, clutching at the stitch in my side. The sun is too bright. All my senses are off-balance, everything tilting away at an odd degree. My vision narrows to a white pinprick.

I'm still struggling to breathe.

I blink hard, and when the world comes rushing back to me again, only one face sharpens into focus. Black hair, pale skin, sharp lines. A strange look in his eyes.

Julius.

He's staring at me, saying something, but the sound is distorted. At first I can only hear the blood thudding in my ears, the thunderous beat of my heart. It's so loud it scares me, and I have a terrifying vision of my heart exploding inside my chest. I swallow down another futile mouthful of air. It goes nowhere.

". . . Sadie. You need to sit down."

Somehow it's his voice that cuts through everything else, the blur of noise and colors in the background, the oblivious cheers of the crowd. Clear as the sky, familiar as my own heartbeat, a line to cling on to out at sea.

I mumble a response, *I'm fine, it's okay, just a little tired*, but

I'm not sure if he can even hear me. If my lips even move enough to form real words.

A crease knits itself between his brows. "Sadie—"

I take another step forward and my knees turn to water. I stumble.

Then suddenly, without warning, his arms are around me. If I weren't so dizzy, I would jerk away. But to my own humiliation, I lean into him. It's nice. It's horribly, disgustingly wonderful, to feel the warmth of his body, the hard lines of his chest. I could sink into this moment forever, could let him hold me and—

No.

The lack of oxygen must be suffocating my brain cells.

"Here." He guides me onto one of the benches in the shade, and the immediate reprieve from the sun is blissfully sweet. The air here feels cooler, gentler. I drink it in like I'm drowning, until my head is light.

"Breathe in slowly." He kneels down in front of me, his hands around my wrists. "Count: one, two, three . . ."

I follow his guidance, counting to five, holding then releasing, then breathing in again. After ten counts, the white spot in my vision begins to fade. Another ten counts and the metal band around my chest loosens.

"Are you feeling better?" Julius asks.

My voice is a dry croak. "Y-yes."

In a flash he drops his hands, steps back, and I feel a pinch of something like disappointment. Like loss. His features are tight when he hisses out his next words. "What's your problem?"

"What's my problem?" My mind is lagging behind, working at half its usual speed. I can only repeat the words foolishly. Wonder at why he looks the way he does, the muscle in his jaw tensed, his gaze cold and sharp and furious.

"Are you trying to kill yourself?" he demands. His eyes cut through me as he speaks, splitting me open from head to toe. "You look like you're about to faint, Sadie. It's not a very pretty image."

My lungs are functioning well enough now that I manage to pant out a reply. "What are *you* getting so worked up for? I'm the one gasping for air over here."

He makes a small, angry sound with the back of his throat, like a scoff and a sigh at the same time. "You don't get it, do you?"

"Get what? What are you on about?"

But he doesn't answer the question. He's talking faster and faster, the words spilling from his mouth. "It's laughable, really. You're always insistent on coming first in everything, but when it comes down to it, you're ready to put yourself last just to please other people—"

"The others need me to," I protest, confused why we're even having this conversation. "They didn't want to race so—"

"Screw the others," he says fiercely. The heat in his voice shocks me. Burns me to the core. "I don't care about them. I only care about—" He cuts himself off. Averts his gaze, stares out at the vivid blue sky stretching over the stadium. The students milling around the water fountain, tearing open packets of dried nuts and chocolate bars. Participants warming up by the fences, bending and straightening their legs out over the grass.

My head is spinning, but I can no longer tell if it's from the lack of oxygen or him.

"Why are you mad at me?" I ask him outright. "You should be happy. There's no way I'll win any of our remaining races. You get to beat me. It's what you've always wanted."

He huffs out a laugh. Gazes back over at me, his eyes a fathomless black, the kind of darkness you could wade through forever and never reach the end. "Good god, you're infuriating."

"And you're making no sense," I snap.

"Why can't you just—"

The shrill shriek of the whistle drowns out the rest of his sentence. The next race will be starting soon: the one thousand meters.

I stand up—or try to. But my legs feel like they've been infused with lead, and the whole world wobbles when I rise, the running track sliding sideways. White stars spark in my vision again. Frustrated, I fall back onto the cold bench.

"My body won't listen to me," I mutter, catching my breath.

"Yes, bodies tend to do that to protect themselves from self-destruction." Julius's tone is scathing. "I believe it's one of our key evolutionary features."

I don't have the energy to argue with him. "I still have to race . . ."

"The one thousand meters, right?"

I blink at him.

"I'll run it for you."

"Wait—what?" I massage my throbbing temples, willing myself to concentrate. To make sense of this.

"I'll be faster anyway," he says with his usual disdain, like I'm slowing him down right now. But the smugness doesn't spread to his eyes. He's watching me, tentative, intensely focused.

"No. Julius, you don't have to—"

"I'll give you the medal as a present," he says, already turning around. "Just wait."

I can't do anything except stare as he goes to the teacher, says something, points over at me. My skin flushes. The teacher nods quickly, claps him on the shoulder, and then he's joining the other racers at the starting line. For most of them, this is only their first race. They're clearly well rested, their hair combed back, shirts smooth, shielding their eyes from the sun, restless energy rippling off their bodies. Next to them, Julius moves with the calculated quiet of a predator. He lowers himself into the correct stance. Fingers touch the red synthetic surface. Shoulders tense. Eyes ahead.

The teacher raises the starting pistol.

Bang.

Cheers and screams erupt from the crowds in the stands as they take off. From the very beginning, he's ahead by a good few feet. I've always raced beside him, only ever been granted flickers of movement in my peripheral vision, the threat of his footsteps next to me. I've never had the chance to observe him in action. He makes it look easy. His every stride is long, deliberate, steady. He runs like there's no gravity, like there's no resistance.

We're typically told to jog the one thousand meters, to save our stamina for the end, but he sprints the whole way without so much as faltering.

"Holy shit," I hear someone yell from the sidelines. "Holy shit, dude. He's going *fast*—"

"What's gotten into him?"

When Julius crosses the finish line alone, the indisputable winner, to wild roars from the spectators, a grin splits over my face.

But I bite it back down when he walks straight over to me. The gold medal swings from his neck, gleaming in the sunlight. He takes it off, then holds it out toward me.

"Yours."

I'd thought he was joking. "You . . . But you won it. You should keep it."

He rolls his eyes. "I have so many of these lying around my house I don't have any room left."

"Okay, you're just openly bragging now—"

"Only speaking the truth."

"I—"

"Just take it, Sadie." He closes the distance between us and hangs the medal around my neck. It's still warm from his touch, smooth against my skin when I turn it over, unable to stop myself from admiring its faint glow, the shine of the gold. The weight of it. It's prettier than any necklace I've ever seen. I open my mouth to thank him, but then he adds, carelessly, "Consider it compensation for all the awards I've taken from you."

My gratitude curdles into a scoff on my tongue, and he laughs at the look on my face.

"You're welcome," he says.

"For being cocky?"

"That too."

But I brush my thumb over the medal, and even though I can't decide what it really means—a gift, a form of compensation, proof of something—it's somehow one of the best things I've ever received.

CHAPTER FIFTEEN

The next day, we're called into the principal's office again.

It's all the same. The same dull carpet, the same two seats pulled up in front of the desk, the same suffocating air. The same nerves coiled in the pit of my stomach. The only difference is the way Julius's eyes catch on mine when I sit down next to him.

"Well, hello, captains," Principal Miller greets us.

"Hi," I say cautiously.

"You're looking great today, Principal Miller," Julius says. I'm almost impressed by his ability to dive straight into such shameless flattery at any given moment. It's way too early in the morning for this. "Is that a new tie?"

The principal glances down at his plain black tie, which looks identical to every single tie I've ever seen him wear. I wait for him to scold Julius, but his poker face breaks into a pleased smile. "Why, yes, it is. Thank you for noticing."

You're kidding me.

"What did you want to talk to us about, Principal Miller?" Julius asks.

The principal refocuses. "Ah, right. I know it's been a while since we had our last conversation about your little . . . *incident*."

His mouth puckers with distaste, as if the incident in question involved us publicly vandalizing his office or undressing the school mascot. "I just wanted to check in with you two. How are we feeling? Have you been enjoying your time with each other?"

"Yes, I've been having a *wonderful* time," Julius says.

When I turn to him in surprise, he tilts his head almost imperceptibly toward the principal, his eyes narrowing.

"Simply incredible," I agree, catching on. If we can just convince Principal Miller his plan worked, we might be able to finally leave the emails behind us and go our separate ways. "We're *so* close now. We're basically best friends."

"The best of friends." Julius nods fast. "We hang out even when we're not at school. She's the first person I think of when something goes well and when something goes wrong. We even finish each other's—"

"Math questions," I say. "He's been a great help in class."

"She's right. I help her all the time."

I let out a high-pitched laugh. "Although, *of course*, I help him plenty as well, seeing as I'm much more familiar with the syllabus than he is—"

"But only because I'm so busy doing the advanced questions." Julius's grin is so wide it looks like it hurts. There's a visible muscle twitching in his jaw. "And because I don't find memorizing the syllabus to be an effective study method, although I concede that it may be beneficial for those with a rudimentary understanding of the content—"

"Which is exactly the kind of thinking that could lead *some* people," I say in a bright voice, squeezing my fingers together under the desk, "to lose three marks on an important test and then complain that the topic wasn't covered, when it was actually stated in black and white."

Principal Miller's brows furrow.

"All of this is to say that Julius is *lovely*," I say quickly.

"And Sadie is the light of my life," Julius says, his lip curling, even though there's an odd note to his tone. Something that could be confused for sincerity. "The sun in my sky, the source of all my joy. She's the reason I wake up every morning excited to go to my classes. Not a day goes by where I'm not grateful that she exists, that she's there, that I get to talk to her and pass her in the halls and listen to her laugh."

I'm concerned he's gone a bit too far with the irony, but Principal Miller looks convinced. No, he even looks *moved*.

"That was beautiful," the principal says, and I have to remember not to roll my eyes. "Truly. I have to admit, I was somewhat skeptical about how well this would work out between you two given the rather intense nature of those emails, but . . . well, I always knew I was a miracle worker. I guess I really *do* come up with the best solutions."

My mouth falls open of its own accord. I can't believe this is the conclusion he's come to.

"I just have one last task for you," Principal Miller says. "The senior trip is coming up soon, and after the less-than-positive feedback we received for last year's trip—"

"You mean when the teachers took the class to a sewage treatment plant?" I clarify.

"Yes." He rubs the back of his head. "Yes. To be clear, that was a case of false advertising and miscommunication, but that is indeed what I'm referring to."

"Got it."

"That's why for this year," he says, "we want more input from the students. I'm going to trust you two to provide a few sensible, budget-friendly suggestions for where you could stay. It would be great if you could get this organized as soon as possible and hand me a proposal tomorrow morning."

"Wait." I exchange a quick look of disbelief with Julius, and for once, the battle lines seem to be drawn before us, instead of between us. *"Tomorrow—"*

"That is correct." The principal makes a hand gesture that's probably intended to be encouraging, but looks more like he's threatening to punch us. I *feel* like I've been punched. "Best of luck, captains."

"You're late," I inform Julius the second he walks in.

I've booked one of the study rooms in the library for us to use throughout our spare period. The pros: There's an arched, stained glass window offering a stunning view of the rippling lawns below, and the walls are perfectly soundproof. There's also a whiteboard for me to stick up photos and details of all the destinations I've gathered.

The cons: It's clearly designed to hold only a single person, which means he has to squeeze his way past the chair to reach the square of empty space available beside me. Which means we're standing much closer together than I'd like. Which means I have to take a deep, steadying breath, forcing myself to focus on the board, to keep my eyes off his face.

"I remember when you used to at least pretend to be civil," Julius remarks as he lifts the coffee cup in his hand to his lips. "You would offer me a terribly fake smile first, then come up with a long-winded way to remind me of the time, like: *Is it just me, or has the school bought new clocks? The minute hand looks really different.* Now you seem to have no problem criticizing me to my face. Real progress."

I carry on as if he hasn't spoken. "You're late because you went to get *coffee*?"

"See." He points at me, as if I've just offered valuable evidence for his thesis statement. "So much more straightforward." He takes another slow sip. "And yes, congratulations, your beverage-detection abilities are impressive. It is, in fact, black coffee."

I wrinkle my nose. The bitter scent is so sharp I can practically taste it. "How do you even manage to drink that without sugar or cream?"

"I find it bracing." The corner of his mouth quirks, his

eyes black and razor-sharp on me. "And perhaps I prefer the challenge."

"Sounds masochistic."

"It does, doesn't it?" he says. Then he turns to the board. Looks over it—my hard work, the resources *I'd* prepared ahead of time, the detailed sticky notes and calculations—for all of five seconds before he tells me, "The beach destination won't work, by the way. We should eliminate that right off the bat."

"Excuse me? Why not?" The beach retreat was the place I'd found most promising. It's only a two-hour drive from here, and the scenery is beautiful: smooth sand and turquoise waves and hammocks strung between palm trees. I'd even started making a list of all the activities we could do, from beach volleyball to surfing to picking up trash, which isn't as fun but is definitely good for the environment. The environment committee could write an article about it for the yearbook.

"Don't get me wrong, it's pretty," he says with a shrug. "But that's also the problem. It's too romantic."

I stare at him.

He sighs. Like I'm being dense on purpose. "Do you know what the teachers' biggest fear with these kinds of retreats is?"

"That one of us will drop dead and the school will end up involved in a long, painful, costly lawsuit despite the fact that they made all our parents sign that form that says in very fine print that nobody is to blame if we're injured, abducted, or murdered."

"Close, but no. If we die, that's very inconvenient for them. If we hook up, that's both inconvenient *and* awkward for them."

I'm pretty sure all my organs stop functioning. "What—"

"When I say *we*, I obviously don't mean—*us*," he clarifies, and despite the taunting note in his voice, his cheeks turn red. He's *blushing*, I realize. It's so bizarre. So unlike him. It's a visible weakness, and I quietly file it away for later use. "I mean in general. I believe there's a scientific equation for it: The probability of teenagers sneaking into each other's rooms and hooking up increases by zero-point-four when you put them in a scenic beach setting."

"You're making that up," I tell him. "You're literally just saying that because you enjoy disagreeing with me."

He rolls his eyes. "Don't flatter yourself. I'm only saying what I know is true." Then he moves to take down the beach retreat flyer from the board.

In one quick movement, I clap my hand over his. Force his fingers to flatten. Ignore the heat of his skin against my palm. "We're meant to *agree* on a destination together. And I don't agree with you right now."

"When have you ever?" he mutters. But he shakes his hand free from mine, which should be more satisfying than hurtful.

"I'm not saying that it wouldn't be an issue if the retreat turned into some kind of . . . matchmaking process," I tell him. "But is the beach necessarily conducive to that? Who says it has to be romantic?"

"I don't know," he says sarcastically, pretending to think. "Only every movie and beach read and song to come out in the past decade." He must see the stubborn disbelief written over my face, because he tilts his head. Sighs again. "Okay, since you're so lacking in imagination, let me set the scene for you. It's sunset, the sky is the perfect shade of pink, the air just warm enough that you can slip out of your sweater and set it down on the sand like a towel. You can hear the waves lapping against the shore, taste the salt on your tongue. There's music playing softly from someone's phone speaker. You're sitting next to the person you've been eyeing for the whole semester, and when a breeze rises and messes up your hair, he lifts his hand and . . ."

And he actually demonstrates, reaching out across the tight space and brushing a stray strand of hair behind my ear, his cool fingertips grazing my skin. It's such a small, brief motion, the lightest touch. It's pathetic that I would even notice it. But I feel a sharp pang echo through my ribs, so intense it almost resembles pain. My whole body overreacts as if I'm in mortal danger, my heartbeat thudding faster and faster until I can't stand it. I squeeze my eyes shut against the emotion, and when I open them again, he's staring at me, his jaw strained.

He swallows, once.

"I—don't see your point," I manage, my voice too loud.

His brows rise, his hand still lingering above my ear. "You don't?"

It requires an incredible amount of strength just to speak.

"No. And—" I push down the odd lump in my throat. Do my best to sound as flippant as possible. "I think you're not giving our—*peers* enough credit. They have *some* discipline, you know. It's not like they're going to try and sneak off into the cabins to make out just because the view's pretty and someone touched their hair—"

"Not even if they did this?" he asks quietly, and he leans forward. All at once he's too close, overwhelmingly close. I'm frozen to the spot as he pauses on purpose, his mouth bare inches from the base of my neck, so I can feel his breath trembling against my skin. "Do you need me to demonstrate further?"

A low, hoarse sound escapes my lips. It could be a protest or a plea; I don't know anymore. I don't know anything.

"What was that, Sadie?" he presses, lowering himself by just another fraction of an inch—

I shove him away. *"I get it."* My heart is still beating at an abnormal rate, heat coursing furiously through my veins. Yet even worse than my fear of what might've happened is the disappointment that it didn't. And the fear that he can somehow sense my disappointment, the itch in my skin from where his mouth had hovered seconds earlier. *Only physical attraction*, I remind myself sternly. It must be some kind of unfortunate side effect left over from the kiss at the party. "I get it, okay? You didn't have to make your case in such a disgusting manner."

Something shifts in his expression. Then he smiles, and it's as smug as ever. "Are you admitting that I'm right?"

"Yes. Fine. Whatever," I spit out. I've lost the argument, but it feels like I've lost something more than that. "Let's hear your proposal, then."

"That's exactly what we should've done from the beginning." He steps back and starts searching locations up on his phone with the brisk manner of someone in a business meeting, leaving me to wonder if I hallucinated the past five minutes. The only evidence of it is the uneven beat of my pulse and the hair tucked behind my ear. "How about this?" he asks, showing me the photo on his screen.

It's a retreat in the middle of the mountain range three hours from here, and all the walls and floors are made of glass. It also happens to be suspended almost two thousand feet above a valley, with an "open-air seating area" available on the rooftop. The main website describes the views as "thrilling," which I mentally translate into "terrifying."

"You realize there are at least five people in our year level who are scared of heights, right?" I ask.

He doesn't even bat an eye. "Then this is precisely what they need. Exposure therapy has been proven to work, hasn't it?"

"How can you be so—so *callous*?" I demand.

"I'm not callous. You're just soft."

I grit my teeth. "Considerate, you mean. Thoughtful. Responsible."

"In futile, stubborn pursuit of making every single person happy, is what I mean," he corrects me.

"And what of it?" I shove his phone back into his hand. "This is the last trip we'll ever have together as a year before we graduate. I want everyone to have the best time of their lives, and that's not going to happen if some people can't even comfortably walk from one room to another. Also, do you see the reviews? You literally need a *helmet* and a *harness* just to climb into bed."

"Which definitely solves the hooking-up problem," he says.

"Don't sound so certain. Some people are into that kind of thing."

He looks, briefly, stumped. Then he bites down on his lip, his shoulders shaking so hard he appears in danger of falling over. His voice is saturated with amusement when he slides forward again. Tilts his head at me. "Wow. I never pegged you as the type."

"Shut up," I grumble. "I was just making a point."

"So was I."

"Your point isn't convincing enough," I say, shaking myself free from his gaze. "Let's go back to the drawing board."

"Your wish is my command," he says sweetly. Sweetly enough that I stare up at him and stumble over my thoughts and fall headfirst into his trap. He starts laughing again as my face overheats. "You really like that, don't you? So you *are* the type—"

I twist my head away and drag my laptop closer toward me like a shield. We spend the remaining period going back and forth on every possible option. I suggest a farm; he says he would like to go somewhere free from the looming threat of accidentally stepping into animal excrement. He pulls up a website for an "affordable" five-star hotel in the city center; I remind him that it would only be *affordable* if the school sold drugs or donated all our kidneys, which leads us on a tangent about which teacher looks most like a potential drug dealer (we both settle on Mr. Kaye, and I observe how depressing it is that this is somehow the only thing we've managed to agree on so far). I then raise the idea of traveling to a national park; he protests that he doesn't enjoy parks.

"Why are you making this so hard, Julius? Didn't you hear the principal? The second we finish this proposal, the torture will stop and we'll be released from each other at last. We won't even have to speak to each other ever again."

A strange look crosses his face. "I know that."

"Then—"

"Let's choose this place," he says, the humor gone from his tone. He points at a lakeside location I'd picked and he'd dismissed because he found the welcome message on their home page *suspiciously friendly*.

I blink. "Really? That's— You agree?"

"Yeah. Sure." He stands up and grabs his coffee cup, all without looking at me. And even though I should be glad we've ticked off our final task, gladder still to be rid of him, I feel more like I've missed a step on the stairs. Before I can put a finger on it, he turns around on his way out and says only, "Congratulations, Sadie. The torture is over."

CHAPTER SIXTEEN

The torture is over.

These are the last words Julius speaks to me in over a month. And they're true. Or they're supposed to be true. After I deliver the completed proposal to Principal Miller, he doesn't bring up any more tasks for Julius and me to work on together. We go back to our own lives, our own busy schedules and old routines. We move like two planets in orbit; both on the same trajectory, but never touching.

The only time he breaks the silence is when we get our tests back in math.

"What's your score?" he asks, twisting around in his seat to look at my paper.

I pin it flat on the table, facedown, and try to conceal my surprise. Try to control my beating heart. It's been so long since we've talked that I feel oddly self conscious, out of sync with our old, familiar rhythm. "Not telling." Actually, I don't mind showing him—I received a 100 percent. I just want to be difficult. I just want him to keep talking to me.

He regards me with an intensity that's surprising. He's gripping his paper so tightly it's starting to crease. "I'll tell you mine if you tell me yours," he says.

"Promise?"

His gaze is sharp. "Of course."

"Fine." I let my face break into a satisfied smile. "One hundred percent."

The corners of his lips cut down—the subtlest of reactions, the smallest sign of irritation—but he simply turns around again.

"Hey." I frown at his back. "*Hey*, aren't you going to tell me yours?"

"I'd rather not."

My blood heats. "You literally promised me, like, two seconds ago—"

"I was crossing my fingers," he says.

"You were what?"

He lifts his fingers to show me. "See? It doesn't count."

"Oh, right." I snort. "Very mature."

"You only have yourself to blame," he says. "Why would you believe me in the first place?"

As utterly infuriating as he's being, part of me is almost grateful for it. *This* is the version of him—of us—I'm used to. Maybe everything is still the same. "Just show it to me, Julius," I demand.

"No."

"Then don't blame me for this." Before he has time to react, I lunge across the desk and snatch his paper out of his hand and flip to the front page, expecting the same score as mine or a 98 at the lowest—

86 percent.

I stare at the number in red, stuck on the impossible discovery. I have to blink fast to make sure I'm not reading it upside down. It's the kind of score someone like Ray would be overjoyed with. The kind of score Georgina's parents would buy her a brand-new car to reward her for. But by our standards, Julius and I both know that any score starting with the number 8 is subpar. It's just above average. It's an abomination.

"Are you done?" he snaps, grabbing his paper back. There's a tendon straining in his neck, and he quickly covers the score up with his sleeve like it's a terrible scar.

"S-sorry," I stammer, at a loss for what to do, how to react. "I didn't know— I was just—"

"You can gloat," he says, an edge to his voice. "Go ahead. Do it. It's what I would do."

Even though it's also what *I* would have done a month ago, I don't feel like gloating at all. "Julius . . ."

At the front of the classroom, Mr. Kaye launches into his next lecture, effectively ending the conversation. Julius doesn't turn around again. And just like that, the silence is back, a heavy curtain falling between us. It lasts for the rest of the class, then the rest of the day, then the rest of the week. Funny how quickly my definition of torture can change.

I keep my eyes on the bakery door, but nobody walks in.

We haven't had any customers so far today, and I can only blame the weather. It's not exactly raining, but every now and then a dark cloud passes, and a few measly drops of water will dampen the cement. Like the sky can't make up its mind.

In the dim, gray light, I stack up the trays and wipe down the glass and line up our new layered strawberry cakes behind the display. My mom's headed off early to meet with an accountant, leaving Max and me here to watch over the bakery. Well, *I'm* watching over the bakery. Max is watching a basketball game on his phone and munching on an egg tart.

"I have to ask," I say. "Do you really just *not* have homework? Ever?"

He replies without glancing up. "Nope."

"I don't believe you."

"Then why did you ask?"

I rub my hand over my face. Usually I'd drop the matter and let him waste time however he wants. But today, I feel a flicker of irritation. "Could you maybe pretend to be productive, then? Or even, I don't know, help out a little around the store?"

"Okay, whoa, dude. You've been in a foul mood recently," Max says, setting his phone aside at last. He wipes the egg tart crumbs from his chin and leans forward in his seat. "Did you get rejected by a boy or something? If you did, just tell me—I can beat his ass."

"I'd rather you scrub a table," I tell him, fighting to keep my expression plain, even when I can feel my skin heating.

"Now, let's not be so extreme," Max says. "And that time I

cleaned a table, you and Mom both yelled at me for using the wrong cloth."

"As in the cloth we use to *wipe the floor*—"

The door swings open behind me, and I spin around instinctively to greet them, my customer-service smile ready—

Until I see who it is.

Julius Gong is standing in the entrance. He's still wearing his school uniform, but he's discarded his blazer, and his tie is undone, hanging loose over his white button-down shirt. He looks different, for a reason I can't quite place my finger on. Maybe it's his stance. Or the crease between his brows. The shadows under his eyes.

"Why are you here?" I blurt out.

He crosses his arms over his chest, but not before some complicated emotion flickers across his features. "Why can't I be here?" he drawls. "I was in the neighborhood and wanted to buy bread. Obviously I didn't know that *you* would be here."

"Obviously," I repeat, embarrassed now by my initial reaction. Of course he wouldn't be here because of me. In fact, I'm willing to bet that if he'd known he would bump into me, he would have driven twenty miles to the bakery on the other side of town just to avoid this encounter.

"Are you going to turn away a customer?" he asks, a challenge in the lift of his brow. "Pretty sure I could file a complaint for that."

I chew my tongue. The idea of having him around while I work fills me with a very specific, skin-tingling kind of dread. But business is business. So I plaster my smile back on again and gesture to the shelves with both hands. "What would you like today?"

"Let's see . . ." He walks up and down the bakery. Past the sweet taro buns and the pizza rolls and the flaking coconut pastries. He pauses, leans closer to inspect the displays. Reaches out, as if to grab something, then retracts his hand. And starts walking all over again.

After ten minutes of this, I lose my patience. "Are you here to select bread or a future wife? What's taking so long?"

His smile is sharp, taunting. "The latter."

"You can't be—" I take a deep breath, remembering every basic customer-service rule I've ever learned. *Be receptive to both positive and negative feedback. Take the time to learn your customers' expectations. Offer solutions, not excuses. Don't push your customer into the stack of mango pudding cups in the corner, even when they're being difficult on purpose—*

"Is that your brother?" he asks, looking past me, to Max.

"I'm afraid we don't owe customers personal details," I say sweetly. "If you could just focus on buying what you need—"

"Yeah, I am," Max says, rising from the chair. *Traitor.* He scans Julius from head to toe like he's sizing him up before a wrestling match. "Who's this guy?"

"Nobody," I say.

"Julius," Julius says. I might as well be talking to air. "I go to Sadie's school. You might have heard about me."

Max scrunches his forehead. "Sorry, bro. Doesn't really ring a bell." Before I even have the chance to feel grateful, his eyes narrow. "Hang on a second—are you the one who rejected my sister? Is that why she's been so mopey?"

"What?" I hiss.

"What?" Julius asks, stiffening at once. His gaze flickers to me.

"Don't listen to him, he's making things up," I say, stepping firmly between them. "Max, just go back to watching your basketball game. And Julius, just . . . get out of the way."

Julius lifts his chin. "What if I also want to watch the game? I'm a huge fan of the—" He pauses just for a fraction of a second, and glances at the phone on the table. "The Hunters too."

I'm completely baffled, but Max's stance relaxes, his face breaking into a broad grin.

"Bro, you should've led with *that*. Come, come, sit down."

"What are you on about?" I mutter out the side of my mouth as Julius moves past me to join my brother. There's no way this is actually happening. There's no reason for him to be doing this except to irritate me. "You don't even like basketball."

He pauses. "People can change," he says, a discernible edge to his voice. "You've changed."

"How have I—"

"You've been moping because of a boy, last I heard," he whispers against my ear. Heat rushes up my neck, gathering around the point where I can feel his lips. "Who is it? Do I know him?"

"I told you, nobody. Ignore my brother."

It's evident from his expression that he doesn't believe me.

"Fine. Think whatever you want," I grumble, twisting around. "I have other things to do."

The sky begins to clear as I sweep the floors and prepare the next batch of egg tarts. The remnants of rain dry up; the clouds float in rose-pink wisps over the sloping horizon, so insubstantial they could scatter with a single exhale. Golden sunlight filters through the windows, warm slants of it falling over the table where Julius and Max sit. Not that I'm looking their way *often*. Not that I'm sneaking curious glances at Julius or noticing the way he runs his hand ever so casually through his hair.

Definitely not.

As the weather improves, more customers trickle in. An old woman with her bags full of dragon fruit and marinated meats. A mother and her two toddlers, who press their faces right up against the cake display. A pretty girl my age, who somehow manages to make a plain white shirt and school skirt stylish. She looks familiar, and it clicks after a moment: She's the one that guy in my year level was stalking during the Athletics Carnival.

She doesn't seem particularly interested in the food. From the second she enters, her attention snaps to Julius, and she drifts toward his table.

I watch their exchange silently from behind the counter.

"Woodvale Academy, right?" the girl asks, pointing to his uniform from such a close distance that it defeats the very purpose of pointing.

Julius lifts his head from the game playing on the screen. Acknowledges her with a faint smile. I grind my back teeth. "That's right."

"I always heard the boys were hotter at Woodvale," she says, brushing her bangs out of her face. "And here I thought they were exaggerating."

Julius laughs, and I feel a hot rush of violence. My fingernails dig into the counter surface as he turns fully toward her.

"I'm not sure if you recognize me?" the girl continues. "A lot of people follow me online. Not saying I'm famous, but I'm not, like, *not* famous either."

"This is my first time seeing you anywhere," Julius says.

She doesn't seem fazed. "Well, it's never too late. If you want to search my name . . ." Then she holds out a hand for his phone.

I expect him to decline. It's not like this is the first time a girl has shown interest in him, famous or not. In year eight, basically everyone in the year level had a crush on him because he was the fastest runner in PE and could open any bottle you passed to him. In year nine, everyone loved him because he was invited to do some kind of fashion shoot for the school, and in the final photos he was enviably beautiful, his shirtsleeves folded, his black hair falling long and soft over his eyes. In year ten, everyone wanted him because he just *was*. Because he didn't seem to care much for anyone, which lent him a cool, unapproachable air. Because he had grown another two inches and his shoulders were broader and his jaw sharper. Because he had a way of speaking like everything he said mattered, meant something.

And while he's always basked in the attention, he's never seemed particularly interested in committing to a relationship.

Which is why I'm stunned to see him take out his phone now and pass it over. His gaze flits to me as the girl types out her name, like he wants to make sure I'm watching, and I remember how much I hate him. It's a physical kind of hatred, the kind that feels like someone's shoved their fist into my chest. The kind that makes my gums itch.

"Okay, so this is my account," she's explaining, as though he's never used a phone before. "I've followed myself for you. These recent pictures on the beach are *so* embarrassing—I mean, I know the comments all say I look super cute, but I have mixed feelings about the bikini—"

"I'm sorry to interrupt, but we're closing," I announce. It's true. Well, technically, we should be closing in two and a half minutes, but all the other customers have already left.

The girl blinks at me. Julius just smiles.

"I guess I better get going, then," the girl says, and shoots me such a friendly look I feel bad. I almost consider taking back my words, inviting her to stay longer if she really wants to—until she grips Julius's shoulder, delicate fingers curling into his shirt, and adds, "Remember, you can message me whenever. Tonight, if you'd like."

Julius is still smiling at me when he replies. "I'll keep that in mind."

Julius doesn't leave.

Not when I flip the sign on the door, or when I turn off the front lights, or when I tell him, quite clearly, "You should leave."

He stands up, but only to lean back against the wall. "Are you going to make me?"

"I can," I say. "You're not a customer anymore. I can do anything."

His stance doesn't change. "Do it, then. Do whatever you want."

Irritation floods through me. I'm seriously contemplating whether or not to drag him out by force when I notice the set of his jaw. The gleam in his eyes. He's goading me. But it's not just that. It's as if . . . he's looking for a fight, or a distraction. I remember how he'd looked when he first entered the shop, and I feel myself hesitate.

But he seems to sense the change in me. In a heartbeat, he withdraws, his expression snapping closed. "Honestly I wasn't planning on staying long anyway," he says, pushing off from the wall. "See you at school."

"Hey—"

He steps out without another word, leaving me staring in his wake, my head buzzing as if I've just been cramming for a final exam. There's too much noise, too many confounding concepts. He didn't even buy any bread.

"He's into you," Max remarks from behind me.

I startle. "Excuse me?"

"He kept looking over at you," he says with a little grin. "At least thirty times. I counted."

"I didn't know you could count that high," I say dryly, to hide my speeding pulse.

"I'm serious. Honestly you could do worse. He's athletic, like you, and he's tall, and good-looking—"

"I'm not having this conversation," I announce. "And for the record, you're wrong. He was probably just staring at some spot behind me; every time *I* looked over, he was watching the game with you." I gesture to the table where they'd been seated, then pause. Julius's phone is still lying there, faceup. He'd been in such a rush to go that he must have forgotten it. I swivel my head around, squint through the window, but he's already halfway down the street, his lean silhouette a shadow in the falling darkness.

"I'll be right back," I say, grabbing the phone. As I do, I can't help noticing that it's still open to the girl's account—but he's unfollowed her already. A stone dislodges from my chest, the resulting rush of relief so strong it's truly embarrassing. Totally irrational.

Yet my whole body feels lighter as I slip through the doorway and run after him, the evening air whipping my hair. Most of the restaurants are still open at this hour, the orange light from inside spilling out in long rectangles.

I turn the next corner and skid to a halt.

Julius is standing in front of a parked sports car. For an absurd moment, I think it belongs to one of the aunties we showed around the school. But no, this car is even more expensive, so new it's gleaming. The windows are rolled down, and I glimpse the unmistakable face of Julius's brother. He's not beaming this time though; his brows are pinched together, irritation written over all the features they share.

"... can't just storm off like a little kid every time you're upset," James is saying. "It wasn't a big deal or anything. Our parents were merely giving you some advice—"

"How did you even find me?" Julius demands. His back is turned to me; I can't see his expression, but the frost in his voice is clear.

"It was hardly detective work, Ju-zi. I saw your search results."

"My—" Julius's frame stiffens. "Those are private."

"Calm down, it's not like you were searching up the closest brothel. It's just a bakery. What are you getting all flustered for?"

The restaurant lights don't quite reach the pavement here, so I step forward quietly, hidden behind an oak tree, my body pressed to the bark. I don't want to eavesdrop. I don't mean to.

But the words fly around my mind like hornets. *Search results. Private.* He'd been searching for a bakery? For *this* bakery?

"You really didn't need to come," Julius says tightly.

"You're still upset," James observes, winding the windows down farther and leaning out. "Why? Just because we wanted to know—for good reason—why you basically failed your last math test? It *is* a little concerning. You keep letting that Sadie girl beat you—"

My heart hits my ribs.

They're talking about me.

"I don't ever *let* her do anything," Julius snaps, and even in the dim light, I can make out the shape of his knuckles when he clenches his fists. "She's smart, okay? She's a formidable force. She does everything she sets her mind to and nothing can stand in her way. Not even me."

"That's all?" James asks. There's something curious about his tone, something that makes my next breath come out too short and fast, makes my heart crawl up my throat.

Julius must have detected it too. "What are you suggesting?"

"I mean, you're sure it doesn't have anything to do with the way you were acting around her at the bookstore? I saw the look in your eyes. I've never seen it before, but now—"

"You're mistaken," Julius says coldly.

"I hope I am," James tells him. "This is your final year of school. This is the beginning of the rest of your life; you need to set the tone right. I don't expect you to get a full scholarship to Harvard and follow in my footsteps exactly, but come on. Our family has standards. I would hate to see you getting distracted and losing your wits over some *girl* and letting all your work go to waste—"

"That's not—"

"Because you'll have plenty of time to date around after you get into your dream school, yeah? Once you enter college, you'll see that there are far prettier girls out there. It's all about timing. About priorities. And look, I understand. I do. If this is just physical attraction— If you need to hook up with her once and get it out of your system in order to focus on what matters, then by all means—"

"Stop talking about her," Julius cuts in, and the threat in his voice almost makes me step back. Even James falters. "Don't drag her into this. I already told you. If I underperformed on a test, that's my own fault. I-I'll study harder—I'll do better—"

"I'm only saying." James taps his fingers against the dashboard. "I never had so much trouble when I was your age. I never came second in anything. If I were you, I would be ashamed."

I can't explain what comes over me.

It's like somebody has lit a flame in my bloodstream, taken control of my body. All I see is the open hurt in Julius's eyes, the shame washing over his face, the way he hangs his head, and I lose my mind a little.

I step out from behind the tree and march straight toward the car, my hands balled into tight fists, my pulse beating fast. "For your information," I say, my voice so loud and sharp it sounds foreign to my own ears, "Julius is one of the best students in the year level."

Julius blinks at me in surprise. "Sadie? What are you . . ." He flushes, his eyes flitting between me and his brother. "This isn't necessary—"

"Shut up, Julius," I snap. "I'm talking."

"Yeah, let her talk," James says, tilting his head and appraising me as if I'm an unexpected bonus question at the end of a test. "It's good to see you again, Sadie Wen. Of course, I never imagined it would be under the present circumstances—"

I speak over him. "You're wrong about Julius. He hasn't slacked off on a single test in the ten years I've known him. He's president of every club he's run for. He's the only one who could get his classmates to give him a standing ovation for a minor English presentation. And if he ever comes in second, it's not because he isn't good enough—it's simply because I'm better—"

Julius coughs. "Is this whole thing building up to a self-congratulatory speech?"

"Are you unable to stop yourself from being irritating when I'm literally defending you?" I hiss.

"Yes, well, you seemed to be getting sidetracked—"

"You're the one getting sidetracked." I squeeze my eyes shut. Rake my hand through my hair. Catch my train of thought again. "What I was *saying* is that despite how annoying Julius is, and how vain, and cowardly, and insincere, everyone who's met him knows he's destined for great things. Through sheer stubbornness and manipulation, he'll find a way to make great things come to him."

James casts Julius a skeptical look. "Are we talking about the same person here?"

"Maybe you just don't know your brother that well," I say coldly. I can't remember ever feeling so angry. So tempted to smash a car with a hammer. No, that's a lie—Julius always manages to infuriate me. The irony is that for the first time, I'm not angry at him; I'm angry because of him. Because the only person who should be allowed to attack him is me.

James is silent for a while. Then he laughs, the sound bright and too cheery, echoing down the street. "How touching, that my little brother has a girl out here protecting his dignity. This is really very sweet."

"It's not about his dignity," I tell him, articulating each and every word. "It's about mine. By insulting my competition, you're insulting me."

He raises his brows. "That's quite the bold statement."

Normally I would shrivel up at this kind of accusation. Blush and back down. Swallow my words, relinquish the space I've earned. But the adrenaline is still pumping through my veins, and it feels different when I'm speaking for the both of us. When—god knows how this happened—we're on the same side. "And what of it?"

James laughs again, his mouth so wide I can see his back teeth. "I guess we'll see if you're right when the end-of-year results come out, huh?" Then he looks over at Julius and beckons for him with two fingers. "Stop sulking now and get in the car."

"Wait," I say, remembering. "Your phone. You forgot it."

I hold the phone out and Julius takes it very carefully, but his hand still brushes against mine, the barest contact somehow torturous. He hesitates. Meets my gaze. A thousand emotions swim in his eyes, one tied to another: gratitude and resentment for his gratitude and something else. "Sadie," he says, quiet, his voice pitched only for the space between us. "I . . ."

The headlights switch on, the harsh white beam of light half blinding me. I block my face with one hand, squinting.

"Get in," James repeats. "Hurry."

Julius's lips part, but he settles for a nod, then climbs slowly into the car. The doors lock; the engine starts. As they drive down the road, I think I catch him turning around in the seat. Looking back at me.

I can't stop thinking about him.

It's mortifying. Unproductive. *Unnatural.* And quite frankly, it's really enraging. He has no right to occupy this much space inside my head. Yet after I go home with Max and lock myself in my bedroom with every intention of completing my history homework ahead of time, I end up staring at my wall for eleven minutes.

"Stop it," I hiss at myself, rubbing my face. "Get a *grip*."

My brain has always been disciplined. Good at compartmentalizing feelings, separating necessary information from garbage, labeling the good and the terrible. Julius absolutely goes into the Terrible folder.

Yet tonight, my brain betrays me. Even when I try to distract myself by doing twice my usual set of sit-ups, hoping the physical exhaustion will quiet my mind, all it does is make my muscles ache.

Like a compulsion, a bad habit I can't change, I keep imagining the ride home for him. Would Julius be fighting with his brother? Would my name come up again? Would he be wondering about me?

Finally I give up and message Abigail. Just two words: *blue dress*.

It's the code we use in every mini emergency, from break-ups to bad grades to boring family reunions. It means: Help. It means: Drop everything and talk to me. We first came up with it when I tore a massive hole through the back of my dress on a shopping trip, and Abigail immediately ran to the closest store to buy me a jacket to cover it up. I'd never seen someone whip out their credit card so fast.

Abigail calls me within two and a half minutes. "Yes, darling? What fire are we putting out?"

"Are you busy?"

"I'm in my room now," she says, and I hear the soft click of the door, the shuffle of her pillows. "So if you're going to tell me that you robbed a bank, nobody will overhear."

"It's not that," I tell her, laughing weakly. I almost wish it were that. It would be a straightforward fix at least. "It's only . . ." I pause, unsure how to articulate what I'm feeling when I can't make sense of it myself. "How do you know if you . . . you know."

"Uh, no?"

I wince. Squeeze my eyes shut. Pry the words from my teeth. "How do you know if you . . . like someone?"

"*Oh.*" Her tone changes instantly. The smile is plain in her voice. "This is one of *those* conversations. It's been ages since you had a crush on someone."

"It might not be," I rush to tell her, straightening in my chair. "I'm only. Confused. And I was standing outside in the cold for a while tonight so there's a chance I could just be exhibiting the early signs of a fever—"

"You don't have to explain yourself. Let me ask you this: Do you think about him a lot?"

"Not, like, *a lot* . . ."

"Your voice always gets squeaky when you're lying," she points out. "This isn't going to work if you're not honest."

"Okay. Okay, so, maybe?" I hold the phone closer to my ear and consider the question like it's one of those twenty-mark short essay prompts on a test. "Like in the mornings, when I'm about to enter the classroom, I do . . . wonder about him. My heart speeds up, and I'm irrationally angry when I do see him, but on days when he's not there, I'm also disappointed. And every now and then—just like every few minutes or so—I might be curious about what he's doing. And after we talk, I always go back and overanalyze everything he's said, and what I've said. I want to leave a good impression. I want to be better than him, but I also want to impress him . . ."

"I hate to break it to you, but that doesn't sound like a basic crush," Abigail informs me. "That sounds really serious, Sadie."

"No," I protest, panicking. "No, it's not— It *can't be*. I mean, wouldn't I feel all those things too if I hated him? How can you even tell the difference between liking and loathing someone? Physically speaking. How do you know if your blood pressure is rising because of how annoying they are, or how attractive you find them? If your hands are shaking because you're holding back from strangling them, or kissing them?"

"Holy shit."

"What?"

"It's Julius, isn't it?" Abigail says. "You're talking about Julius Gong."

I choke and wonder if it's possible for someone to die from sheer embarrassment. Even the sound of his name is apparently too much for me. My pulse is racing so fast I can feel the blood in my veins. *Pathetic*. I could kick myself. "Um . . ."

"Oh my god," she says hoarsely. Repeats it over and over in a hundred different variations, like she's trying to reinvent the phrase. "Oh my god, oh my god. Oh. My god. Oh my *god*—"

"At this rate you're literally going to call God down to earth," I hiss, pressing a hand to my burning face.

"No, no, you know what, darling, I'm not judging. Not at all," she says. "I was genuinely attracted to a cartoon lion at thirteen. Like, something about his claws really worked for me."

"I can't believe you're drawing parallels between these two bizarrely different situations," I say. "First, Julius is a *person*—"

"He's also been making you miserable for ten years," she cuts in. "Don't you remember when you were assigned to the same group project, and he secretly worked ahead of you so he would look more prepared in front of the teacher? Or when he beat you in the spelling competition and followed you around the school just to rub the trophy in your face? Or when he got all those roses for Valentine's Day and put them in a vase right above your locker to taunt you for not receiving any?"

"All fond memories, yes," I say. "I remember clearly. But . . ."

But I also remember the softness of his blazer around my shoulders. The look on his face tonight, the quick violence in his voice when his brother spoke of me. His breathing, quiet beside me, as he swept confetti from the floor after the party. His hands, firm but warm around my wrists after the race. The shine of the medal, the light in his eyes, the curve of his lips. So beautiful and infuriating and confusing. So ready to split me open with a single word, stitch me up again with a fleeting touch.

"Do you think there's any chance . . ." It feels so foolish, even asking it out loud. "Any chance he would like me?"

"Wow, yeah, you're in deep," she says. "And I don't see why he *wouldn't*. You're the whole package. You're smart and good at everything and you're totally hot in this kind of successful future-executive way—"

I snort out a laugh despite myself. Then I come to a sobering realization. "But you're not factoring in the emails," I tell her. "You should've seen how upset he was when he first received them. I don't think he's forgiven me for them yet. I don't know if he ever will."

"Right." She pauses. "About those emails—"

"Like, would you ever want to be with someone who once expressed to you, clearly, in written text, that they would *rather listen to someone perform slam poetry about corporate income taxes in an auditorium without ventilation on the hottest day of summer while a baby plays tug-of-war with their hair from behind* than have to sit through your speech for school captain again?"

There's a long silence. Then, in a voice of forced optimism, she says, "Maybe he'll wake up one day and lose half his memories."

"So it's pointless how I feel." I slump back in my seat again. "Because he'll never be able to move past this."

"You can't be certain," she insists. "You can't be certain of anything unless you tell him, face-to-face."

I cough. "*Tell him?* Tell him what? *Oh, hi, I know we've hated each other's guts for a decade and you find me insufferable, but I think we should make out."*

"It's a pretty convincing pitch," she says. "And you know what? The retreat will be the perfect time to do it. You'll be in the same place, and you'll have time to yourselves, and there won't be as many teachers around. The only shame is that the retreat isn't set at, like, a beach or something. It would be *so cute*—"

"It was going to be," I say grimly. "But Julius rejected the idea on the terms that it would be too romantic—and yes, I know, the irony is occurring to me as we speak."

"He really shot himself in the foot with that one, huh?"

"Or saved himself," I tell her. "Maybe he was protecting himself in advance from the chances of someone cornering him with a confession. Maybe he's, like, opposed to relationships in general, and even more opposed to a relationship with me, specifically."

She clucks her tongue at me. "Where's your confidence disappeared to?"

"You realize that, according to the laws of physics, something can't disappear if it never existed in the first place, right? Matter can't be created or destroyed—"

"Just *talk to him*, Sadie. Really. What's the worst that could happen?"

I sigh. Grip the edge of my desk to steady myself against the overwhelming tide of possibilities. "Everything," I say. "He could laugh at me. He could weaponize my feelings against me in every test and competition to come. He could mock me for the rest of my lifetime. He could recoil with horror and disgust—"

"Or he could surprise you with his response," she says. "Just consider it, okay?"

I chew the flesh of my cheek until it stings. Somehow, I feel even more disoriented now than I did at the beginning of the call. "Okay. I will."

CHAPTER SEVENTEEN

There's a trick to writing a good history essay.

Most people assume that you start with the contention. You read the prompt and instantly form your stance on something, like whether the sansculottes in the French Revolution ought to be considered a mob, and then you search through your memory for evidence to back yourself up: quotes from famous historians, dates, statistics. But I always start with the evidence first. I go through the information I already have, the facts I find the most compelling, that will most likely stand out to an examiner. Only after that do I pick my argument. Otherwise it's a futile practice, a waste of precious writing time; it doesn't matter what you believe in, or want to believe in, if you're not supported by the data.

I know this. I *should* know this.

Yet after I hang up, I can't help hoping that Abigail's right. That maybe, miraculously, Julius could feel something for me other than bitterness or annoyance. And even though it's not the logical thing to do, I find myself abandoning all my tried-and-tested study techniques and scrabbling for evidence to prove it.

Evidence like: He ran the race for me when I felt like I was dying. Like: He stayed behind with me after the party, and he's never shown any particular interest in sweeping floors before, so there must have been another reason. Like: Max said so when he came into the bakery after school, and didn't his brother say that he'd been searching for *our* bakery? Like: There was a very brief moment four and a half weeks ago when he gazed over at me so tenderly I felt my breath catch.

It probably isn't substantial enough to convince any examiner, but it's enough for me to convince myself by the end of the night. I'm going to do it, I decide. I'm going to tell him, and I'm going to pray he won't reject me on the spot.

"I'm going to be sick," I inform Abigail when I slide into the bus seat the next morning.

She's sipping a drink that's more whipped cream than actual liquid, her bag crammed into the space between us, her denim jacket draped over her lap like a pillow. Never one to let herself sit in discomfort, even if it's just for a one-hour bus ride into the woods. "You look like you didn't sleep at all last night," she says, studying my face.

I grimace. "I didn't. I was busy strategizing my next move."

She almost spits out her drink with laughter. "My darling, you're not planning to go to war here—you're just telling a boy you like him—"

"Keep your voice down," I hiss, scanning the bus. There are still students shuffling their way down the aisle, others standing up to search for their friends or shove their luggage under the seats. "Someone will hear you."

"Nobody could possibly guess who we're talking about. Like, I barely believed you when you *told* me. And he's not even here yet," she says lightly. "Also, if we're really focusing on strategy, I feel like you should kind of ease into it. You know, considering your . . . history and all. You don't want to startle him by launching into an impassioned speech straightaway."

"Huh?" I'm still craning my neck, checking every face that passes. I feel physically nauseous, and it's only partially because I skipped breakfast altogether this morning. I feel almost as sick as I did before my school captain speech, before our end-of-year exams, even. Is *this* what liking someone should be? Because contrary to common description, there's nothing warm or gentle about it at all. This is a violent intrusion, my own body revolting against me. There are no butterflies in my stomach, only scorpions.

"Maybe just act friendly first. Or at least like you don't absolutely *loathe* the guy," Abigail advises. "Plus—"

"Oh my god, he's coming."

After wasting so much time thinking about him since yesterday, it's a surreal experience to see him just standing a few feet away. There, right there. The sun streaming in through the bus windows and hitting his face.

But if I look like I didn't sleep last night, he looks like he hasn't slept in weeks. Tired, blue-gray circles are smudged around his eyes, and his hair is rumpled for once, messy strands falling free over his forehead. Then he catches me staring and stares back.

The scorpions inside my stomach crawl up to my throat.

"Remember: Be friendly," Abigail hisses under her breath.

This is entirely counterintuitive to everything I've learned over the past ten years. As natural as jumping backward, or sticking your hand into a boiling pot, or running headfirst into a flaming building. But I force the muscles in my face to relax. The corners of my lips to lift. A high-pitched, strangled sound escapes my mouth.

His brows furrow. "Sorry?"

"I was just—saying hi," I say brightly. "In greeting. Hello."

He shoots me a weird look and walks right past me without another word.

And I've decided I would like to stop existing.

"Okay, to be fair, that could have gone a lot worse," Abigail says once he's settled into the back of the bus. The doors slide closed, and the teachers do a final head count before we start reversing out of the school parking lot. "It's not like you *completely* fumbled the birdie."

I'm hitting my head very slowly against the window.

"Maybe stop doing that," she tells me.

"Don't worry, I'm not doing it hard enough to risk impairing my cognitive functions."

"No, I'm worried because Ms. Hedge might see and force us

to watch that seventy-minute video about the importance of self-love again. And also because Julius is currently looking in your direction."

I freeze. Feel all the heat in my body refocus in my cheeks. "Are you sure?"

"Quite," she confirms somberly. "But I'll handle it." Before I can even ask, she speaks up in a loud voice, so loud it drowns out the rumbling engines. "It's great to see that the windows are so sturdy, Sadie. Thank you so much for testing that out for me. I'm now inclined to believe that the news article I read about that twenty-year-old who crashed headfirst through the bus window and left a human-shaped hole in the glass was most likely fake."

I don't know whether to burst into tears or laughter. "Is he still looking?" I whisper.

"Nope. All safe now."

I heave a sigh and slump back in my seat. "God, I *detest* this."

"You still have the whole trip," she says, popping in an earphone and offering the other up to me. "Just wait until we get there."

We don't talk much for the rest of the ride, except to change the music every few songs (our tastes are starkly different; Abigail listens to what she refers to as *sad music for hot girls*, or music you can wail to, while I prefer music you can study to). It's one of the many reasons I love being around Abigail. We can talk on the phone for five hours straight in the evenings, stopping only to grab our phone chargers or a glass of water, but we can also just sit together and watch the changing scenery through the window. Soon the roads narrow into a single winding lane, and the rising sun glimmers through the trees on both sides. The malls and gas stations and busy cafés disappear. Everything disappears, until we're venturing deep into the mountains, and all the colors are some variation of gold and blue and green.

And then we're not the only ones silent, drinking in the view. The other students quiet down too. Even the athletes have stopped their competition of who-can-throw-their-empty-sports-drinks-higher-without-accidentally-hitting-a-teacher, which is pointless anyway, because there are no clear rules or rewards.

"Wow, it's pretty," Abigail murmurs, and I agree.

Lake Averlore looks exactly the way it does in photos.

From the handcrafted cabins at the base of the mountain to the wisteria and lace wildflowers to the great elm trees fringing the lake bank. We round the corner, and the lake itself comes into full view, vast and beautiful, the emerald water so clear it glows in the daylight, reflecting the scattered clouds in the sky. The place feels like its own secluded world, a retreat in the true sense of the word. It's almost enough to help me forget about Julius, about the emails, about everything that's happened these past couple of months.

But then the bus jolts to a stop, and I'm yanked back to reality. Or maybe some weird, alternate version of it. Because as everyone starts unbuckling their seat belts and reaching for their things, Ray Suzuki stands up from his seat and turns to me. "Hey," he calls. "Did you choose this spot?"

I straighten Abigail's earphones and hand them back to her. Look up warily. "Yeah?"

"It's not as bad as I expected," he grumbles.

I'd think I had hallucinated it if Abigail wasn't wearing a similar expression of disbelief.

"Oh. Um, I'm glad," I say, still waiting for the catch. Maybe the follow-up sentence is: *It's still a lot worse than I'd hoped.* Or, *I was imagining a literal pit in the flames of hell to match the inside of your soul.*

But it doesn't come. He just nods, clears his throat, and joins the other students crowded down the bus aisle.

"So you're blushing and stuttering over Julius Gong, while Ray Suzuki is being sincerely appreciative of you," Abigail remarks, her brows raised. "Bizarre. Truly, absolutely bizarre. Next thing you know, Ms. Hedge is going to start advocating for underage drinking and Rosie is going to declare that her lifelong dream is to become a nun."

"Don't be so dramatic," I say, laughing, but I can't help feeling like she has a point.

We're given half an hour to settle into the cabins.

It's very nearly perfect. The interior is designed like something from a fairy tale, with vintage couches and stacked bookshelves and a blazing fireplace. The local staff have laid out tables of homemade scones with fresh whipped cream and strawberry jam to welcome us; within minutes, they're all gone, not even a crumb left on the porcelain plates. The teachers are given raw salmon appetizers and mocktails that smell suspiciously like cocktails, and I've never seen Ms. Hedge look so happy. The bunk beds are comfortably wide too, the sheets fragrant with the scent of flowers from outside.

The only problem is—

"Naked clowns," Abigail says, her voice a mixture of horror and pure disgust.

All the other girls gather around her, staring up at the paintings on the wall. As in, paintings, plural. Because for whatever cursed reason, there are *multiple* paintings of naked clowns hung up in every room, right on open display for everyone to see. Above the beds, next to the mirrors, over the doors. Perhaps it would be better if they were done in some sort of abstract art style, but they're unforgivably realistic, the tiny brushstrokes capturing every detail.

"This shouldn't be allowed," Georgina Wilkins says, shaking her head. "That's just—what's the word? Diametrical? Diagonal?"

"Diabolical," I correct her automatically, then wince. I know from experience that this is one of my less popular traits.

But Georgina just throws me a grateful look and says, "Right. Exactly." Which proves how bad the paintings must be.

Abigail drags a hand over her face. "My eyes feel like they're being physically attacked. To be more specific, like they're being kicked by a kangaroo and then dragged through cut glass and then set on fire."

"God, I'm sorry," I tell everyone. "I swear this wasn't included in any of the photos on the website when we were picking out locations . . ."

And maybe it's true what they say, about unlikely alliances forming from common enemies—even if the enemy is a two-dimensional clown who should be arrested for public indecency—because Rosie comes to stand next to me. "What are you apologizing for?" she asks, flicking her hair over her shoulders. "It's not as if you put the paintings up there yourself."

I open my mouth. Then close it again. I'm so used to taking responsibility for everything, to apologizing to her and everyone else, that it feels wrong *not* to say sorry.

"You're so strange sometimes, Sadie," Rosie continues, though she doesn't sound like she's being unkind. "You know most people rush to push blame away instead of taking all of it themselves, right?"

I blink. Try to find my bearings again. "I— Right. Well . . . it might not be my fault, but I do know how we can fix this. Temporarily, at least."

"Please," Abigail says. "Anything."

I rummage through my bag and pull out the spare jacket I packed, then drape it over the painting frame so it covers the clown completely. "There," I say. The others quickly join in, grabbing loose dresses and oversized sweaters, and soon we're running from room to room, giggling, lending one another our clothes to block every single painting from view. The hysteria fizzes on my tongue like alcohol, and when I turn around at one point, I catch Rosie's eye. There's no malice in her expression. We're both doubled over, laughing at the absurdity of the whole situation, and for the first time in a while, I don't feel like the year level's number one villain. I don't feel like the perfect student either; I'm just one of them.

We're still laughing when we stumble outside onto the lakeshore, into the sunlight.

The first activity for the day is canoeing. Two canoes have already been set down over the pebbles, the green lake water shimmering behind them. A tanned, buff guy with beaded bracelets around his wrists and ankles introduces himself to us as David, But You Can Call Me Dave. Then he dives in right away, showing us how to hold the canoe paddle and adjust your body position while Ms. Hedge sips her cocktail-mocktail and watches from under the trees.

"We'll split you off into two teams," Dave says, rubbing his hands together. "And then, just to make things interesting, we'll do a little race. The first person to the other side of the lake wins. Got it?"

Most of us nod. Abigail slaps a mosquito on her thigh and mutters into my ear, "I was hoping we wouldn't have to do any physical exercise. When can we do a race to see who falls asleep the fastest? I bet I'd win that without even—"

"You," Dave says, pointing at her.

Abigail jerks her head up. Smiles without any shame. "Yeah?"

"Since you're feeling so chatty, you can lead the first team. And . . ." He looks around, sizing each of us up before his eyes land on Julius. "You look like leader material."

"Well, he is school captain," someone volunteers.

"Oh, is that right?" Dave asks.

Julius nods with barely concealed smugness, crossing his arms over his chest.

"Perfect. You can lead the other team, then," Dave decides. "Both of you choose your members."

"I would pick you," Abigail whispers to me, nudging my ribs, "but I'm going to be generous and let you join his side."

"That's if he picks me," I whisper back.

"Of course he will. Based on athletic ability alone, he should."

I shake my head and smile like the idea couldn't be further from my mind, but secretly, humiliatingly, I am waiting for Julius to turn to me. To at least *consider* me, if not choose me. I'm waiting for him to take his time, to meet my eyes. My stomach flutters from the sheer anticipation, and my heart—my heart is beating unbearably fast, the suspense of the moment so disproportionate to the stakes I want to laugh at myself.

And then I want to slap myself. Because he doesn't hesitate, or even glance once in my direction. Instead, he waves Rosie forward.

"Oh my god, *yes*," she says, grinning wide and making her

way down the shore like a pageant queen. "We'll make the perfect team."

Julius grins back at her. My nails dig into the soft flesh of my palms, my hurt hardening into rage. It's not Rosie I'm angry at though. It's him. It's always him.

He doesn't choose me next either. He chooses Ray and Adam and Georgina, who gets out of swimming lessons every year by claiming she's allergic to chlorine. It's like I don't even exist to him. Like last night never even happened. Or maybe it didn't. Maybe I've been spinning it into something it's not.

By the end, I'm one of the last two people left. Me, and that boy in our year level who talks to nobody.

Julius's eyes flicker between us. His expression is passive, careless, when he nods once at the boy. He doesn't even appear sorry. It's not as if I was ever certain I could be his first choice. But knowing that I'm his last choice—it's a twist of a knife in the gut.

Humiliation stings my throat. I'm no longer planning to confess to him; I'm planning to choke him. But for the sake of my own dignity, I act like it doesn't matter. I move over to Abigail's side, my head held high, my fists clenched to stop them from shaking.

"Great. Now, who wants to race first?" Dave asks.

"I will," Julius offers, rolling up his sleeves.

Dave's sunburned face splits into a beam. "And who thinks they can take him in a one-on-one—"

"I'll go," I say loudly, marching forward, not even caring when the freezing lake water sloshes over my shoes. "I'll beat him."

There's a beat of surprised silence. Dave blinks at me. "Oh! Oh, okay. Really loving the confidence here. Now, the paddle might be a little heavy for you—"

I pick up the paddle easily, tightening my grip around the rough wood. "Just teach me how to row this thing."

I've always been a fast learner.

It takes me only a few minutes to push the canoe into the lake, strap on my life jacket, and get used to steering with the paddle. Then I start paddling.

Wild geese startle and soar over my head, their white wings flapping as the canoe makes its way through the water, foam forming from the ends of the paddle. The earthy scent of the air fills my nostrils, coats my tongue. The lake itself is serene, tall grass rising over the opposite shores, the sun's reflection rippling outward. I can make out the trees in the distance, their smooth, pale bark gleaming, their golden-green foliage swaying with the breeze.

If I wasn't competing against Julius, I would probably admire the view more. Let myself sit in the rare silence and watch the light playing over the water, the wilted flowers floating across the surface.

But all I can focus on is his canoe in my peripheral vision.

I lean forward, dig my paddle deeper into the water, my muscles burning from the effort. It's still not enough; he's pulling ahead. I dig as hard as I can, but I apply too much force on one side and the canoe lurches unsteadily. Cold sprays my face, soaks through my clothes.

"Slow down," Julius calls from beside me. He sounds irritated. "You're going to fall into the water like that."

"*You* slow down," I snap at him.

He doesn't. Of course he doesn't. He clenches his jaw and pushes his canoe onward with renewed vigor. Without looking at me, he asks, "What are you getting so angry for?"

I choke out a harsh laugh, the sound only half-audible over our splashing paddles. "Unbelievable."

"What?"

"I'm not angry," I say coldly. My arms are starting to weaken, and I can feel the wood rubbing open the skin on my palms, but I ignore the sting. "Why would I—" A sudden gust of wind tears through my hair, creating waves in the water, one bigger than the next. The canoe wobbles again, this time more violently. "—be angry?" I grip the edge of the canoe for support, grit my teeth against the emotions fighting for room inside my chest. "It's not like we owe each other anything."

He makes a soft, frustrated noise. "See, you're saying that, but your tone strongly suggests otherwise."

"And since when did my *tone* matter to you? Last time I checked, you didn't even want to look my way."

"Are you kidding? I—" His sentence dissolves into a muffled curse as my canoe slams against his, the sudden impact jolting both of us out of our seats. "Seriously, Sadie, watch out—"

"I'm not doing it on purpose," I interject, pushing myself upright with a huff. "Maybe if you gave me more space—"

"I can't control the speed of this," he says. A shameless lie. He just doesn't want to risk losing to me.

"Well, then, neither can I," I say, paddling faster. *I'm winning*, I think. We're more than halfway there, the opposite shore close enough for me to see the shine of damp on the stones, the grass tall enough to reach my knees. *I'll make it before him.* But then my paddle gets caught on something in the water. A weed, maybe, or a net. I try to yank it free, but I lose control, and it's like everything unfolds in slow motion. I can only stare in horror as my paddle swings out sideways—as Julius attempts to duck, but leans too far backward, and crashes into the water, sending a great wave rushing toward me—

And my stomach drops, gravity slipping out from under my body as my canoe flips upside down.

CHAPTER EIGHTEEN

The water tastes absolutely disgusting.

Like fish and seaweed and mud. It pours into my mouth when I gasp, choke, flounder in the cold. My bones feel like stone, heavy, clumsy, and my clothes are cemented to my skin. It's hard to move, impossible to breathe. For a few moments I can't see anything except the darkness stretching down, can't feel anything except the chill of the lake and the silt sticking to the back of my teeth—

And then I break through the water, gasping, blinking hard. Color rushes back to me first: the stark blue sky, the aureate sun melting into the clouds. Then sensation in my fingertips. Then sound. My pounding heart. The distant yells from the shore, telling us to stay put or swim, Ms. Hedge's shrill voice rising over the others. But we're too far away from them to wait for their help.

Julius is already pulling himself back into his canoe. Water leaks from his hair, onto his cheeks, and I make the most absurd observation: that his hair is even more intensely black when it's wet. He's breathing hard when he collapses safely over the canoe seat, soaked all the way through, leaves sticking to his shirt. Then he turns to me, his dark eyes narrowed.

I kick hard against the water, seized by the sudden fear that he might not help me up. That he'll just watch me struggle and thrash like an utter fool from the comfort of the canoe. I wouldn't put it past him.

He pauses. His expression is inscrutable, the sharp planes of his face giving nothing away. One excruciating second passes. Two. Three—

He extends a hand.

Both shame and relief fill my lungs. I take it, or try to, my fingers slipping against his. But his grip is firm, secure, and in one movement, he drags me up, out of the water. The only problem is that our combined weight pulls me over the side too fast; I crash gracelessly against him inside the canoe, his body pressed to the seat, mine pressed to his.

"Sadie," he manages, with a small, breathless sound, a suppressed groan. "Sadie—you're—"

"I know, I know, sorry," I say, my face warming as I struggle to rise. My hands keep sliding over the wood, failing to find purchase.

"Won't you *hurry*—"

"You don't think I'm trying?"

"I think you're awfully close to me—"

"Not by choice," I protest shrilly, even though he is right. We're far too close, the space between us nonexistent. I should be freezing right now, but his skin is shockingly hot, burning underneath my chest.

He squeezes his eyes shut. The muscle in his jaw stands out. "This is your fault—"

"*My* fault?"

"I told you to be more careful. You didn't have to go that fast."

"We were racing," I say, by way of self-defense. It's the one thing that we've always been able to agree on, the one principle we've always stuck to: Nothing matters as much as winning.

I can feel the thud of his heartbeat beneath me when he demands, "Haven't you beaten me enough times already?"

"No," I say, my voice fierce. "No, it'll never be enough."

He shakes his head. Mutters under his breath, "You make my life so difficult."

I finally manage to sit up. The cold air immediately encircles me, and I almost miss the warmth of his body.

"Aren't you going to give me a hand over here?" he asks, still lying back in the seat, the lower half of his body pinned down by my knees. "You were the one who pushed me into the lake to begin with."

I scoff. Deliberately place my hands on my hips. "For the record, I didn't *push* you—"

"You hit me with your paddle—"

"The paddle went right over your head—"

"Only because I ducked," he argues.

I roll my eyes, but I mirror his motion from earlier and offer him my hand. He shifts into sitting position, then drops my hand quickly, like it burns him. Stares out instead at where my canoe is still overturned, bobbing over the lake surface like a dead body, my paddle floating farther and farther away from us. The water laps against the side of the boat, casting intricate silver patterns over the cedar.

"This wouldn't have happened if we were on the same team," I say. I mean for it to sound like an angry jibe, an accusation, but my voice decides to be a traitor and wavers violently.

His gaze swivels to me. He studies my face for a long time. Too long. "You've never wanted to be on my team before."

I wring the water from my hair, twist it a few more times than necessary, just for something to preoccupy my body with. "I would have liked the option."

Silence swells between us like a solid thing. The shouts from the shore have died down too. I can hear only the rippling lake, the drops of water splashing onto the wood, the birds chirping from far away. My own volatile breathing.

"Why are you doing that?" The sudden sharpness to his tone startles me.

"I'm not," I say, confused. "I'm not doing anything—"

"You're acting nice all of a sudden," he continues forcefully. "Smiling at me on the bus. Acting like you would rather be on *my* side for this ridiculous race than your own best friend's. Defending me last night—" He shakes his head. Stares down at his own hands.

My heart is beating painfully fast, my breath snagging in my throat. He's found out. He must have detected it. He knows I like him and he's appalled, furious, disgusted—

"You don't have to pity me," he says in a low voice, and my brain goes blank. "This is why I didn't want you to meet my brother, and you shouldn't have been listening to our conversation to begin with. You shouldn't take any of the stuff he says seriously, especially the stuff about you. I really—" His fingers form closed fists. "There's nothing—*nothing* I resent more than when people feel sorry for me. Because I don't need it. I'm fine. I'm perfect."

"Oh my god," I say. In my shock, I forget that I've just been in the lake, and rub my eyes with my wet palms. Now I'll probably walk away from this cursed conversation with both a headache and an eye infection. "You can't be serious."

"I am," he tells me without looking up. "I would much rather you go back to insulting me than tiptoeing around me—"

"You want me to insult you?" I actually laugh. I laugh so loud the geese circling us overhead squawk with alarm and fly higher. "Oh, well, that's easy. You're so self-absorbed, Julius Gong. You really think you know everything— You act like you've got me all figured out—"

"Don't I?" he says, and he sounds perfectly confident in himself, his skewed judgment. "You're so fixated on being nice, aren't you? The obedient girl who needs everyone to love her." Mockery drips from his every word like acid rain. "The perfect student who never says no to anything, who goes out of her way to cater to everyone's needs, who would dance on flames just to keep everybody entertained. You just have to be seen as undeniably *good*; you have to do the right thing all the time, or at least appear to. That's your whole personality—I get it. All I'm asking is for you to spare me."

It feels like I've fallen headfirst into the water again. I'm choking, suffocating, the cold flooding through my blood, freezing my bones until they're so brittle they could break with one touch.

Neither of us is even attempting to steer the canoe. It's drifting on its own over the lake, directionless, the water and sky stretching out wide around us. I've never felt so small.

"Take it back," I tell him quietly, amazed by my self-control. What I really want is to shove him out of the boat, to throttle him with my bare hands. "I'm going to give you one chance to take everything you said back."

His jaw tightens, but he doesn't say anything.

"*God*, Julius—" I cut myself off, bitterness creeping over my tongue. There's something so presumptuous, so condescending about it, that he would twist my sincerity into some sort of *charity*. That while I've been trying to see the best in him, he's been assuming the worst of me. "You know what? I hate you," I breathe, because it's easier to say *I hate you* than *you hurt me*. Because both options might shatter my heart, but at least one of them leaves my pride intact. And maybe because I simply crave the sharp, perverse pleasure of hurting him back.

His gaze snaps up to me. Something flashes across his face, and he leans in abruptly, his eyes fierce and dangerous and on fire. I can feel the heat of his breath against my lips when he says, "I hate you more."

"That's impossible."

His smile is a sneer. "I promise it isn't."

I'm shaking, I realize dimly. My teeth clenched with the effort of restraint, of holding back from him, of refusing to shrink away. His eyes could cut me open as they drift down lower, linger on my parted mouth. They darken, turn wholly black, until I can't tell the pupils from the irises.

For a shameful second, I think he's going to grab my face and kiss me, the kind of kiss you feel down to your toes, all heat and hunger and wild intentions. And for a split second, I need him to, I'm *dying* to, if only for a chance to sink my nails into his skin, to find a spot of vulnerability somewhere in his body.

But he stays still. The light reflected off the lake bleaches his skin and sharpens the cruel lines of his face, and right now, in this very moment, I can't believe I ever imagined him capable of softness. Julius is who he's always been, who he will always be: selfish, ruthless, conceited. To expect anything else of him is like expecting flowers to bloom from a blade. Like walking into a snake's embrace.

"You're the worst," I tell him, my lips bare inches from his, neither of us retreating. It's torture, blistering agony. It feels like

I'm being burned alive. "You make me sick. You make me so violently *angry* sometimes, I could—" I want to continue, but the burning sensation spreads to my eyes, my nose. *I won't cry. I won't be weak in front of him.* My fingers curl hard into the collar of his shirt, to make the sentiment clear where words fail me, and I see him swallow, the rising bump in his throat. *Go on*, I urge myself. *You have the upper hand now.* But all I can get out is, "You're so mean to me."

It's laughable. Pathetic. It's an exchange between children on the playground. It's not what I meant to say, not at all, but something about it unravels me. My anger abandons me, my last remaining weapon against him dropped, and I press my lips together to stop them from trembling. Blink rapidly to stop the tears from falling.

His expression morphs into something else at once. He jerks back, his brows furrowed. Lifts a hand, the aim unclear. "Sadie," he says. Tentative. Tender, even. "I—I didn't mean to—"

"Start paddling," I say stiffly. "We should go back."

Then I duck my head so he can't see me cry.

Neither of us speaks on the way back.

There's no point; we've already said too much. The instant the canoe bumps against the shore, I'm jumping off, barely noticing when the water splashes my legs.

"Had a little fall, did we?" Dave says, grinning, somehow

oblivious to the tension simmering between us. "Don't fret. It happens pretty often—"

"You both need to change," Ms. Hedge interrupts, looking far less amused. She's even set her cocktail-mocktail down. "Go shower and put on some warm clothes—god forbid someone gets pneumonia on this trip. You can meet us back here after."

"Thanks, Ms. Hedge," I say, genuinely grateful for the opportunity to escape. But as I walk past Abigail, she catches my wrist and pulls me a few steps back, out of earshot from the others.

"What happened out there?" she whispers. "Have you been *crying*? Did you tell him you like him? What did he say?"

I almost laugh. "No. I told him I hate him, and he told me he hates me too. So that's that."

"What?" Her jaw drops. "But I thought— That wasn't the plan—"

"It was a terrible plan," I say. "I don't know what I was thinking."

"Okay, wait. Wait. Just—hang on." She shakes her head. "I'm still trying to understand how you went from wanting to confess to him to fighting with him—"

"I guess old habits die hard." I try to make it sound like a joke, like it's already behind me. But maybe it's true. Maybe, by this stage, we've both been hardwired to hate each other. Maybe it's a fundamental part of our internal coding, and there's no way to reprogram it without self-destructing, setting everything on fire. Maybe it's for the best this way.

"Are you okay?" she worries. "Do you want me to punch him for you?"

"No, no, I'm okay." My mouth strains into a smile. "Really."

I *am* okay. Completely okay. I'm okay when I stomp up to the cabin bathrooms and stand under the hot spray of the shower, letting the heat melt the ice from my bones, scraping the mud from my skin with such force it leaves behind angry red nail marks. I'm okay when I slather my hair with too much shampoo and close my eyes against the water like it's pouring rain; when I sob into the palm of my hand, alone where nobody can hear me. And I'm definitely okay when I towel myself dry, change into a faded knit cardigan and skirt, and head back to the lake. Julius Gong is dead to me, I vow silently. If I think about him again— If I so much as *look* at him, then I deserve to be pelted with ice.

I deserve to be pelted with ice.

In my defense, I manage to hold it together all throughout lunch and after it too. The teachers split us off into our two teams for the afternoon activities, which means I don't have to worry about stumbling across him. We're taken to the other side of the lake to fish and bird-watch and color in illustrations of the mountain ranges. Everything's going well.

But later, we all gather back inside the warm air of the cabin and dim the lights, and my self-control rapidly deteriorates from there.

The screen unfurls. The projector flickers on. Around me,

people are lying down, getting comfortable on faded cushions and beanbags and pink wool blankets. Someone's snuck in a bag of gummy worms, even though we're technically not allowed snacks, and the candy is passed discreetly from hand to hand like drugs.

Abigail saves me a pillow, and I lean back next to her, dropping my head on her shoulder. That's when I notice Julius on the other end of the room. The sharp line of his shoulders. The glint of his hair. The cold planes of his profile. He's changed his clothes as well, discarded his button-down shirt for a dark V-neck that exposes his collarbones.

"What are you looking at?" Abigail whispers. "The movie's starting."

"Nothing," I say hastily, ripping my gaze away. *Stop it*, I tell myself. *I think we've established by now that it's a bad idea.*

"It's not scary by your standards, I don't think," she adds. She knows my incredibly low tolerance for blood or gore. She, on the other hand, likes to fall asleep to horror films. Claims she finds the suspenseful music relaxing. "But if it is, you can use my arm to cover your face. Just don't pinch me too hard like you did last time."

I shove her with the pillow. "I told you, I couldn't help it—"

She pushes the pillow back. "There wasn't even any blood. It was just one dude kicking the wall—"

"Aggressively," I supply.

The movie's some kind of tragic romance dating back years ago, and Abigail's right: It isn't scary at all. I think there's a dog involved. And maybe a boat. I don't really pay close attention, if I'm being honest. As the colored images move over the screen and the soundtrack plays, my eyes are drawn back to Julius. Like instinct. Like always.

It's easier to watch him while he's watching the screen. Though I'm not sure how much of it he's actually absorbing; he doesn't laugh or gasp when the others do. He just stares ahead, his expression blank.

I study his features carefully, hungrily, like I'm piecing together a puzzle. I can't prevent myself from drinking in the sight of him. From hating him and wanting him all at the same time, one point of tension bleeding into the other until it's impossible to separate the two. The blue glow of the projector sweeps over the curves of his cheekbones, and even though I've sworn against it, I feel a rush of fierce, reckless longing. I imagine going to him now, after all the ugliness from this morning, after he made me cry. I imagine stroking his hair, his cheek, his collarbones, the way the shadows do, then wrapping my hands around his throat.

Without warning, he turns his head a fraction, his eyes cutting to mine like the crack of a whip.

I flush. Look away. But I can sense his gaze on me for the rest of the movie.

It's the longest movie I've ever seen.

CHAPTER NINETEEN

Dinner is a combination of roasted marshmallows and chicken kebabs and creamy potato salad.

It looks so good that even though I don't really have an appetite, I join my class around the campfire, stacking my paper plate with as much food as it can physically carry. Then I drape my cardigan over the log and sit down on it, inhaling the sweet smoke and the scent of the lake nearby, content to chew and stretch my legs out and lick the melted sugar off my fork.

The teachers are meant to eat with us outside too, but Ms. Hedge is the only one of the three who appears. She's barely sat down when her face pinches, her skin turning a concerning shade of green, and she dashes off in the direction of the cabins, a hand covering her mouth.

"What's up with her?" Ray asks.

"Must've been the raw salmon from earlier," Georgina says, with the firm authority of someone who's suffered through food poisoning multiple times in the past. "On my way out, the other teachers looked like they were dying too."

Sympathetic murmurs travel around the tight circle, but nobody makes a move to check up on the teachers. Instead everybody relaxes in the absence of any adult authorities. The air seems to lighten, the conversations around me rising in volume, whispered jokes and muffled giggles turning into full-body laughter. It feels less like a school retreat and more like a massive party—except, unlike the one at my house, I can almost bring myself to enjoy it. To eat the melted marshmallows and watch the sun start to slide its way down the horizon, lending a pink glow to the sky.

"You know what the moment calls for?" Rosie speaks up.

"Spin the bottle?" Ray says instantly.

I drop my fork. *No. Absolutely not.* I think I'll die if I have to kiss Julius again, and I'll die if I see him kiss someone else. "How about scary stories," I suggest, with perhaps more fake enthusiasm than I've ever summoned in my life.

To be honest, I expect Rosie to shoot down my idea right away and call it childish, but she considers it for a second, then nods. "Sure," she says, crossing her ankles elegantly, as if the log is a throne. "Do you have one?"

"Oh . . . I guess." I straighten, trying to make something up on the spot. "Okay, okay, here's one: Once there was a girl called . . . um, Skye. She was very smart and very organized. She had a habit of keeping all her homework notes and certificates and important files in a special compartment inside her locker. Then one day . . . she discovered that her locker was empty."

This is meant to elicit gasps of shock and horror, but all I get are blank, perplexed stares.

"Sorry, is that meant to be scary?" someone asks at last.

"Her certificates are *missing*," I emphasize, frowning. "Her records of achievement are *gone*. She may have to redo *all her homework*."

"Okay, do we have any non-homework-related stories?" someone else asks.

"I have a ghost story," Julius offers, and all heads swivel to him. He lowers his voice so it's just barely audible over the dry hiss and crackle of the campfire. "A *real* ghost story. Actually, it's set right in the woods, not too far from here."

"Sure it is," I mutter.

But everyone's already listening closely, hanging on to his every word.

"There used to be a house in these woods," he begins, soaking in the attention. "A young couple and their two children: a boy named Jack, and a girl named Scarlett. The boy was healthy and always happy; everyone who saw him adored him. But Scarlett was born . . . *strange*." He drags out the word in a whisper. "As a baby, her father claimed that her eyes would flash red. It was quick, so quick it could've been confused for the light, but it happened too many times for it to be a coincidence. He even took her to the doctor once, wondering if it was some kind of rare disease, and the doctor said there was nothing wrong. Nothing that they could find anyway."

On the other end of the circle, one of the girls shivers and wraps the wool blanket tighter around her shoulders.

"There were other things too," Julius continues. "Like she

would be running, and her shadow would disappear. Or she would throw a tantrum, and within an hour, a bird would drop dead outside their yard. Or she would get into a fight with her little brother, and he'd wake up in the middle of the night claiming someone was choking him. Over time, her parents started to suspect that she was cursed. Perhaps a demon incarnate, or a monster."

It's a silly story. Typical. Certainly no better than *mine*, which is rooted in realism. But in the falling darkness, by the crimson light of the fire, I can't help the pinch of fear in my gut.

Julius catches my eye across the circle, and one side of his mouth lifts, as if he can read my mind. "On Scarlett's thirteenth birthday, there was a sudden, terrible storm. It was as if the sea was falling from the sky. The whole house was flooded. The parents didn't even have time to pack; they just grabbed what they could and fled into the night. But whether by accident or not, they forgot about Scarlett. When they came back, almost everything was destroyed. The wood was rotted through, the furniture in pieces, the windows shattered. They looked around, and they couldn't find any sign of Scarlett. There was no body. Not even any of her old clothes or toys. It was as though she'd never existed."

He pauses for dramatic effect. In the same instance, a heavy wind picks up, blowing through the trees, and more than a few people startle and glance around them. The sky is no longer rose pink but graying, clouds forming in the near distance.

"They were rather attached to the woods, so they rebuilt their house in the exact same place," Julius says. "But every time it rained again, they could hear . . . crying. It sounded like a child. Like Scarlett. They tried to follow it, but it seemed to be coming from *within* the house, within the very walls. A year later, there came another storm. Much tamer than the first. Almost everyone survived it; the water levels didn't even rise above the knee. Except Scarlett's family was found drowned in the living room the next morning, all of them lying facedown."

"And then?" someone whispers.

"That's it," he says smoothly. "They all died."

Heavy silence follows in the wake of his words.

Then, somewhere in the distance a door slams, and Ray lets out such a high-pitched shriek I briefly wonder if a chicken has broken loose.

But the spell is broken. Everyone's too busy laughing at Ray to linger on the details.

As the campfire burns on, people split off into private conversations, friends huddling together on the log. I'm cleaning my plate when I feel a weight lower itself next to me.

Rosie.

I instantly stiffen.

"Chill, Sadie, I'm not here to bite your head off," she says, seeing my reaction. She's smiling, which is very alarming. "I just wanted to chat."

"About what?" I ask.

"I've been thinking about the email you sent me, and you know what? I was really, *really* pissed off." She brushes her hair over her shoulder. "Honestly, when I first read it, I was ready to slap someone."

I shift back, out of slapping distance.

"But I kind of deserved it. I *did* copy your science project." She exhales. "I didn't plan to. I don't know what I was thinking. Or, well, I guess . . . Everyone knows I'm gorgeous, right? Sometimes when I'm walking past a mirror, I have to stop for a few seconds because I can't believe how stunning I am. Like, damn."

I officially have no idea where this conversation is going.

"I'm proud of it," she adds. "It takes a lot of work to look this good all the time. But I was just . . . curious. What it's like to get great grades and have people compliment you for your intelligence. To be you."

This is perhaps the most bizarre statement I've ever heard. Even more shocking than Abigail's prediction about Rosie devoting the rest of her life to being a nun.

"I was planning to apologize," she goes on, crossing her legs. "Except I feel like we'd only be going in circles with our apologies. I'm sorry I copied your project; you're sorry you wrote that email. I'm sorry I proceeded to snap at you in front of the year level. So I guess what I'm really trying to say is—thank you. For being understanding, and for all your help in general." She lets out a little laugh. "Funnily enough, it wasn't until I made it a point to ignore you that I realized how often I turned to you for notes and stuff. You didn't have to do that, but you did."

It takes me a minute to remember how to speak. "Um. You're—welcome?"

She laughs again. "So we're good?"

"Yeah. Yes. Very good," I say, still stunned.

"I'll miss you when we graduate, you know," she adds. "I can't believe this will all be over soon."

"Yeah," I repeat softly, gazing around the campfire, at all the familiar, laughing faces. "I can't believe it either."

"She actually said that?"

"I know," I tell Abigail that evening, plopping down on the bed. We're lucky enough to have been assigned one of the smaller cabin rooms, made for only two people. Some of the girls have to share with three or four others. "I was so certain that she would never forgive me for the emails, that she'd spend the rest of her life hating me. That the damage would be irreversible. I've literally been sick to my stomach for weeks, *months*, thinking about it, and now . . . Thank god." I release a laugh, shaking my head.

She turns back to me from the dresser, a strange little smile on her lips. "Were the emails . . . that bad? I mean, did it . . . affect you so much?"

"That bad?" I snort. "They were catastrophic."

"Right." Her smile wobbles. "I didn't realize— I knew you

were embarrassed, obviously, but you never talked that much about it."

It's true, I guess. I haven't *really* talked about it with anyone. Not my mom, because I don't want her to worry. Not Max, because I don't think he'd understand. And not Abigail, because I don't want her pity. But maybe it's also habit by this point. The summer when I was eleven, we had flown to China for a large family gathering, and as everyone was trading stories and laughing and clinking drinks in the crimson glow of the restaurant, a fish bone had gotten lodged in my throat. Instead of making a big deal out of it and trying to cough it out in front of thirty-six people I was directly or indirectly related to, I'd chosen to swallow it inward, to quietly absorb the pain as the bone scraped its way down while I sat there and smiled. Nobody could have guessed that something was wrong.

It was only years later, when the event had long passed, that I had even thought to bring it up with my mother as a joke. She was horrified. *You could have choked to death*, she'd scolded me. *You should've said something.*

But you were chatting with laolao, I'd replied. *I was afraid of bothering you.*

She had been silent for a long time. When she finally breathed out, her eyes were so sad and heavy I'd regretted bringing it up in the first place. *Why are you this way?* she kept asking, until I didn't know if she was directing the question at me or herself. *Since when did you become this way?*

"Sadie," Abigail says, yanking me back to the cabin, to the present. "There's something . . . something I've been keeping to myself. I didn't mean to, I swear—I know I should've said it way earlier, but . . ."

I stiffen, my pulse accelerating immediately. "What's wrong?"

She wrings her hands. Steps forward, then stops a few feet away from me. Abigail Ong is never nervous, not before delivering a class presentation, not before a date, not before any major test. Except she's nervous right now, her eyes flicking to the dark clouds rolling in beyond the window, then back to me. "The emails," she says. That's all she says at first.

I blink at her, not understanding.

"I sent them."

I don't process the words. There's a faint ringing in my ears, all sound distorted, muted. I feel like I'm falling away from my own body, like those scenes in the movies where the camera zooms out and out from the person to the sky above them.

"Not on purpose," she says, speaking in a rush, like she's scared I'm not going to give her the chance to continue. "Not all of them. I was just—I was reading the draft you wrote to Julius, and I knew that he'd been bothering you for ages, and in that moment I thought . . . I don't know, I was tired of seeing people walk all over you. It was only one email; it was only *supposed* to be one email. But then you had, like, hundreds of tabs open, and your laptop was lagging, and when I hit send, nothing happened, so I kind of just—I kept clicking and trying to send it, and then suddenly *all* your drafts were being sent out, and I couldn't undo it . . ."

I'm frozen in place, rooted in my shock. "Wait," I croak out. Squeeze my temples. "You sent the email? *When?* No, hang on . . ."

It's all coming back to me, the details sharpened, everything different under a new light. When I'd rushed outside the classroom and come back to find my laptop moved. "Oh my god," I say. Part of me still refuses to believe it. Waits for her to tell me she's joking, she's making it up.

"I shouldn't have gone behind your back," she whispers, her face pale. "I know. I'm sorry—I'm so sorry. I take full responsibility. I'll—I'll write an explanation to every single person who received an email from you. I'll do anything. Just . . . please don't be mad at me."

"I don't get it," I say slowly, even as my heart pounds at breakneck speed, each thud painful. "Why didn't you say anything earlier?"

"I tried to, I swear." She holds up a hand as if making an oath. "But there never seemed to be a good time, and, well, I was convinced that I was doing what was right, in the long run. My whole life, I've believed that I know what's best, but when the thing with Liam happened . . . It sort of occurred to me that my gut instinct might not be as reliable as I thought." She pauses. Swallows. Eyes on the floor.

And even through all my shock and fury, I still feel a spasm of sympathy deep beneath my sternum.

"Plus for a while there," she continues, "it seemed like everything would work out on its own. People started treating you differently, pushing you around less. And you and Julius had grown closer—"

The sound of his name strikes me like a whip. "He's exactly why those emails should have never been sent."

I'm shaking now. It feels like I'm *being* shaken, like there's some invisible, overpowering force grabbing hold of my bones and nerves and muscles and jolting everything out of place. My teeth chatter; my fingers tremble. All this is so unnatural I don't know what to do, whether to stand or sit down or march out of the room or scream my throat hoarse. Abigail and I never fight. She's too chill about everything, and I'm too afraid of confrontation. The most heated argument we've ever had before today was over whether potatoes should qualify as vegetables.

"If he'd never read them, we wouldn't have been forced to do all those ridiculous tasks and spend so much time together, and I wouldn't have had to throw that party, and I wouldn't have had the chance to like him. And now I do, god help me, and it—it really—it feels like—" I fumble around for the right words, the most sophisticated way to express the ache in my chest. "It feels like *shit*."

"Okay, whoa." For a second, Abigail seems to forget we're

fighting. Her mouth falls wide open. "I thought you had, like, a firm no-swearing policy—"

"It's horrible," I continue furiously. "It's revolting how much I care about him. Even now. I shouldn't want this. I shouldn't want him."

Her jaw drops farther, her gaze catching on something behind me. "Um, Sadie—"

But I'm too angry to stop. "Out of all the people in this school, it somehow *has* to be the one person who called me up just to taunt me when I had a fever and missed out on practice—"

"Sadie," Abigail says again, louder.

"It's like I've been poisoned," I go on, my palms itching. "It's like a sickness, and somehow, the cause and cure of it is him. I hate it so much, but I can't even control my own brain—"

"Sadie."

I freeze. Because this time, it's not coming from Abigail. It's a low, male voice, coming from behind me.

My whole life seems to disintegrate before my eyes as I turn around on my heel, and I'm praying it's not him, it can't be him, *please* let it be anybody but Julius—

"Sorry to interrupt," he says. He's holding out my cardigan in the doorway, and I can't read any of the emotions on his face as he stares at me. "You left this behind at the campfire . . ."

It's somewhat difficult to hear him over the sound of my dignity splintering into a thousand pieces. I consider dismissing the whole thing as a joke, or maybe a reenactment from a very dramatic play about modern feminism, but I can tell from his expression, from the terrible, sweltering silence in the room, that the damage has already been done.

There's no taking it back now.

"Thank you," I manage to say, which is a miracle in and of itself. I keep my eyes averted as I grab the cardigan from him, my skin searing hot.

"Not at all," he says with equal politeness.

This is probably the most polite we've ever been around each other.

And then—nobody speaks.

I'm staring at a fissure in the wall, and in my peripheral vision, Abigail is staring at the clouds outside the window, and Julius is still staring at the side of my face. It's excruciating.

"Well, thanks a lot for visiting," I tell the spot under Julius's shoes when I can't stand it anymore. "This has been very fun. If that was all, please feel free to go whenever—"

"No," he says quickly.

My head jerks up against my will. This is what I mean about the sickness, because only somebody who is utterly unwell would hear that one word and wonder: *No*, what? No, there's more? No, he doesn't wish to leave? No, he doesn't like me?

But before he can elaborate, a deafening clap of thunder startles all of us, so loud it makes the floor tremble. I glance outside just in time to watch the skies split open, water pouring down to flood the earth. It's almost breathtaking to witness the rain come in, the droplets shattering the lake's surface like hundreds of tiny knives. Within seconds, the pavement has darkened to black, the wild grass submerged under rapidly growing puddles.

Then, from inside a cabin, someone starts yelling.

CHAPTER TWENTY

Ray is trembling.

Whimpering, really. He's standing in the middle of the hall in his polka-dot pajamas and clutching his arm, and he looks so alarmed, so horrified, that my first reaction is to search for blood. His clothes are damp and plastered to his skin, but there's no trace of red. It's only water.

"The roof is leaking," he gasps. "I was doing my skincare routine and I felt a splash of freezing water on my *arm*."

"Since when did you have a skincare routine?" Jonathan Sok grumbles behind me.

Unsurprisingly, his screams have drawn everyone out of their rooms; one quick glance around and it's clear half my classmates are in their pajamas too. Georgina even appears to have come running straight out of the shower. There are still shampoo bubbles in her hair.

Ray narrows his eyes. "What's wrong with it? You're just jealous you don't have beautiful, shiny skin like me."

"Hey," Jonathan protests. "My skin is already very shiny—"

"Yeah, well—"

But Ray's voice is drowned out by the violent rush of rain

outside. Within seconds, water starts trickling through the ceiling and pooling over the floors.

"*See?*" Ray yelps, lurching back. "It's everywhere."

"Oh perfect! It's exactly what I need." Georgina steps forward until her shampooed hair is positioned right underneath one of the leaks. "This is what you call being resourceful."

I have to admire her outlook on life.

"What do we do?" someone asks.

More voices chime in, all of them speaking over one another, over the pouring rain:

"My clothes are going to be wet. This blazer is dry-clean only—"

"The water's freezing—"

"I can't sleep like this—"

"Someone take me home *right now*—"

"Where are the teachers when you need them?"

"I heard they all have food poisoning—"

"This is exactly how all horror movies start—"

There's an ache building in the back of my skull. I want to join them. I want to yell and complain and wait for someone else to clean up the mess. But the water is spreading rapidly, and I know the rot will set in if we don't do something fast. There was a storm just like this a few years ago, and our bakery barely survived it.

I force myself to clench my fingers and unfurl them again. Deep breaths.

One.

Two.

Three.

"Someone go get Dave," I speak up, my voice ringing out in the room. Everyone falls quiet. "Does anyone know where he is?"

"I, uh, think he's asleep," someone offers. "Pretty sure I heard him snoring on my way over here."

"Go wake him up," I instruct. "There should be mops in the cleaning cabinet, but only he'll have the keys. In the meantime, everyone go grab buckets or containers from the kitchen or anything you can find to collect the water—"

An audible snort cuts through my sentence.

I swivel around and my stomach turns. Danny is hovering in the back corner, his arms crossed over his chest. I can see those awful words again, as if written in burning red: *Sadie Wen is a bitch*. "Seriously?" he asks. "Even when we leave the school, you're bossing us around?"

Ice crawls through my veins. "I'm not—"

"What, just because you're the captain? Or because you're a good student or whatever?" He rolls his eyes. "You think you're *so* important, but honestly, we're all sick of you, Sadie. We don't have to do anything you say."

I can hear my heart pounding, detonating inside my chest. I wouldn't be surprised if everyone in this room could hear it too.

"This really, *really* isn't the time," I manage. "I know you hate me, and that's fine, but the cabin is literally leaking as we speak—"

"Don't change the topic."

"You're the one changing the topic," I say, incredulous. "I'm just saying that there's a much more pressing issue at hand. If you have a solution, I'm always happy to hear it, but if not, you could at least cooperate—"

"Stop acting like you're better than us," Danny snaps. "You're the type to write shady emails about people behind their backs."

"And you're the type to write *Sadie Wen is a bitch* on a bike shed," I shoot back.

There's a collective, sharp inhalation from the crowd. "Damn," somebody mutters.

I can't even believe the words coming out of my own mouth, but it feels good. I'm so tired of playing nice, of smiling as people walk over me. What I'm realizing is that if you're quiet about the things that hurt you, people are only going to mistake your tolerance for permission. And they're going to hurt you again and again. "Yeah, I know it was you," I say coldly, folding my arms across my chest.

Danny stares at me. "You know? So *you* were the one who sent Julius to punch me?"

The whole room screeches to a stop. The world freezes on its axis.

Now it's my turn to stare. "Julius punched you?"

"Julius punched him?" someone else whispers in the background. "But I thought he and Sadie hated each other."

"But they kissed each other," someone says. "At that party, remember?"

"Wait, Julius and Sadie *kissed each other*?" someone asks. "Why am I so behind on the gossip? How did I miss this?"

"Yeah, well, seeing as she sent him a bunch of emails—"

"Technically, Abigail sent it."

"Abigail sent it? Sadie's best friend, Abigail?"

"Sorry, I was walking past their dorm room and kind of overheard a bit of their conversation—I left just as Julius showed up to her room though. So I'm guessing he likes her."

"Whose room?"

"Abigail's room."

"Wait, Julius likes Abigail?"

"No, Julius likes Sadie. They just share the same room."

"Him and Sadie?"

"*No*— Oh my god, this is why you're so behind on gossip."

I'm breathing against the knot in my chest and scanning the room, but I can't find Julius anywhere. I have no idea where he is or what this means or why I'm doing exactly what I'd accused Danny of doing earlier: forgetting the issue at hand. It's so bizarre how our brains work, how our priorities are organized by emotions instead of actual significance. This cabin could be flooded soon and still we'd be standing around gossiping, too fixated on our own petty grievances and grudges and crushes to notice the sky falling.

"Just. Stop," I say to nobody in particular. "*Stop*. If you disagree with me, I can't force you to do much. But if you do agree, then please, listen to me."

I don't expect anything.

For a long time, it seems that I'm right not to. Nothing happens. Nobody moves.

But then Rosie nods and flashes me her best smile. "Okay, I got you. Buckets coming right up." It's like magic. For the first time, I think I truly understand the term *influencer*. Because with a few simple words, everybody has been influenced. Her friends leap into action right away, and someone whips out tape to stop the smaller leaks. The water has already progressed through most of the room, but we manage to stop it from flowing into the corridor.

Just when I think the worst of it is over, the bulb above me suddenly flickers. There's a loud buzzing sound, like an insect caught in a trap.

And the power goes out.

The corridor is pitch-black.

I fumble my way alone through the darkness, away from the others, feeling the hard, cool plaster of the walls for support. Outside, the rain is pounding harder than ever. Water slams against the roof and churns through the old pipes. The wind shrieks through the trees, and it sounds eerily like the wail of a child.

The bare skin on my arms turns into gooseflesh. I'm sharply

aware of every hiss through the cracks in the window, every tremble in the floorboards. I swallow, rub my hands together to warm them, but the wind picks up again, louder. The back of my neck prickles.

Stop it, I command myself, cursing Julius for telling that horrible story. *It's completely made up. He just enjoys scaring people.*

I take another careful step forward—

And a cold hand wraps around my wrist.

I let out a hoarse shriek. All rational thought abandons me. My fight-or-flight instincts kick in, and because there's nowhere to run, I can only fight. I jerk back, squirm and punch and kick out like a wild, cornered animal. *Oh my god*, I think hysterically as my fist connects with something hard. *I'm about to be murdered by a ghost girl in a cabin in the middle of nowhere. The school isn't even going to take responsibility because they made us sign that form—*

"Sadie. Stop it—*ow, stop*—"

It doesn't sound like a vengeance-seeking ghost girl. The familiar voice registers a beat too late. *Julius.* My body doesn't understand even though my mind does; I'm still thrashing, swinging my fists around. Then the long fingers around my wrist tighten. He grabs my other wrist. Locks both of them together with one hand, pins them to the wall behind me, high above my head.

"Hold. Still."

I go still, but my heart continues hammering so hard I can

hear the blood rushing through my veins. For more reasons than one. Because soon my eyes have adjusted enough to make out Julius's face, bare inches from mine. He's breathing hard, the muscles in his arms tensed from holding me in place. One step closer and our lips would touch.

Everything floods through my brain at once. The look on his face when he stood in my doorway. The idea that he'd punched Danny for me. The fact that he heard me state very clearly that I like him so much it feels like a sickness—

Shut up, I tell my brain.

"Why did you have to sneak up on me?" I don't know why I'm whispering. "I thought you were Scar—" I stop myself, but he's already heard.

"Scarlett?" His smile is sharp in the darkness, like the gleam of a knife. "I'm flattered you found my storytelling skills so convincing. If you're afraid, you can tell me."

"I'm not." I am. Scared breathless. Terrified. But I can hardly admit that it's him I'm scared of now. Being alone with him. Being in this position. I try to wriggle free, but his grip doesn't loosen.

"Promise me you won't hit me again," he says.

"Julius—oh my god, just let me—"

"Promise," he insists, his voice pressed close to my ear, the heat of his breath fanning my skin. Goose bumps spread over my body.

I manage a nod, and he releases me at once but doesn't step back.

"I wanted to talk to you," he says.

My pulse skips. *Hope.* Foolish, irrational hope takes root inside me. But I wipe my voice clean of it, because there are countless directions this conversation could go. He could be here to talk to me about the math test next week. About weather patterns. About how pretty Rosie is. About how they've run out of buckets. If it's not what I so desperately want it to be, at least I can save myself the embarrassment of anticipating anything. "Why?"

He huffs out a laugh. "You're too smart to act this slow. You know why. We both do."

"What, are you going to accuse me of pitying you? Of being too nice?" I ask. It's a challenge. This is what we do, I realize. We talk in circles. We give each other riddles, confounding clues, half answers. Everything and anything but the truth.

"No— No, I'm sorry for that," he says quickly. Swallows. He's never sounded so nervous, so unsure of himself, and I find my anger bleeding out of me. "I didn't mean to say those things. I shouldn't have assumed . . . There were only two possible explanations for why you were acting the way you were, and the other seemed too unlikely. And I was—scared."

"Scared?" The last of my frustration vanishes like smoke in a breeze. It's almost funny; nobody else infuriates me like he does, but nobody else makes it this difficult to stay mad. "Of what?"

"Losing," he whispers.

I stare.

"You have to understand . . . If you knew the effect you had on me, how often I think about you, the things I would do for you . . . I wouldn't stand a chance against you ever again. You would have taken everything from me," he goes on in a rush, like the words are burning him from within, like he has to get it out before the pain becomes overwhelming. "Not just a debating championship or some points for a test or a fancy award or a spot in a competition—but my whole heart. My pride. God, my *sanity*. It would be all over. You would annihilate me."

I keep staring. I'm afraid to so much as blink, to breathe, afraid it'll shatter whatever wild fantasy or lucid dream this is. He can't possibly be saying these things to me. *About* me.

"I mean, nothing has even really happened between us," he says hoarsely, "and already it's hard for me to concentrate whenever you're around. My brother was right, in a sense, about you being a distraction, except you're so much more than that. I can't pretend to care about the things that once interested me. I can't fall asleep. I play through every look you've ever cast in my direction. I read through your emails over and over until they're carved into my memory. You did this to me," he says, and there's a rough, bitter edge to his voice now, nearly an accusation.

My knees buckle. It's too much to absorb. I feel myself slide down against the wall, sink onto the floor.

"You had to write those awful emails," he continues, lowering himself down next to me. Except he's kneeling, and he's still too close. I'm convinced he can hear my heart thrumming. "You had to kiss me, then kick me, then fill my head with your voice.

You made it clear—so terribly clear—how much you hate me. That I'm the last person in the world you would ever consider. But I kept looking for signs that would suggest otherwise. I kept wondering if it was still possible. Because I'm willing to lose everything," he says, his eyes blacker than the surrounding darkness, than the sky outside, "so long as I don't lose you."

I'm stunned.

It can't be a fantasy—I'm certain of that now. My own imagination couldn't conjure something like this.

"Of course, if you . . . if you don't want to," he says into the silence, sliding his gaze away from me, "I can accept that. I won't bring it up again. I know I'm not . . . I know what I'm like. That I'm infuriating. And selfish. And cruel. I know I'm not perfect the way my brother is, and I manage to disappoint my parents every time. It's okay if you don't choose me, really—I never expected to be the first choice. I wouldn't blame you—"

"I do choose you."

He doesn't seem to hear me at first. He's still talking, rambling really, the words flowing out like rainwater. "I can't always say pretty things, and sometimes I tease you when really I just want you to look my way, and— Wait." He stops. Even his breath freezes in his throat. "What . . . did you just say? Say it again."

"I choose you," I say quietly, glad for the shadows concealing my flushed cheeks. For the support of the wall behind me. "You'll always be my first choice, Julius Gong."

"Really?"

"Really."

His eyes widen, and he leans in, lips parted, his fingers trembling like moth wings over my cheeks. It's clear what he wants, and I almost let him. But I'm not going to make it *that* easy.

I twist my head away. "I recall you saying you would rather die than kiss me again."

He lets out a soft, half-stifled groan, and the sound shoots straight through my bloodstream. Makes my pulse quicken. "God, you really know how to hold a grudge."

"They're your words, not mine," I tell him, refusing to sway.

"You're killing me now," he murmurs against my neck. His lips graze my skin, and his other hand slides up, tangles in my hair, his nails lightly scraping my scalp. Despite myself, I feel my resolve buckle. "Isn't that enough?"

"No." I try to ignore it. The heat in my veins. The crisp scent of him, peppermint and rain. For once I have all the power, and I'd be a fool to let it go without putting up a good fight—no matter how badly I want him to just kiss me.

"Fine, then." His breath warms the shell of my ear. Tickles my cheek. "Please."

I can feel my heart pounding. "What?"

"Please, Sadie. I'm begging."

A triumphant grin splits over my face. "All right. I suppose, in that case—"

He doesn't even give me a chance to finish my sentence. His mouth is on mine in an instant, desperate, urgent. And I cave in. I hate surrendering, but maybe it's different when you're both surrendering to the same thing, because this doesn't feel awful. The opposite, actually. My brain is buzzing, but all my thoughts are floating, nonsensical fragments as he deepens the kiss, wraps a hand around my waist, forces me farther back until my spine is pressed flat to the wall. Thoughts like:

If you told me this would happen a year ago, my head would explode—

I swear to god if anybody hears us—

Maybe the emails weren't such a disaster after all—

His lips are so soft—

His hands—

Julius—

Julius.

"Julius," I gasp.

I feel him smile against my lips. His voice is raw silk. "Yes?"

"N-nothing. I just—" It's hard to focus. I squeeze my eyes shut. "It just doesn't feel real."

He shifts back, and the sudden absence almost feels like physical pain—until he kisses the curve of my neck. Murmurs, "I know. Even when I was imagining it—"

"You imagined this?"

He pauses, which feels like unfair punishment. Then he brings his lips firmly up to mine again. "Do you always pay such close attention to everything people say?" he demands between short, uneven breaths.

"No. Only what you say."

A sharp intake of air. "You have to stop doing that, Sadie." His hand tightens around my waist. "I won't survive it."

I'm not sure how I'll survive *this*, this overwhelming jumble of sensation, the want blazing through my body like wildfire, the need for more overriding all impulse control—

He kisses me harder, and I can barely get out my next words. "Wait—Julius, wait—"

With what seems like immense difficulty, he pulls away by just an inch, his eyes black and heavy lidded. He looks nearly intoxicated, delirious. I touch the base of his neck, feel the pulse striking his veins. The way it picks up beneath my fingertips. "What is it?"

"What if we're bad at this?" I ask in a small voice.

In response, he only moves close to me, wonderfully, terrifyingly close, his mouth traveling over my jaw, and everything is spinning, spinning out of control, my heartbeat racing ahead of me. I almost forget how to speak. How to breathe. "Does this feel bad to you?"

"No, I don't mean—" I tilt my head back without thinking. "I mean, you and me. We've hated each other for ten years, made each other's lives difficult—how do you know—" I will myself to stay focused as he brushes a thumb over my lower lip. "What if we're bad at—liking each other? What if we don't know how to be—civil—or nice—"

"I'm not planning on being particularly nice," he whispers. "And I don't expect you to be either."

"But—"

"It's *us*, Sadie," he says, like that's answer enough. "When have we been bad at anything?"

He has a point. A very good one. And in either case, I don't have the strength to argue any further, because he's kissing me again, and it's everything. It's so satisfyingly perfect. It's as if I've been suffocating in silence for days, months, years, and now I can finally inhale. Nothing has ever made as much sense as his hands on my waist, his heart hammering against my rib cage, the involuntary sound he makes when I adjust my posture, slide my hand farther down his neck to the hollow of his collarbones. He says my name, whispers it like it's sacred. And just when I'm wondering how we could ever stop this, how I could ever do anything except listen to his sharp intakes of breath, let him kiss me until my head goes fuzzy—

The lights come back on.

I blink, half-blinded, and jerk away from him. It takes a second before my eyes stop watering and my vision clears. An immediate flush races up my neck when I see Julius. His lips are swollen, his black hair rumpled from where I ran my fingers through it.

It feels like that surreal moment in the cinemas, when the credits start rolling and the doors open and the strangers around you rise from their seats, gathering their popcorn buckets and switching on their phones. And part of you is still reeling, still immersed in another world, your heart caught in your throat, struggling to tell which part is real life.

Then I find Julius watching me nervously. Like he's waiting for me to tell him. To take it all back, now that the cover of darkness is gone and I can see him clearly for the first time.

My heart throbs.

I want him to know he looks more beautiful than ever in the light, up close. I want to kiss him again, until all his doubts dissipate to nothing. I want to take away everything that's ever hurt him. But for now, I simply smile at him. Hold out my hand. "Come on. Let's see how bad the damage is."

CHAPTER TWENTY-ONE

It's already midnight when I trudge back to my room.

Abigail is waiting for me. She's practically in the same position, in the same spot as when I left her, and I'm struck by an overwhelming sense of déjà vu. It's as if time has stopped, yet so much has happened. I can still feel the ghost of Julius's hands around mine.

"Are you . . . still mad at me?" she asks.

I sit down and pat for her to sit as well. Am I mad? I search myself for any remnants of anger, but there's nothing. I don't want to argue with her. I just want to be around my best friend.

"This is what my mom always does when she's about to lecture me," she mumbles.

"I'm not going to lecture you," I say. "I only have a few questions."

Her eyes widen in horror. "That's *also* exactly what she says."

"I mean it. I'm genuinely curious . . . Why did you do it?" I ask. It's the one thing I can't let go of, can't fully wrap my mind around. "What was going through your head?"

She hugs her knees to her chest. I can't be sure what I'm waiting for her to say, but it's certainly not: "You know how I used to pour boiling water into plastic bottles before you stopped me and told me it could release dangerous chemical stuff?"

"Uh, yeah," I reply.

"Or how I once almost touched mercury, thinking it was just a funny-looking form of silver?"

"Yes."

"Or that time I convinced myself I could write a five-thousand-word essay during our lunch break?"

I shudder just recalling it. I had nearly broken out into stress hives for her. "Definitely."

"Yeah, well, I've never really been smart-smart or particularly talented. I've always known that. I can't even imagine what it's *like* to come in first in a race or be praised by teachers. My kindergarten teacher literally called my parents to the school to tell them I wasn't making as much progress as everyone else." She lets out a quiet laugh. "And guess what my parents did? They called the teacher narrow-minded and judgmental and stormed out of the office, and then they picked me up early and took me to get strawberry ice cream. They never made me feel insecure. But there are times when I still want to feel . . . *useful*. Needed, the way everyone needs you. And I mostly get that feeling when I'm giving advice to people or helping them work out the things going on in their lives. Does that make even a little bit of sense?"

"Kind of," I say.

Abigail rests her chin on top of her knees, her platinum hair falling around her. "So I'm being totally honest when I say that I wanted to help you, and I thought I *was* helping you. I didn't mean to go so far. I won't ever meddle again, I promise," she says. "But I'll also understand if you're still angry and want to drop me or violently smash a cake in my face—"

"I assure you, I've never once been tempted to smash a cake in somebody's face," I snort. "It's a tremendous waste of food."

She pauses, a faint, tentative smile touching her lips.

"And I assure you that I'm not going to drop you," I tell her, giving her a light shove. "Even if I were mad at you, you can be mad at someone and still love them."

"You mean it? We're still— We're cool?"

I nod. Raise my eyebrows. "Who else am I supposed to talk to when I've just kissed someone in the corridor during a rainstorm?"

I watch the understanding sink in. Her jaw unhinges. Her eyes light up. She grabs my hand, squeezing hard. "You don't mean . . . You and—"

I can only nod again, unable to help the grin spreading over my face.

"Holy shit," she yelps, and all the tension between us thaws as she springs up fully on the bed, and it's like every sleepover we've ever had, giggling into our pillows and whispering with the lights out. "Okay, you have to tell me *everything*. Don't spare any details—actually, no, you can spare certain details, but, like, was it good? Was he good? Are you together now?"

I'm laughing so hard my stomach hurts, and even though I know we'll both be exhausted tomorrow, we stay up talking until four in the morning, and when I finally do fall asleep, I feel lighter than I have in years.

· · ·

"How was your school trip?" Mom asks from behind the bakery counter. I had braced myself for a mess when I first walked in, imagining burnt bread and invalid receipts and spilled jam and a thousand other mini disasters to sort through after my time away. But everything is in perfect order. The SORRY, WE ARE CLOSED sign has already been hung up on the front door, and most of the shelves have been cleared.

I set my bag down on the spotless floor, then seat myself at an empty table. My arms are still sore from the camp activities, and my shirt is all wrinkled, and my left shoe is damp from when I'd accidentally stepped into a puddle on my way to the bus, but I feel a smile drift up to my face, like it's the most natural thing in the world. Like I can't think of a single reason why I *shouldn't* be smiling, why I haven't been doing it more my whole life. "Good. Great, actually."

She assesses me for a few beats, her eyes warm. "You look very happy."

"So do you," I say in surprise, studying her too. It's hard to place what, exactly, is different, only that it is. Maybe it's something about the evening light streaming in through the windows and softening her features, or the relaxed line of her shoulders. Or just how still she is. In all my memories of her, she's moving around, restless, rushing to get from one place to another.

"Because you are," she says. "Also, Max has good news. He's been waiting for you to get back to tell you himself."

I crane my neck. "Good news?"

The second the words leave my lips, Max pops out from the back room. "Surprise," he calls, beaming wide.

I'm instantly wary. "Is this one of those jokes where you say you're the surprise because your presence itself is a gift?"

"No, though I'm very flattered you think so," Max says, pulling out the chair opposite me with a drawn-out scraping sound. "I have something better than that." He pauses dramatically and clears his throat. "You might want to be seated for this."

"I'm already seated."

"It's a figure of speech," he says, annoyed. "Cooperate, please."

"Aiya, just hurry up and tell her, Max," my mom urges, stepping out from behind the counter to join us. She even takes her work apron off, which is how I know that whatever's coming is a big deal. I've seen her fall asleep with that thing on.

"Okay. So basically, a scout for the Hunters—yes, *the Hunters*—has been coming to a few of my games and . . . in short, they're interested in recruiting me. Like, super interested. Like, if this were a marriage, they're already shopping around for the ring. And it's occurring to me as I speak that that's a weird analogy, but, like, whatever, because they're *interested*."

My jaw drops. "I— Oh my god." It's all I can think to say. "Are you—are you for real?"

He grins at me. "Obviously."

I'm still fumbling around for proper words to express how

elated I am, how relieved, how shocked, so I slap his arm instead.

"Hey!" he yelps. "Why are you hitting me—"

"When *was* this? Why didn't you say anything sooner?"

"I mean, it's kind of been a developing situation for the past few months, and I didn't want to get your hopes up too quickly in case you were disappointed . . ."

Past few months. I'm aware that I'm gaping, but I can't help it. This entire time I've been worried sick about him and his future, desperate to solve every problem to come up, because I thought that he wasn't worried at all. That he simply didn't care enough. But he's okay—far better than okay. And this bakery is okay too. And, somehow, so is my mom, who's smiling at both of us, her eyes bright.

And I have to wonder when things changed. Or if it's been like this for years, but I was buried too deep in my own guilt to look up and see for myself that everything is really, truly fine.

My chest aches at the thought, joy and sadness mingling together.

"I'm happy for you," I tell Max. "Genuinely."

He wrinkles his nose, but he also bumps my shoulder. It's what we used to do when we were on the same team in basketball and won a game against our dad. And I've missed that. Not just our dad, but being on Max's team. "Don't you dare go all sappy on me," he warns. "Save it for when I break a world record."

"Fine. Then I'll save you the speech and go do something productive." I look around for a cloth. "Have all the tables been wiped already? Because I can—"

"No," Mom says.

"No?" I repeat, confused.

"You just got back," she says. "Rest. Relax. Do whatever you want to do."

I hesitate. "Are you sure?"

"Go," she insists.

I'm sorry. The words rise instinctively to my lips, but I push them down, seal them shut with the part of me that believes everyone else's happiness should come at the expense of my own. Try something different for once. "Thank you," I say quietly. It feels foreign. Strange. Yet it tastes sweet on my tongue, like forgiveness, like the rising spring air, like the lingering scent of strawberry shortcakes.

Like a beginning.

On the bus ride home, I take the window seat and compose a brand-new email:

Julius,
I'm writing this to inform you that you're the most infuriating person I've ever met. You, with your smug, razor-sharp smiles, your mocking eyes, your arrogance, and your vanity. Your

voice when you call my name, your hands when they wrap around mine. I'm not so familiar with vices—I like to think I have none, but if anything were to count, you would be my only one. It must be an addiction or an obsession. I have never known anybody as completely as I know you, and yet I still want to sit next to you, draw close to you, closer. I want you to tell me every story, want to listen to you speak until the night sinks in the sky and the stars fade out. I want you to hold me like a grudge, keep me like a promise, haunt me like a ghost. You're so beautiful it enrages me.

Maybe you're expecting an apology after all this time, so I'll cut to the chase: It's not coming. I apologize far too much—I'm working on it, I promise—but I'm not sorry for those emails.

You know that evening when I stumbled across your conversation with your brother? All right, not stumbled—followed. That's beside the point. Afterward, I could track the hurt in your eyes, and everything in me burned. I'm not sure if I expressed myself clearly enough then, if I'd convinced you enough. If not, then let me establish for now and forever that you will never be second. You will never be inadequate. You will never be anything but good.

Because you care how your parents see you. Because you will talk about anything except the things that actually hurt you. Because you never commit to something if you can't see it through to the end. Because you are brutally hard on yourself, and you have never gone easy on me in a competition or test. Because you challenge me, you distract me when my brain is being cruel, you sharpen my edges when the world tries to wear them down. Because every time I tired during class, I would catch your eye across the room, and remember why I needed to keep going.

Since I've decided to peel back my pride for the length of this email, let me tell you a little secret. When I was fourteen, I would stare up at my bedroom walls and wonder what it was like to fall in love. Most of my inspiration came from songs and the movies. But still, I imagined it. What it would be like to be someone who had somebody else. I would imagine tenderness. The concept of infinity. Of endless patience. Imagine them chasing after me even when I run. Cradling my sorrows in the palm of their hands. Imagine them caring, trying to understand.

And now there's you. This whole time, it's been you, and I didn't even realize. In retrospect, it makes sense, doesn't it? In order to beat the enemy, you have to understand them intimately. You have to observe them, learn their weaknesses, memorize their every word, track their progress, predict their next move. For ten years I thought I was preparing to destroy you, when really I was preparing to love you.

All of which is to say I really hope this finds you.

And I hope you find me too.

Sadie

I receive his reply within ten minutes. It's only two sentences:

You were right, Sadie Wen. I am completely, helplessly obsessed with you.
Love,
Julius

ACKNOWLEDGMENTS

This book could not have found its way to you without the talent and efforts of the following people:

My eternal thanks to my extraordinary agent, Kathleen Rushall. Thank you for always making me feel so seen and supported, and for being there throughout this entire journey. I may have trust issues, but I would trust you with my life. Thank you to the incredible team at Andrea Brown Literary Agency for your support.

A huge thank-you to Maya Marlette, for understanding the heart of this story and for helping me shape it into what it is today. It is such a tremendous joy and honor to get to work with you on another book. Thank you to Maeve Norton, Elizabeth Parisi, and Robin Har for all your work on the beautiful cover. Thank you to everyone at Scholastic for your enthusiasm and expertise, including: Elizabeth Whiting, Caroline Noll, Melanie Wann, Dan Moser, Jarad Waxman, Jody Stigliano, Jackie Rubin, Nikki Mutch, Savannah D'Amico, Lori Benton, John Pels, Rachel Feld, Erin Berger, Lia Ferrone, Avery Silverberg, Daisy Glasgow, and Seale Ballenger. All my thanks to Janell Harris, Priscilla Eakeley, Sarah Mondello, Jody Corbett, and Jessica White for playing such an integral part in preparing this book for publication. Thank you to the fantastic Emily Heddleson, Lizette Serrano, and Sabrina

Montenigro. My heartfelt thanks to David Levithan, Ellie Berger, and Leslie Garych.

I am deeply grateful for Taryn Fagerness at Taryn Fagerness Agency. Thank you for helping bring this book to more readers around the world, and for all that you do.

Thank you to everyone in the US and abroad who has championed this book throughout the publication process and beyond.

Thank you, forever and always, to my readers, for being so kind and generous and wonderful. Getting to share these stories and characters with you is truly one of the most meaningful experiences of my life.

Endless thanks to my friends both in and outside the publishing industry, for your warmth and wisdom, and for making everything better.

Thank you, of course, to my sister, Alyssa. Thank you for always being my earliest reader and biggest cheerleader, and for not getting too annoyed when I ask for your opinion on very small, specific things, or when I ask you questions like "What should I write about for your part in the acknowledgments?" I'm extremely grateful for your company and reassurance and humor—so grateful that I almost don't even mind you being the taller sibling.

To my parents: Thank you for supporting me in more ways than I can count. Thank you for encouraging me to read and write when I was a child, and for not freaking out when I decided I wanted to read and write for a living.

感谢我的家人对我一直以来的支持和鼓励：姥爷、小姨、小姨夫、南华小姨、大大、大妈、二大大、二大妈、和姑姑.

Keep reading for a sneak peek at Ann's next unforgettable rom-com!

The last thing I want is to make a dramatic entrance at my cousin's wedding.

Actually, the last thing I want is to *attend* this wedding. It's not that I have anything against my cousin Xiyue; she's seemed like a lovely person from the brief times we've spoken, even if most of those conversations consisted of me communicating via elaborate gestures instead of Mandarin while she stared in faint confusion.

But that's exactly what I'm dreading.

Once she says her vows, the event will become an intensive, three-hour-long version of those awkward exchanges, with all our relatives and family friends and strangers grouped together in one hotel ballroom. There'll be small talk. Jokes. Questions—none of which I'll be able to answer without slipping into English. And while I'd been clinging to the possibility that I could keep a low profile and slip in and out without anybody noticing, those hopes have now been left to rot somewhere on the road behind us.

"We're going to be late," I warn, leaning as far forward in the backseat as my seat belt will allow.

"Nonsense," my mom says. She lifts one hand off the steering wheel to point at the massive, white-domed building ahead of us, rising elegantly above the rows of palm trees and picket fences. "You can already see the hotel."

"We've been able to see it for the past ten minutes," I say. When she ignores my very valid observation, I catch my dad's eye in the rearview mirror. *Help*, I mouth.

He clears his throat and adjusts his spectacles, though they immediately slip down his long nose again. "We could afford to go just a little faster," he says, in the gentlest tone possible.

Three cars rush past us as he speaks. Someone honks.

"I'm going very fast already," my mom snaps. To be fair, for someone who generally seems to be on a mission to prove that walking is more efficient than driving, she is. At least we're not so far below the speed limit that we're at risk of being fined, like last time.

"You've made a convincing case," my dad says at once. "There's no rush. No rush at all." He shoots me a helpless look over his shoulder, which I return with a sigh. This is about as far as either of us will ever get to arguing with my mom. He adores her too much to ever accuse her of doing anything wrong, and I simply don't like to invest energy into battles I know I'll lose.

Besides, I've upset her enough in the past week.

So I lock my jaw shut, will away the slow churning sensation in my gut, and refresh my makeup for the third time since lunch. No matter what products I use, they tend to melt off my face within an hour, and it's always worse when the air is as hot and humid as it is today. Every makeup artist I've worked with has pointed this out. That, and the "lack of real estate" around my eyelids, and the sallowness of my complexion, and the thinness of my lips.

Not that it's an issue anymore, I remind myself, feeling a pang behind my sternum. It's another reason why I don't want to draw any unnecessary attention to myself at the wedding, but there's no way I'm avoiding my fate now.

We're running half an hour late by the time my mom pulls into the crowded parking lot. I yank open the door and jump out onto the pavement in my stilettos, then smooth my dress out over my knees, ready to bolt into the hotel—

Except Mom pauses on her way to the front steps,

scrutinizing me with her hand on her hip, her mouth pursed. I've never seen her in court before, but I imagine this is how she appears before her clients. Focused, serious, and slightly frightening. "You look pretty," she says.

I release an internal sigh of relief. It doesn't matter how often I hear it—I still want the confirmation that I can be beautiful. Crave it, chase it, like an adrenaline junkie craves their next high. If too much time passes without getting *some* kind of positive feedback about my appearance, I imagine myself shriveling away, all the work I've put into my face and my body gone to waste. "Thanks," I tell her. "That's very nice—"

"It's not meant to be nice. Why are you so put together?" she demands. "You're going to upstage your cousin."

"I'm not trying to upstage anyone." And I'm really not. My goal is never to look better than other people—it's just about making sure that I don't look bad. Still, I tug the bottom of my dress even farther down. It's a fairly straightforward navy piece, with a modest collar and basic lace design on the side. A model scout once told me in passing that darker tones suit me better, and I haven't worn anything else since.

"Maybe tie your hair up," she suggests.

"Fine." I attempt to follow her advice, scraping my hair back with my nails. "Is the ponytail better? I mean, well, worse?"

My mom pulls my dad over onto the sidewalk. "What do you think? Does she look uglier?" she asks hopefully.

"Our daughter is perfect. She could never be ugly, no matter what," my dad says, which is both really moving and unhelpful.

"She's certainly suited for modeling," my mom says, then catches herself. Remembers, once again. It's hard to describe the emotion on her face. Disappointment? Anger? Resentment? I feel all of it in my throat, and more, an ache I can't get rid of.

"Let's just go inside," I say, walking well ahead of them before either can continue. I could run in five-inch heels, if I wanted to. Every now and then, at my high school friends' gatherings, they'd ask me to demonstrate it as a party trick, and the response would be overwhelming.

I pick up my pace, my heart beating in sync with the sharp, satisfying *clack* of my shoes against the marble floor when I step inside.

Even though I'd much rather not be here, I do have to appreciate the venue. Lilies and violet orchids bloom in vivid clusters all the way down the wide corridor, and a six-foot-tall poster of my cousin and her fiancé is perched before the entrance. In the photo, they're gazing at each other on a balcony, both beaming, their skin near perfect thanks to some combination of the golden hour light and professional airbrushing. There's a sign, too, but it's written in Chinese characters—the only one I recognize is the *Zhang* from my own family name.

Judging from the sounds of tinkling laughter and shuffling footsteps and rumbling voices, the wedding must be well underway by now. My heart rate spikes the way it always does before I'm about to enter a crowded room, and I have to consciously steady my breathing. It's an old trick, picked up and perfected two years ago at two different schools, when the simple act of grabbing a salad from the cafeteria or finding my seat in class was something I had to brace myself for.

Breathe in for four.

Hold.

Out for four.

Good.

You're good now.

Or I'm supposed to be. But when I walk through the doors, the noise drops away.

It's like I'm back at my old school again, the very last place I'd ever want to return to.

The stares. The raised brows. The exchanged glances. Even though the people here don't have a reason to dislike me the way my classmates did, there are still way too many of them, filling up almost every single table in the ballroom. Countless faces turn, assessing me, and I get that pit-in-my-stomach feeling I've always hated, this sense that I'm looming over everyone like a dark cloud, a giant in the metaphorical and, at five feet ten, literal sense, unable to blend into any crowd, incapable of fitting into any room. I can only stand here and let them stare as my face grows hot and my fingers go clammy.

There are times when I agree with my mom that maybe I *was* cut out to be a model, that maybe it's the only thing I can ever be cut out for—standing still and looking pretty—and I've wasted that, played my cards wrong. Then there are times when I'm convinced I was never suited for it, that it was ridiculous I'd ever believed otherwise. That the past two years were the true waste, because how can you be a model if you loathe the feeling of being looked at?

"Leah!"

More eyes flicker up as Xiyue strides over to us. The wedding poster really didn't do her justice. She's glowing. Gorgeous in her joy and in her qipao, which seems to have been designed just for her. Each delicate silver thread gleams as she moves, weaving together images of peonies and phoenixes that wrap around her shoulders and waist. She's everything you'd imagine a happy bride to be, with her red dress and rosy cheeks.

I open my mouth to tell her that I'm sorry for being so late, but the only Mandarin words I manage to recall on the spot are: "I'm sorry."

This comes out much more ominous than I'd hoped.

"Sorry?" She frowns slightly.

My mom jumps in with what I'm assuming is an explanation, and then she spots Xiyue's mother behind her. Her face tightens for just a second before her already-wide smile stretches farther into a beam so beatific it can only be fake, her arms stretching out with it.

"Jiejie," she coos, pulling my aunt into a polite hug, neither of them really touching.

I stay quiet as they exchange loud air kisses and step back to study each other. My aunt hasn't changed since I last saw her at the Spring Festival dinner a couple years ago. Same expensively coiffed, pitch-black hair, same stern, thin brows, same powdered skin pulled taut over high cheekbones. I actually don't think she's changed at all since I *first* saw her when I was a baby. The woman is walking proof that genes can only get you so far when it comes to anti-aging, because while she looks like she's been sipping from the Fountain of Youth every morning, I was helping my mom pluck out the white hairs near her temple just the other night.

The bizarre thing is that in almost any other family, my mom would be the favorite child. The success story you brag about at events like this one. Good grades, good house, good career, happy marriage. Unfortunately for her, my aunt just happens to be one of the youngest and most esteemed professors in the Department of East Asian Languages and Cultures at Stanford, and a Grammy-nominated composer on the side, because being good at just *one* thing is too primitive. The family legend goes that she's so accomplished she caught the attention of NASA, who wanted to send her into space, but she declined because she was too busy. Like, too busy *for the moon.*

"Hey," I say, when my aunt turns toward me with an expectant look.

My mom tugs at my wrist harder than she typically

would. "You don't say *hey* like you're bumping into a friend at the mall. You say *xiaoyi hao*," she hisses.

"Xiaoyi hao," I amend, but I seem to have already failed some kind of test. And I fail it again when my aunt asks me something in Chinese. I look helplessly over at my mom, who answers for me in a strained, high-pitched voice, then waves me off to a table in the corner.

It's the kids' table, I realize. Piles of candy have been laid out around the crimson rose centerpiece: chocolates in the shape of hearts and peanut brittle and strawberry swirls and pink marshmallows. There's even the corn-flavored jelly I remember from my childhood, as artificially sweet as it is bright yellow, yet so good I could never stop eating them.

A few of the kids have started digging into the sweets already, the shiny wrappers crinkling in their little fists. As I sit down in the only empty chair left, I recognize two of them as my very distant cousins, but everyone else at the table is a complete stranger—

No.

My gaze catches on the person next to me, the only boy here who's also seventeen, and I feel my heart drop.

It can't be him. It *shouldn't* be.

Yet there he is, with his dark hair falling like silk

over his forehead, the angles of his face so finely rendered it's almost a taunt to contemporary sculptors, the softness of his lips a lie. He looks like he hasn't smiled once in the two years since I last saw him. He's definitely not smiling right now. His eyes are pinned on me, and though they're the exact same shade of brown—the kind that turns to liquid amber in the light, and black onyx at night—there's something different about them. Something heavier and melancholy.

"Hello," he says, and his voice is different too. Low. Leveled.

I never thought I would hear it again.

I'd prayed I would never have to.

"Hi," I say. Or I attempt to say, the effort of that single word exhausting. My whole body is numb. The moment doesn't seem real, but I can feel moisture gathering over the bare nape of my neck.

I like to consider myself a reasonably amiable person. I've never gotten into a heated argument or physical altercation with anyone before. I have a healthy number of friends, and though we're not exactly drive-across-the-country-at-midnight-to-help-you close the way I wish to be, at least we're you-can-borrow-my-sunglasses close. And I might dislike a number of people, or disagree with them on multiple points, but I don't *hate* anybody—

Except for the boy sitting down beside me.

Cyrus Sui.

ABOUT THE AUTHOR

Photo by Alyssa Liang

Ann Liang is the *New York Times* bestselling author of *I Hope This Doesn't Find You*, as well as the critically acclaimed YA novels *This Time It's Real* and *If You Could See the Sun*. A graduate of the University of Melbourne and born in Beijing, she grew up traveling back and forth between China and Australia, but somehow ended up with an American accent. When she isn't writing, she can be found making overambitious to-do lists, binge-watching dramas, and having profound conversations with her pet labradoodle about who's a good dog. You can find her online at annliang.com.

Don't miss the first rom-com from the world of Ann Liang!

When Eliza Lin's essay about meeting the love of her life unexpectedly goes viral, she lands newfound popularity and an internship at her favorite magazine overnight. The only problem is that Eliza made her essay up. She's never been in a relationship before, let alone in love. All good writing is lying, right? All she needs is a fake boyfriend to help her hide the truth... and there's no one better than the famous actor in her class, the charming but aloof Caz Song.